Apocalypse End

Apocalypse End

Reign of the Dead

Len Barnhart

iUniverse, Inc.

New York Lincoln Shanghai

Apocalypse End
Reign of the Dead

iUniverse, Inc.

For information address:
iUniverse, Inc.
2021 Pine Lake Road, Suite 100
Lincoln, NE 68512
www.iuniverse.com

ISBN: 0-595-27165-0

Printed in the United States of America

To Carol

I have looked across majestic mountain ranges in
    awe.

I have marveled at the stars in the night sky
    and the secrets they hold

In the simplest of things in nature I have seen
    complexity.

But dearest to me is when I look to my side
    and know you will always be there.

Contents

Acknowledgements

Many people have helped me in one way or another since I started this book so I would like to give some of them special thanks.

Michael Shiley, you were a big help at the Pittsburgh Comicon. It is a pleasure knowing you and for all the times you've gone above and beyond to help me, I thank you.

Don Pedicini, at imajicastudio.com who is currently working on the illustrated version of Reign of the Dead. You do great work and I am looking forward to the finished product.

Editor; Marilyn Pesola, For the past five years I've counted on you for insight, advice and the betterment of my work. You've been there at every milestone and your help is deeply appreciated. Thank you. You put the cherry on top of my sundae.

Leonard Lies, I should've known you sooner. I can't think of a better person to work beside me to find a place for "Reign" in the world of film. In the short time I've known you I have come to call you 'friend' and I am sure that it will be a lasting friendship.

George A. Romero, Where would vampires be without Bram Stoker? Where would zombies be without George Romero? Your contribution to the genre cannot be overstated.

PART

I

Tangier

1

Leon Baltimore walked into the storeroom of the makeshift armory on Tangier Island and stopped dead in his tracks. Jacob DuBois, a recent immigrant from Louisiana, was swaying back and forth on his knees, chanting a rhythmic cadence. His face was upturned and his arms were outstretched, palms up.

"You think that'll conjure up some big miracle?" Leon asked. "That those bastards will just drop dead again and go away with a little Who-do Voodoo?"

Jacob stopped swaying and looked at Leon's black face. "'E's powerful stuff, man. If 'e can raise de dead, 'e can work de udder way, too," he said with a heavy Cajun accent.

"Well, how about keeping your little rituals at home, Swamp Man?" He pushed past the kneeling man. "Jesus Christ, just what we need here, another freak!"

Jacob got to his feet and walked out of the room, determined not to lose faith. Not now, when he had been delivered for this long. He would hold on to his beliefs no matter what.

Leon set about the task that had brought him there; another recon mission. He hated them. They always ended the same way, with dead air, dead cities, and wasted time. Washington, D.C., and all of the suburbs within flying distance, had been that way for some time now. For the life of him, he couldn't figure out why they still bothered to look.

Leon unlocked the gun cabinet and opened it. The armory was damp and without the aid of a controlled environment, metal was more prone to rust but he'd seen to it that his weapons were clean. A misfiring gun would not be the cause of his death.

"I put my faith in you," he cooed, stroking the barrel of his favorite rifle.

His thoughts returned to Jacob. What the hell was he doing in the armory, praying? It didn't seem right.

Leon locked the gun cabinet and walked out, ready for battle.

There are two ways to get on or off Tangier Island, which is located off the coast of Virginia: by air or by sea. The ferry no longer ran its daily route and as long as sick and dying were closely monitored, Tangier was safe.

The heavy armory door swung open and Leon stepped out into the cool March sunlight. He tilted his face to the warm sun, then rubbed the tense muscles on the back of his neck to relieve the tension. What he really wanted was a pair of pretty black hands to massage his troubled thoughts away. He wondered what Halle Berry was doing these days. Since movies weren't made anymore, maybe she would help him out. He smiled at the ludicrous thought.

The past two years had been more than most people could cope with, and they'd had more than their share of trouble, but they had managed to survive. They were safe enough for now from the walking plague of death that had invaded a thriving world and turned it into an endless quest for survival.

Now he was ready to leave the safety of Tangier Island again for another fruitless search for survivors. How he hated returning from the hell out there with nothing to show for it except a dark mood.

Leon slung his rifle over his shoulder and made his way to the local tavern. He still had time to get a glass or two of Julio's apple wine before the trip, enough to ease the stiffness in his neck. It wouldn't hurt to calm his nerves, either.

The bright blue sign on Julio's Bar proudly declared it to be the most popular social club on the island, never mind that it was the only one on the island. Money was no good anymore. Barter was the new order of business.

Julio opened the tavern at his leisure, sometimes early, sometimes late in the evening. Ten this morning was not at his leisure, since the door was locked when Leon tugged on it.

The anticipated tang of Julio's apple wine teased the back of Leon's tongue but he pushed the thought out of his mind. There was plenty to think about with another impending trip into the wasteland. He would come back when he returned.

*   *   *

The helicopter was readied for flight on the pad in front of the airport's main building. It was a modest airport, with one main terminal and several maintenance buildings. Only one landing strip was long enough to handle smaller planes. Two hundred yards away, the tides of the Chesapeake Bay licked the sandy shoreline.

The chopper's rotating blades created a strong, steady wind that tore at Leon's clothing with a ferocity equal to the tropical storm they had experienced a week ago. The chopper's military green skin was dull but clean. Great care was taken with the equipment on the island. There was no replacing anything without great danger to those doing recognizance.

Leon saw Hal Davidson and Jack Lewis in the doorway of the main structure. They would be going on this futile expedition with him. Hal would fly the big green bird and, as usual, he and Jack would do the grunt work.

Leon tried to shake off his aversion for the trip and smiled at the approaching men.

2

Jim Workman stared hopelessly at the guts of the communication console in front of him. He had devoted countless hours to get it operational again and refused to accept defeat. It was ironic that the most powerful and advanced communication setup within fifty miles had failed shortly after their arrival at the Mount Weather Underground.

For more than a year he had pulled, poked, and pounded at it in a futile attempt to get it operational. He had finally succumbed to the reality that it would never work again. The simple truth was that vital parts had burned out and there were no replacements to be found.

Jim reclined in the swivel chair and glanced up at the video monitors that lined the wall in front of him. Four of the screens were dead and displayed blank screens. Two were still live. One had a clear view of downtown Moscow, a desolate place. The only movements were walking corpses.

The other monitor was of Washington, D.C., and that scene was no better than Moscow's. The other four screens had ceased to function, one at a time, months before. More than likely the satellites had spun out of their orbits or had simply stopped working. In any case, they were cut off from anyone who might still be alive outside of their safe haven.

Dr. Sharon Darney, their resident expert on the plague, had once told him that the walking dead could remain mobile for ten years, maybe more, before decomposition made movement impossible.

Two years had passed and he couldn't wait another eight to find out if anyone else still lived. They had survived; others, too, must have survived.

Jim knew it was time he stopped being as stale and stagnant as the air they were breathing in the underground complex. He needed to do something. Complacency had set in and it had become too easy to shut out the outside world and hope for the best. Surely there were survivors out there banding together to regain control of the situation. It was time now to go and find them.

Amanda would be against the idea. After all the horrors they had been through, she would be content to stay right where she was and to hell with any other survivors. As they had all learned, it was not just the well-intentioned, kind, and honest people who had survived the plague. They'd all had more than their fill of the other kind of survivors.

Being cooped up in the massive hole in the ground was finally catching up to him. It was time to make a move. Surviving was not living.

*   *   *

Amanda sat at the corner table in the cafeteria, pushing powdered eggs around on her plate. She had forgotten what real food tasted like. She had forgotten much the past two years—her life before the plague, old friends, and old loves. She thought it better that way, at least for now. Dwelling on the past only brought sadness with it.

When Amanda looked up, she saw Jim and motioned for him to join her. He sat down across from her in the familiar manner of old lovers.

She couldn't help but notice that his mood had not changed. Lately he had become jaded, at times distant and isolated. He would hide away in the war room for hours without so much as an appearance for food or water. She was becoming worried about him. This sullen behavior was such a stark contrast to the person she had fallen in love with. The caring and compassionate leader that he was only months ago had become reticent and even a bit callous. She feared not only him but also for herself. She loved him and now she may be losing him. The worst part of it was, she didn't know why.

Amanda finished chewing a forkful of the bland eggs and hoped that a little small talk might coax him into a meaningful conversation with her.

"Anything new?" she asked, expecting the usual answer.

Jim squirmed in his seat and then replied the same as always. "No."

He fell silent, leaving Amanda to think up a new topic to keep him talking. Anything was better than another silent meal, she thought, stirring her eggs once again.

"That radio's never going to work," she said finally. "Have you thought about looking for other survivors? There hasn't been a creature near the complex in months. It should be fairly safe."

Jim's eyes widened and an exhilarated look washed over his face.

"Yes, I've thought a lot about it. Tangier Island." He said. "I want to go to Tangier Island."

Amanda's jaw dropped. Well, you've done it now, she thought. This was not the conversation she had hoped for when she began asking questions. She had opened a big can of smelly, walking-dead worms.

"No, no. That's not what I meant. Not Tangier Island, Jim, it's too far." How quickly he had turned this around. "It's too dangerous and, besides, it's been a year since you got that message. How do you even know that the person who sent it is still alive? For God's sake…"

"I *don't* know. That's the point. They never acknowledged our reply. I don't think the radio was sending, even then."

Amanda dropped her fork with a clatter that mirrored her jangled nerves. She had suddenly lost what little appetite she'd had. Her head was spinning and now she had to win an argument with one of the most headstrong men she'd ever known.

"So that's it? You want to risk your life and what little happiness may be left to us because you're stir crazy? Jesus, Jim, why?"

"If there's someone alive there, I have to know," he said. "We all do. We can't go on forever here. Eventually, we will run out of supplies. Tangier Island would be the ideal place. If there are survivors, there's a good chance they'd be there, maybe even hundreds of them. We have to know. This is important."

"No, goddamn it." Her voice quivered as she stood up "*We* don't have to know anything, *you* do!"

She stormed away and left a perplexed Jim sitting there all alone.

3

The helicopter rose in the crisp spring air and Leon felt the familiar churning in his gut return, as it did every time the bird took off.

There was no approval or clearance for takeoff. The sky was free of traffic. Not so much as a single airplane had been seen flying over the island since the first couple of months. No planes, no cars, or people where they were going. No living ones, anyway. They were going into the pits of hell once again. God how he hated this part.

The airport diminished beneath them as they rose higher. Leon stared out of the window, hoping it would relieve his upset stomach. It finally settled down after the chopper leveled out for their flight to the mainland.

Leon watched the island as it dropped away behind them, noticing for the first time how green everything had become since winter. The blue-green waves of Chesapeake Bay glimmered in the sunlight and occasionally a wave caught the sunlight just right and sent flashes of brilliant, blinding light up to him.

"Where today?" Hal asked, glancing at Jack who was seated next to him, a pen clenched between his teeth, reading some maps.

"Go up by Crisfield, "Jack said, "then turn west toward St. Mary's County and follow the coast north for a while. We'll see from there." His eyes never left his maps. He turned them to the left, then to the right, as though trying to find the best angle to view them. He flipped from page to page trying to find the right one.

Leon rolled his eyes in disgust. He'd seen this same scene played out many times before. No wonder they hadn't found anyone yet. They'd be lucky to find their way home.

Jack finally threw the papers aside and drank from the cup of coffee hanging in a cup holder next to him. His creased face and graying hair showed every bit of his fifty-two years. He had become hard like a rock since the plague but his strength wasn't with calculations. He was a soldier, an unstoppable force once he got started, Leon thought, though not the sharpest knife in the drawer. If there was anyone he'd want in a foxhole next to him, it would be Jack. Just don't ask him to count the remaining bullets.

Leon had been on many missions like this one with Jack. He knew when to take chances and when not to. But when someone needed help, Jack was the first one to offer it. He'd give up his life to save another. Salt of the earth and everyone knew it. Leon was always glad to have him along.

The chopper continued to fly north along the path Jack had laid out until they reached Crisfield. The familiar sight of the Mormon temple came into view, its tall golden steeple still as pristine as it had been two years before. The rest of the building was in shambles, like most churches now. When things had gotten bad and people were left with nothing else, they had turned to the churches, temples, synagogues and mosques, hoping their religion would save them. It had only made them easy prey for the bloodthirsty ghouls that surrounded the buildings like dogs herding sheep to be slaughtered.

Leon thought that religion had caused the situation to get out of hand as much as anything else. Many held the outlandish idea that God had somehow willed the dead to rise to attack the living, that it was the resurrection foretold in the Bible. Religious zealots had whipped the easily-led masses into a frenzy of Bible-thumping idiots shouting, "God's will!" Faithful flocks refused to properly incapacitate the bodies of the dead. They saw it as a contradiction to "God's will." Others thought resurrected family members or friends were still, at least on some level, themselves. Nothing was farther from the truth.

Those misguided herds of humanity had, in large measure, caused the downfall of mankind with astonishing speed. It had taken a mere two months for eighty-five percent of the world's population to be annihilated, most of whom then joined the increasing numbers of walking dead. It was a desperate situation. But they were safe on Tangier Island, at least until the ghouls learned to swim.

Leon shifted in his seat. He didn't want them to set the chopper down. Sometimes they did, sometimes they didn't. He was hoping this was a time that they wouldn't. It was never a good time on the ground. You could never really tell from the air what was below. They had been nearly overwhelmed on two past occasions when a safe landing had looked feasible but then hordes of the things had emerged from buildings and filled the streets.

Leon was in no hurry for another adventure. He breathed a sigh of relief when they flew by Crisfield and turned west toward St Mary's City.

Their flight path took them over Smith Island. The view created a sense of normalcy in this world turned upside down. Traffic moved on the island roads below, mainly bicycles because there was a shortage of gasoline. But life moved on with at least some of the past's regularity. People strolled the sidewalks and slipped in and out of trade shops in a manner impossible to do anywhere else, at least not anywhere that they had found.

A group of no-nonsense locals on the island had been the first to take things in hand to rid the place of the walking dead. Once the situation had been handled, they began broadcasting Ham radio messages, searching for other survivors. The island's population began to grow as the harrowed and haggard masses clung to the hope that this was a safe place and made their way here by boat and helicopter. A group had even clung to a half dozen lashed-together inner tubes and kicked and paddled their way across the bay to the island.

Early on, making a stand on the mainland would have meant certain death. There were just too many of the demons over there. They needed better odds to survive. Tangier quickly became overcrowded and a team was organized to go to Smith Island to repeat the feat they had accomplished on Tangier, giving their little community a chance to expand.

Smith Island was a bit more complicated to conquer than Tangier. It was much larger, meaning more ghouls to destroy, but eventually it was accomplished. Later, they would take the Bloodsworth and Hooper Islands, an area totaling approximately forty miles in length located between Virginia and Maryland in the Chesapeake Bay.

Things were still far from normal as Leon could attest to but from fifteen hundred feet in the air it looked much better than where they were going.

The chopper flew along the coastline toward St. Mary's City. Leon's stomach began to churn as his anxiety mounted. This was not the coastline of an island but the state of Maryland. Real danger lurked below. If they set down there, they'd be putting their lives at risk.

Hal turned west and the chopper moved inland. St Mary's City was a typical town on the bay, with lots of seafood restaurants, shopping centers and buildings on stilts. Before the plague, tourism had flourished. Families and friends arrived by the hundreds each week during the summer months for the sites of the bay, deep-sea fishing, and vacation bliss.

Gleeful tourists had been replaced with uncaring monsters that aimlessly roved about in large numbers, not sure of where to go or what they were there for until some unfortunate person happened to stray into their field of vision.

If there were survivors there, they were hidden well; a simple flyover wouldn't bring them out. The easy task of extracting them from rooftops had long since ceased. If the truth be known, they hadn't found anyone to save in more than a year.

Jack pointed to a cloud of gray smoke that billowed into the sky several miles ahead. It seemed to be coming from the area of Lexington Park. Hal tilted the stick and the chopper increased its speed.

Leon knew what they were hoping, that someone needing assistance had set the fire, that it could be a smoke signal for help.

Leon began checking his gear in the event they'd have to get out of the craft and set out in a ground fight. Adrenaline spiked his chest as though liquid steel ran through his veins. His breathing became faster and perspiration beaded his forehead. He found himself not so much afraid as exhilarated at the thought of making the trip meaningful. Finding just one person out there still alive would make all those fruitless trips over the last year worthwhile. He began to get his hopes up again.

Hal flew the chopper counterclockwise about three hundred feet above and outside of the column of smoke above a strip mall that housed several small businesses. One of the businesses in the middle of the mall had caught fire. In a few minutes the whole mall would be burning.

Leon watched closely, waiting for that person or persons to flee from the flames, their arms flailing about so the saviors in the helicopter would see them. Anytime now they would rush to the ground and lay waste the ghouls that were smart enough to stay away from the fire and wait for their prey to come out, then load the chopper with grateful occupants and give them a new home, a home that was safe. Anytime now it would happen...

Hal kept the chopper in a circular path around the building. All eyes were focused on one spot as they waited for someone, anyone. They waited until the flames spread from business to business and consumed the entire mall. The roof caved in from the center out and sprays of sparks shot upward. The heat was immense.

A burst of heated air exploded above the inferno and the chopper rose fifty feet in a matter of seconds. For a moment it seemed that the aircraft would spin out of control and crash to the ground as the sudden rush of heated air pushed them upward too fast for Hal to maintain control. He fought with the stick in what seemed like an eternally as the chopper swung left to right, then dived forward and backward, all the while bouncing its occupants around in their seats, pondering their fate. Then he regained control and it settled again. Hal turned the stick and pulled the chopper further away from the blasting heat and hovered there.

Hope dwindled as the building burned. The ghouls moved in. Seeing no one to attack, they dispersed and moved on, ignoring the green bird overhead. The occupants of the chopper watched silently, then moved on themselves.

Leon's stomach churned again.

4

Jim Workman spread the maps onto the table in the conference room. He was looking for the fastest and safest route to Tangier Island. Staying away from the more populated areas whenever possible was a given but as he stared at them, it was becoming all too clear that there would be no safe way to get to his destination. From this particular map, he couldn't even tell if there was a bridge that led to the island or if he'd have to take a boat.

Route 17 would take him most of the way but it would also take him through several small towns. The fact that it was such a straight shot outweighed the danger that would get him as far as Tappahannock. From there he'd have to take 360 to the coast.

Tangier Island looked to be about twelve miles off shore. If there wasn't a bridge, and that seemed to be the case from what he could tell, it seemed logical that there'd be boats docked in or around Smith Point. It was the closest tip of land to the Island.

Jim studied the small island on the map and searched his mind for details from the static-filled message he had received a year before: *This is Tangier Island, off the coast of Virginia. Is anyone there?* The message repeated several times before it stopped. He would have missed it completely if not for the fact that he'd forgotten to turn off the radio when he left the room and had returned to do so.

He had tried for weeks to get a response, day in and day out, to no avail. In the pit of his gut—in his soul—he knew they were still there. Somehow, he knew. Though they never received the message again after that one time, it remained in the back of his mind until he had become obsessed with finding out once and for all.

The total trip was over one hundred and sixty miles. He was sure he could make it. He'd go it alone. There was no reason to have someone else to look after. If by chance something did go wrong, there was no reason to also put them in danger.

*   *   *

An outer lobby and floor-to-ceiling windows gave Felicia an excellent view of the front lawn and the Easter lilies in full bloom. It was a beautiful day and happy thoughts flooded her mind. She enjoyed the green foliage and the leaves that gently blew in the breeze. She enjoyed it so much, even from the inside looking out.

If Felicia could only step through the door and stand outside, she'd let the fragrance of those flowers and spring air fill her senses, but she knew better than that. It was best to stay hidden away. They'd learned from past mistakes that it was vital to remain unseen and unheard. One blunder could bring a world of trouble upon them.

They had been quite safe at the Mount Weather complex since arriving a year ago, tucked away underground in the seven-story city built by the government to maintain control in the event of a national crisis. When the crisis finally arrived in the form of an Armageddon-type day, the tenants had been done in by their own selfish desires for power and ill-advised procedures. It left the way open for the sixty-eight survivors, counting Felicia, to find a new and safer refuge.

How long they would have to stay in this place didn't matter to her now. She had become comfortable with her surroundings and, most importantly, they were safe as long as no one stepped outside. She could get no closer than the lobby to the smell of those flowers but she was content to look at them from her chair.

Felicia turned at the sound of the elevator door sliding open. A year ago a sudden noise that broke the silence like that would have made her jump from her skin, but not now. The premonitions had left her and calmness reigned.

The grimace on Amanda's face made it clear that she didn't feel the same way. Amanda walked over to the window and stood beside Felicia.

"It's pretty outside, isn't it?" Amanda said.

"Yes."

"It looks so peaceful, so calm. Do you think it's this peaceful out there beyond the safety of the mountain?" She turned to face Felicia and a lone tear slid down her cheek.

"I don't know. Maybe."

Amanda brushed the tear away and focused on the lawn outside. "I hope so," she said, then fell silent.

"He's going out there, isn't he?" Felicia asked. "Jim, I mean. He's going on a search for others to Tangier Island."

Felicia knew it would come to this, even if Amanda didn't. Jim Workman was not one to sit idle for too long. She was surprised that he had stayed cooped up this long. Everyone in the complex knew of the message from Tangier Island last year.

"Yes, he is."

Felicia thought of a way to console her friend. She felt Amanda's pain. If Mick came to her and announced a plan like this, she wouldn't take it too well, either. She would quickly lose the contented feeling she had been experiencing. A terrible thought suddenly came to her.

"Mick's not going with him, is he?"

"No. Jim's going alone."

Amanda's answer eased Felicia's mind and she released a long sigh. Mick wasn't the adventurous type. He was a coordinator, a layer of plans. He would be perfectly happy to make sure everything was just as it should be at home. Felicia was glad of that.

"Amanda," Felicia said. "Jim has a purpose. If it weren't for him, we would have all perished long ago, before we even got here. He saved us all. God or whoever is controlling this world gone crazy, has things in store for him. That's what I believe. Who's to say he isn't helping someone else to survive now?"

"That's a lovely little scenario but we don't know that for sure. All I know is, the man I love is leaving me on a very dangerous whim. I may never see him again and I think I'm beginning to hate him for it."

"What if you're right, Amanda? What if you never see him again? Do you really want to spend your last moments with him full of hate? Go to him. Let him take your love on this journey with him, to keep him company, to keep him safe. You'd be surprised how much something like that can serve to keep one safe. If you don't, you'll regret it forever if something does happen."

Amanda fell into Felicia's arms and sobbed. Once again her world was falling apart. In the beginning, when the walking death had stripped her of everything she held dear and now, with Jim leaving, once again her life was being turned upside down. She felt helpless and afraid.

5

Mick was tightening the last bolt on the access panel to the backup generator when Jim found him. Mick hadn't seen Jim enter but he sensed him there and turned. He brushed his blond hair away from his face and huffed a sigh of completeness upon finishing his job. Matt Ford lugged the tools away.

"All done." He wiped his hands on a towel draped over his shoulder. "That's the last one. This equipment is still in good condition. We may never need to use the backup stuff but it's good to know it will work should we need it to."

Jim nodded his agreement as he watched Matt put the tools they had been using back into the cabinet on the far wall of the utility room.

Mick leaned over and picked up a forgotten tool lying on the floor and tossed it to Matt.

"You don't know what's out there, Jim," Mick said.

Here we go again, Jim thought, another sermon on the dangers outside. Word of his planned trip had obviously traveled fast.

"That's the point isn't, it Mick? None of us do. No one's been out there since we got here."

"Yes, we do know. Have you been ignoring those monitors in the war room? One satellite is still pointed at Washington, D.C. It looks to me like those bastards are still out in full force."

"I'll stay away from D.C."

"They're not just in D.C., they're everywhere. And in case you've forgotten, one bite from those things and you're infected. And you know what that means."

"I know what it means. I'll be fine."

Matt, who had been listening, said, "I'll go, too. It'll be—"

"No!" Jim snapped, cutting him off. "I go alone."

"But—"

"No buts! I won't risk another life."

"There," Mick said, "you see? You do realize the danger. Why risk it at all? Let those people take care of their own."

"And us ours?" Jim asked. "We're fine here. Those things couldn't get down here even if they had the brains God gave a chimp, and they don't. What if there are people there and they need help? It would be selfish not to try. Besides, eventually we'll need a new place."

Mick had had this conversation with Jim before and he had never come out the winner. Jim was going to do what Jim wanted to do and that was that. Still, he felt it necessary to convince him of what he thought was the most prudent decision.

"I've got it all figured out," Jim said.

Mick noticed the satchel Jim was holding.

"Let me show you," Jim said. "It may make you feel more at ease."

Jim withdrew some papers from the bag, selected the map he intended to use for the trip, and laid it out on a nearby workbench. He had used a yellow Hi-liter to trace the route he would take from their location all the way to Tangier Island.

Mick studied the map. He was familiar with the route Jim had outlined. "It should be smooth sailing until you get to Fredericksburg," he said, pointing out the spot, "but you'll have to be very careful there, and again once you get to Tappahannock." He traced his finger along the yellow line as he spoke. "From there on, you'll have your hands full all the way to Smith Point."

Mick turned to Jim. "How do you figure to get there?"

"The Humvee up top."

"What if it breaks down?"

"I'll throw a motorcycle in the back. If the Humvee has problems, I'll use the motorcycle."

"Where are you going to find a motorcycle?"

"There are several in the warehouse at the far end of the property up top.

"You've been up there?" Mick asked.

"I have."

Mick's eyebrow rose in surprise. Even he had not ventured up top for fear of attracting unwanted guests.

"All right, then. It seems like you've got it all figured out.

"I do."

"Well, I guess the only thing left to say is, good luck."

Jim smiled and they shook hands.

Matt began a plan of his own.

*   *   *

Sharon Darney was the resident expert in the field of virology. When the dead phenomenon began, she had been sent to the Mount Weather Underground to assist in finding an answer for the sudden plague of living dead that rose to epidemic proportions in a matter of weeks. Her work had been in vain.

Before she could unravel the mystery, war broke out between the two differing military factions running the complex. They finally killed each other in the final moments before her escape amid a flurry of gunfire.

One hundred soldiers and staff members lay dead, though they hadn't remained that way for long. Before she left the compound, they had reanimated, forcing her to leave through the ventilation system. It was later that she found Jim Workman and the rest of the survivors who now occupied the underground complex with her. They had briefly taken control of a prison for asylum from the marauding dead until that, too, had proven unsafe.

Ironically, she was back where she had started from with the sixty-eight survivors from the prison, but her return raised new questions. The hundred soldiers who had reanimated before she left were once again dead, sprawled motionless on the floors of the compound when they had arrived. It puzzled her. She thought that by now she would've had answers but she was still in the dark for a cause as ever.

Complicating matters further was the fact that her private lab specimen still functioned. She did have one clue. The reanimated soldiers had never gotten to ground level. They had never seen the light of day.

Was something in the atmosphere responsible for keeping the dead going? It certainly didn't have anything to do with their ability to reanimate or they wouldn't have. From the amount of decay, Sharon figured they had ceased to function after only a month or so, though it was hard to be sure.

Once reanimated, the decomposition rate slowed drastically but varied from case to case. All evidence showed that the bodies infected early in the plague decomposed at a slower rate than those infected later. That made for a difficult conclusion.

Once again she had spent the majority of the day pouring over old data, hoping to suddenly see something she had missed the first hundred or so times, with no luck. In the thirty-seven years of her life she had never been so frustrated. Sometimes she felt like packing up all of her lab equipment and simply riding the whole thing out without even trying anymore. It would ease the headaches but not the desire. Sharon Darney was passionate for answers.

Why did dead bodies suddenly reanimate? How could they continue without the slightest sign of blood flow, need for nourishment, or water? Then there was the eeriest thing of all: Why did they feel the urge to consume living human flesh? It was definitely not to sustain them; it was more like some deep, dark primal urge that drove them to such horror.

Somewhere in the back of their malfunctioning brains a very dark evil urge lurked. Cannibalistic urges. With little or no reasoning power it was their main drive, their only motivation. Sharon had wondered early on if some new virus was responsible for the dead plague. Maybe a virus was responsible for the agonizing death one suffered from the slightest bite from one of those things, only to reanimate minutes after death themselves.

Lately she wondered if God himself didn't put the whole thing into motion. If a person died for any reason, they would revive. Contact with the unknown virus was not needed. It was beginning to seem like a greater power *was* at work.

Sharon removed her lab coat and hung it on a metal hook close to the door leading from the lab. Her research day had come to an end. Maybe she should just give up her work altogether and sit down with a good book for a while. At least take a break. In seven or eight years the problem would take care of itself.

The decomposition rate, though slowed, would eventually take its toll on the reanimates by refusing to allow their brains to function. The state of their bodies would become so decayed they would no longer be able to move; they would literally fall apart.

Sharon opened the door and came face to face with Jim Workman. The sudden encounter startled her and she stumbled backward into the room, clutching her chest as though to calm her pounding heart.

Jim grabbed her by the shoulders, thinking she might fall faint. Sharon raised her hand to show she was able-bodied and Jim released her.

"I didn't mean to scare you like that," he said.

Sharon straightened her disheveled hair. "It's okay, Jim. What can I do for you?"

"I'm going on a little trip and I need your advice."

Sharon wasn't aware of any planned trips to the outside. It wasn't any of her business but, still, it seemed a little bold.

"Where are you going?" she asked.

"Tangier Island."

"Ah, yes, the message. Did you get another one?"

"No."

"A little risky, isn't it?"

"If I'm not careful, it could get hairy."

"Indeed. What is it you want to know?"

Jim tried to think of specifics. "Is there a way to not attract attention to ourselves as far as those things are concerned? What I mean is, is there a way to keep them from noticing us as prey?"

"Silence is key. Movement, too. Don't let them hear you or see you. Maybe they can smell us. For all I know, we could give off a bright glow to them, like a lit up Christmas tree. They can tell us from one of their own, you know."

Jim nodded. "So that's it? No real secrets revealed yet?"

"I'm sorry, Jim. I wish there were, but the truth is that I just don't know. The safest way to go is not to go."

6

Leon sipped from his glass of apple wine and let it trickle down his throat, savoring each drop. He was belly up at Julio's bar, enjoying the company of friends and the sounds of music. A song by Credence Clearwater Revival spewed from the small stereo in the corner.

I see, the bad moon risin' I see, trouble's on the way.
I hear earthquakes and lightnin' I see, a bad time today.
Well don't come 'round tonight
Cause it's bound to take your life.
There's a bad moon on the rise.

The words echoed in Leon's ears as part of the room's background noise. He was preoccupied with the apple wine and Julio, who was talking rather harshly to his wife in his native tongue. She threw her arms up and screamed something back at him and stormed off into the restaurant kitchen.

Julio was five-foot-two and Leon was amazed that his wife, who towered a good six inches over him, hadn't retaliated yet for his constant tongue-lashings. It was a safe bet that one day she would pick up something and beat him over the head with it, putting an end to his verbal barrages.

Julio calmed down but spewed his displeasure by flailing his arms about in comic fashion behind the bar. Leon chuckled at the little man's tantrum.

"Julio, I swear, she's going to get you one day," Leon said with a laugh.

"She gets me now!" Julio howled. "Right here!" He patted his rear. "She's a pain in my ass!" He released a stream of Latin curses, waving his arms once more.

"It's impolite to speak anything but English when in the company of others who can't understand you. Don't you know that?" Leon teased.

"I'll tell you what is impolite, my friend," Julio fumed. "It is impolite for me to say what I say to her so that you do understand. That is impolite."

Leon downed the last of his wine and pushed it toward Julio for a refill. Julio filled the glass, then went back to wiping the bar clean of cracker crumbs and peanut shells that littered its surface.

Leon took a sip and rolled his eyes in pleasure. "This is some good shit here, Julio. You damn sure can make some tasty apple wine."

Julio smiled. "You like it so much because it is all there is, but I can make good wine from lots of things." Julio dumped the peanut shells and crumbs he had gathered with his rag into a trashcan behind the bar.

"I could make good wine from the moisture in this dishrag if it was all I had to work with, my friend. And even if it wasn't good, you'd like it because it is all there is."

Leon grunted. He doubted it but he smiled and took another sip.

Hal Davidson took a seat beside Leon. He removed his baseball cap and laid it on the bar in front of him, then motioned for Julio to bring him the usual. In a flash, a glass of wine was placed beside his cap.

"I thought we had something out there today," Hal said, taking a sip.

Leon remained silent, swirling his wine around in his glass, ignoring Hal without so much as a look to acknowledge his presence.

Hal tried again. "One day we're gonna find someone, you know. It's just a matter of time."

"That's bullshit!" Leon snapped, and then looked around to see how much attention his outburst had drawn. "That's bullshit," he repeated, lowering his voice. "There ain't no one out there to find. They're all dead and you know it. If there are people alive, they sure ain't gonna be anywhere around that city over there. If there's someone out there, they're not in our flying range. You can bet your ass on that. You know what I think? I think we're wasting our time and the fuel it takes for you to fly that bird, that's what I think. Besides, what the hell do you know? You don't get out of the chopper long enough to let it get to you."

Hal was agitated and it showed on his face. He wasn't particularly fond of making the weekly trips over to the mainland either but if it meant the possibility of saving one single life, then it was worthwhile. He thought Leon took it all too personally. Either that or he was trying to get out of work. Whatever the reason, it was pissing him off.

"Fine, Leon," Hal said. "Then don't go anymore. You just keep your ass right here on this island, on that barstool, for that matter, and Jack and I will go it alone."

"Fine," Leon said and marched out of the bar, leaving his half full glass of wine.

Leon walked down the street toward his house, half mad at Hal and half mad at himself for saying what he had said. He should've kept his mouth shut. It was a noble and good thing they were doing, it was just that he couldn't take it anymore. He couldn't take what he saw each time they went over there. The city was in decay. The walking corpses were in decay. Hideously mangled and disfigured, they roamed about in groups, searching for prey.

On one occasion in particular, they had put down near Waldorf, Maryland. There was a commotion below and they assumed there might be survivors who needed their help. What they had found was a pack of wild dogs that had dragged one of the ghouls to the ground and were tearing at it as it squirmed to get free.

The dogs quickly dismembered it and moved off with the appendages to gorge on the rotted meat. Head and torso were left lying in the middle of the street, alive and writhing in their own rotten stew. He would've put a bullet through its brain and ended its miserable existence if not for the fact that the noise would've attracted more attention to them. So they left it lying there and made their way back to the chopper.

A bullet to the brain did it. Kill the brain, kill the ghoul. It was elementary school education these days. His life would be so much more enjoyable if he could just stay on Tangier and not have to look at that sort of thing. Maybe then the nightmares would stop.

The walk to his house was a dark one. There was no moon, which made for an uneasy and lonely journey. If they had more electricity they might have streetlights but, like most things, electricity was in short supply. It wasn't hard to figure out why Julio bothered to open the bar and make his apple wine. He did it for the company of friends and for some sense of normalcy.

It was hard to keep one's sanity in a world gone mad. The Islands gave them their own little niche away from that madness but it had taken some doing to get there and make it safe. The fact that it could all come swiftly crashing down was never far from anyone's thoughts. How'd the old saying go? *A running man in the night can slit a thousand throats?*

The same applied here. One quiet zombie could create a hundred more in one night. One makes two, two makes four, and so on. Yep, come crashing right down, he thought. Still, it was the safest place to be. If there was a death, the bodies were quickly disposed of by fire.

Leon pressed the button on the side of his watch and a green light flashed on. It was eleven-fifteen. As tired as he was, he thought it was later than it was. It would feel good to crawl into his warm bed and stretch out for the night.

His house was a nice one. The population living on the islands was much less than what it was before the plague so they pretty much got to pick where they wanted to live. He had chosen a large three-story Victorian style home with an octagonal tower attached to the side. It was white with a wraparound porch and plenty of shade trees in the front yard. It was the kind of house he's always dreamed of living in but his delight was diminished by the small detail that it was obtained at someone else's expense. Whoever had owned the house before must be dead or they'd still be living there. It was his residence but not his home.

Leon turned down Appleway Avenue, the street where he lived, obviously named for the abundance of apple trees lining the street. His house was another hundred yards ahead.

The hard heels of his boots clicked on the asphalt and echoed off the houses as he walked past them. Each step drew him closer to his warm bed.

A loud crash nearly made him jump out of his skin. His heart thudded heavily in his chest as he drew his pistol from its holster and pointed it in the direction of the sound. He squinted to find a target but it was too dark. He couldn't see more than thirty feet and the noise was twice that far.

His mind raced as he turned around, fearing of an attack from that direction. The way was clear and he whirled back toward the noise.

"Who's there?" he demanded.

There was no response. After a few seconds, he repeated his question. Again there was no answer. He moved to replace the pistol in its holster when another crash split the quiet air. Leon raised his gun again.

"Who's there?" he demanded, louder.

When no response was forthcoming, he eased forward in the direction of the sound. His hands shook slightly as adrenaline pumped through him.

The sound came from the side of old man Grady's house. He lived four houses down from Leon in a two-story home with green trim. Old man Grady was in his seventies and the possibility that the old man had died in his sleep crossed Leon's mind. Damn this, he thought. Life on the island was supposed to be free of this type of thing.

Leon reached the corner of the house and stopped. He peered around the corner. He didn't see anything out of the ordinary, just a couple of trashcans and one of the lids lying on the ground. When the lid fell, it would have made the sound he had heard.

Leon began to feel stupid. A breeze had apparently blown the lid around. He relaxed his grip on the weapon and lightly kicked the lid. It clanged against the side of the can. A flash of movement streaked from behind it and ran across his foot.

Surprised, Leon fell backward into the trashcans and sent them rolling, creating an immense racket. He got quickly to his feet, pointing his gun at the culprit that sat on old man Grady's front porch, licking its front paw. A small black and tan cat.

Leon exhaled the breath he'd been holding. The porch light flashed on and the old man opened the front door. He held a double-barreled shotgun.

"What the hell is going on out here?" he shouted, when he saw Leon. "Sounds like you're tearing up the neighborhood." The old man cocked his head to one side. "You drunk or something?"

Leon put the gun back in its holster; glad he hadn't fired off a shot. He imagined himself being made to carry bullets in his shirt pocket like Barney Fife to avoid further accidents.

"Sorry, Mr. Grady. I heard something and thought it could be trouble. It turned out to be just a cat."

The old man looked down at the cat, then picked it up and tossed it inside the door. "Don't you go shootin' my cat now, ya hear? I've had that mangy thing for thirteen years. Keeps the mice away."

Leon walked up the street to his house. It would take him a while to get in the mood to sleep again.

7

Jim Workman selected the motorcycle he wanted to use and parked it in the middle of the warehouse floor to give him the needed room to work. Most of the batteries had lost their charge but it was a simple task to rectify the problem with one of the battery chargers stored there. While he was at it, he'd change the oil. The bike had been idle for quite some time.

Matt walked down the long isles of equipment in awe of what he saw. The aisles seemed to stretch to eternity in the largest warehouse he'd ever seen, everything neatly parked in straight lines like tin soldiers primed and ready for battle.

"Why the hell didn't you tell us what was up here, Jim? Christ, this place is an armory!" Matt said, pointing to a line of large army tanks. He counted twelve. Besides the tanks, there were also trucks, Jeeps, armored personnel vehicles, and an assortment of heavy weapons.

Matt jumped onto the tracks of one of the tanks and climbed up to open the hatch. He peered down into the dark compartment, then turned back to Jim, who had begun removing the battery from the motorcycle.

"Man, we could kill a lot of those things with this stuff," Matt said. "Blow 'em right back to hell." He jumped from the tank, then walked around the vehicles, touching each one like a child in a toy store, not sure which toy to buy. "How long were you going to wait before you broke out the heavy stuff? Holy shit, Jim, we could have our own army."

Jim put the battery on the floor. "And what would we do with it, Matt?"

The question caught Matt by surprise. What else would they do with the stuff? There was only one answer to that question. "Kill those son of a bitches, that's what. Go out there and hunt 'em down," he said, matter-of-factly.

Jim walked over and eyed the tanks. "You mean like the U.S. army did? Like they didn't try? It didn't work for them and they were a lot better trained and equipped than we are. What makes you think it will work for us?"

Matt shrugged and continued to explore.

Jim had scouted out every inch of the compound property. He knew everything that was there. Something else he knew but had decided not to share with anyone was the location of the missile silos over the hill. Not just any missile silos, these contained nuclear missiles. He had used a Geiger counter to check for possible radiation leaks but had found none. There was no reason to inform anyone of their presence. It would cause too much uneasiness.

"Well, it seemed like a good idea." Matt pulled himself away from the tanks and joined Jim by the bike. "I suppose using one of those tanks to go down to Tangier is out of the question then?"

Jim placed a pan under the bike to catch the old oil.

"Yep. They use too much fuel and are too slow. More trouble than they're worth."

"How's Amanda taking this?"

"Not too well but she's accepted it." The old oil had emptied out and Jim replaced the plug. "There's some oil for these bikes over there on that shelf," he said, pointing. "Get it for me.

Matt grabbed some and brought it to him. Jim cracked the seal on a bottle and dumped it in as Matt watched.

"No, she didn't take it well at all," Jim said. "Like I said, she accepted it, she doesn't like it."

Matt listened. He was a good listener. He learned from just listening. He was still alive because he had listened to Jim and had learned to keep his head in bad situations. Jim had saved him from starvation more than a year ago when he had come to clear the way for the others to move into the prison, which was safer than where they had been, a run-down rescue station hastily put together in the middle of a crisis.

Matt had been on the verge of joining the rest of his prison mates, who had all perished and were pacing their cells as the undead. They had been left to die by a prison staff who had either died themselves or had made a run for it. Another day or so and he wouldn't be standing here now.

"You can't blame her for that," Matt said.

"I don't. I feel for her, I really do, but I don't plan on going out and getting myself killed."

Jim tossed the empty oil bottle to Matt, who turned around and pitched it into a trashcan made from a fifty-five gallon metal drum. "Two points!" he said as it bounced off the rim and fell inside.

Jim smiled and wiped the excess oil from the bike's motor, then picked up the battery charger. "Get the battery and let's go see if we can get the Humvee started."

Jim and Matt walked up the hill to the main gate where the Humvee was parked, about a quarter mile from the giant ware-house. Matt got his first good look at the sprawling lawns, now grown thick with tall grass, and the rows of office buildings. A high fence surrounded the mountain top complex.

"FEMA was here before all hell broke loose," Matt said. "Up top, anyway. Look at it, Jim. They're gone and we're still here. Didn't do 'em one damned bit of good to have the inside track."

Jim took a sweeping glance of the area, more to check for unwel-come guests than to speculate how FEMA had fallen. A thick forest bordered the fence in all directions and made advanced warning nearly impossible.

"I imagine that the personnel working up top deserted their posts when things got bad," Jim said. "They weren't part of the sta-tion below. I doubt many of them ever saw the underground or knew much about it because it was a secured area. They'd probably have gotten shot if they tried to get in."

"You mean to tell me that if atomic bombs were about to fall on their heads, they wouldn't be allowed to get to safety down there?"

"That's right."

"Well, I gotta tell ya, that blows!"

"Keep it down," Jim cautioned. "We have neighbors we don't want to invite to dinner."

"That blows," Matt repeated quietly. "Those shits downstairs deserve what they got."

Jim switched hands to carry the heavy charger and picked up his pace. "Whether they deserved it or not, they got it because they were stupid. They had it made and blew it because they couldn't agree on what to do. They split into two factions, one who thought nuking the cities was the best solution and another who didn't. They went to war and killed each other."

"I'm glad they didn't nuke the cities."

"Me, too," Jim agreed.

The Humvee was a wide, squatty-looking thing, larger than a Jeep and more rugged in appearance. This one was outfitted with reinforced windows and heavy bumpers to deflect objects from its path.

Matt admired the hard, powerful exterior. It was the perfect vehicle to take on the trip. Not too large to get through a tight squeeze and not too small to plow over a crowd.

Jim placed the charger beside the Humvee and walked into the guard shack at the main gate. Matt followed.

Documents and fax sheets littered the floor of the tiny room. A calendar on the wall displayed a date of almost two years before. Jim pulled it from the wall.

"Look at that," he said, and handed it to Matt. "According to the date, this post was abandoned a couple of months after it all started."

Matt gave it a quick glance and let it fall from his hand. "Yeah, either that or they just didn't bother to turn the page. I know the last thing on my mind, with everything happening, would be to keep that calendar up to date."

Jim picked up a fax sheet from the floor. "The fax machine panicked, too," he said.

Matt took the paper from him, read it, and crumbled it into a ball when he saw the same month dated near the header.

"Didn't waste any time, did they?" Matt grumbled.

"Would you?" Jim asked. "Stuck up here, away from your family and not allowed to go below ground where it was truly safe? I'm surprised they stayed that long. There probably wasn't much left for them to go back to at that point. They'd have been better off to stay. They're probably dead now."

Matt nodded, acknowledging their probable fate.

"Check that cabinet over there and see if you can find the keys to that Humvee," Jim said. "I'll look in the desk drawer."

Matt rummaged through the cabinet, slinging items to the floor to break or clang when they hit the concrete. He winced each time, peeking over his shoulder, expecting a scolding from Jim for making too much noise.

He found two walkie-talkies and held them up by their straps for Jim to see.

Jim held a ring of keys and jingled them. Matt lowered the radios.

"Are they the right ones?" Matt asked.

Jim flipped the keys around and gripped them in his palm. "I won't know that till I try," he said, and walked out to the Humvee.

Matt considered the radios, then surreptitiously pocketed a set of handcuffs lying on the desk, and followed.

Jim studied the key ring. There were about forty keys on the hoop and he didn't feel much like trying each and every one before finding the one that fit, if it was on the ring at all.

He thumbed through several before deciding on one. He inserted in into the ignition. It was a fit. The engine roared magnificently to life. Jim smiled and reclined in the seat, pleased with his choice.

"Put the charger in the back," he said. "I'm going to take this thing down to the warehouse so I can load up the motorcycle."

Matt opened the back door and tossed the two radios in before getting the charger.

"What do I need the radios for?" Jim asked.

Matt bit his lip. "You never know."

8

"I have sworn to uphold the Constitution of the United States and oppose tyranny," George Bates reminded the young officer. "The situation changes nothing. We will continue as our forefathers intended and wipe clean the moral decay that caused this great nation to fall asunder and rebuild."

His tall stature and no-nonsense style made Lt. Col. George Bates the practical successor to Col. Hart, who had been killed six months earlier. Rugged and strong, Bates never gave up and fought for what he believed to be right.

The Virginia Freedom Fighters had been around long before the end of society. For years they had trained for a racial war, a civil war, or perhaps the day the United States government handed supreme governing power over to a world leadership, the so-called New World Order.

What that really meant was an end to personal freedom. Their organization stood as a bulwark against such tyranny at home. They had trained for many such scenarios but nothing could have prepared them for what had happened. Still, it changed nothing. Their goal remained the same: They would continue to uphold the Constitution the way it was intended to be, unchanged.

Bates handed the orders to the young officer.

"Take these to Lieutenant Hathaway. Tell him to meet me here in my office ASAP. I have something to discuss with him."

The young officer saluted and walked out.

Pressure had been mounting lately. The former commander had procrastinated, possibly too long. The time was ripe for a move. If they didn't do something soon, things could revert to what they'd been before the plague and once again they might be on the verge of totalitarianism. More recruits were needed. To take back the nation, they needed more, many more.

If they could unite all the organizations spread across the country it would be easy but long distance communications were out. Attempts to contact them with scouts had always met with failure. They had most likely found their fate at the hands of the flesh-eating ghouls. There were just too many pockets of humanity left.

Once the plague was over, they would reunite and return to that post-cold war style of thinking of a one-world government, in turn abolishing the Constitution. It was unimaginable that they had such a golden opportunity as this one to set things right and then fail to take advantage of it.

Lt. Robert Hathaway straightened his disheveled attire and knocked lightly on the Colonel's door, quickly running a hand through his hair.

"Come in!" the weighty voice on the other side boomed.

Hathaway entered the room and tried to not look like he had just dragged himself out of bed and stood at attention in front of George Bates' desk.

"At ease," Bates said, motioning for him to sit.

Hathaway slipped into the black leather chair, eyes forward, trying to appear alert. His shift started in an hour but he hadn't had time yet to get himself properly together.

"There's a matter of importance I need to discuss with you, lieutenant. It requires that you leave camp and go east, toward the coast."

Hathaway's eyes widened.

"We've received several communication signals from the coast and the radar onboard the carrier we commandeered in Norfolk last year has picked up air traffic in the region."

Hathaway leaned forward.

"I need you to put together a party of about ten men," Bates continued, "and find out if it's our own flying around up there or if it's a foreign, possibly hostile, aircraft.

Hathaway studied the Colonel. It was odd that he'd send his second in command on such a dangerous mission. Could it be that he wanted him out of the way? Maybe my presence threatens his command. That must be it, he thought. He would have to be very, very careful with this man in charge.

"Sir, going on these missions is at best risky," Hathaway said in his most respectful voice. "Do you think it wise to do this?"

"I think it's necessary," Bates said with a raised eyebrow. "I want answers. You know what we're here for and more than ever we all know what's at risk—"

"But, sir," he interrupted, "the coastal areas were heavily populated and are surely overrun with those putrid monsters. May I remind you that not one of our search parties has returned from their assignments?"

"Those search parties had to travel over twenty-five hundred miles to reach their destination in Montana. You'll be going less than two hundred. I've looked over the map and laid out the route I want you to take."

Hathaway's lower jaw began to hurt and he realized he'd been gritting his teeth. He didn't fear the trip; his years in the army had made him strong and fearless. It was the audacity of Bates that angered him. Who was he to put him in such danger?

He couldn't quite figure out why Bates was so highly regarded. Bates had served in Vietnam but that was a lifetime ago. Where was this great leader when he, Hathaway, was inhaling poisonous gas and sweating the Middle Eastern heat in Iraq? Here in Virginia, that's where, playing army with a bunch of over-the-hill wannabes. In their small minds they were saving the United States of America from the bleeding-heart liberals who wanted to give it all away. Hathaway sucked in a jagged breath at the thought.

"Yes, sir," Hathaway said.

George Bates studied Hathaway and began to doubt his ability to lead this mission. "You have the specifics in the orders you received," he said, then stood and opened the door. "I want no con- tact made. This is to identify only. Is that understood?"

Hathaway felt a surge of anger return. Not only was this mission unworthy of his talents, belittling him, now he was being ordered to do it half-assed.

"Yes, sir!" he replied and forced a halfhearted salute.

He would certainly remedy part of the problem. The Colonel wanted him to lead a dangerous mission into the bowels of hell on some wild goose chase for invading armies. Well, that was fine and dandy, but he'd do it his way, with men he chose to take.

If the Colonel wanted to play hardball, then Hathaway could do that, too. He'd show him by executing those orders with complete success and return in one piece. Then where would the Colonel be? He'd be right back where he started, that's where. Bates outranked him but he sure couldn't out think him. He'd have to find another way to do away with him. Bates would be wise to watch his back from now on.

Hathaway continued to fume as he walked down the corridor. Two guards by the door saluted him as he walked past. Hathaway ignored their salute and stepped out into the brisk morning air.

Morning drills had already begun and well-trained units exer- cised in groups of forty. A row of eight wide and five deep did jumping jacks on the main lawn to his left. Another unit did squats on his right. A third unit jogged the perimeter, singing silly rhymes as they ran.

Hathaway watched in wonder. A year ago they had been on the verge of total defeat. The Virginia Freedom Fighters had been low on morale, food, and personnel. Throngs of the undead had besieged their ranch at Roanoke. They'd lost many good men in that battle.

Then they joined up with the militia from West Virginia there at Big Meadows, on the Blue Ridge mountain range in the Shenan- doah National Park, and had remained ever since. Now they were strong again. They were more organized then ever and boasted almost twice their original numbers.

Big Meadows had been a good choice to hold camp. On the top of the mountain, it was more than twenty-five hundred feet above sea level and adequately equipped with cabins for shelter, stores of food, and other things. Wildlife thrived. Deer, bear, squirrels, and rabbits were plentiful. It was total seclusion from the catastrophe miles away.

Hathaway followed a gravel walkway back to his office to prepare. There were many things to be ironed out before the mission could take place, so many decisions to be made.

Bates would need to be taken care of once and for all. The only question left was how to do it.

*   *   *

As the sun sank low in the western sky, Lt. Hathaway inspected his troops. He shook each one of the ten men's hands as he made his way down the line. Most of them were his men, his friends, hand picked specifically for this mission. They would follow him to the ends of the Earth if asked, the ends of the Earth this time being Norfolk, Virginia, a large urban area on the Atlantic Ocean, also home to the country's largest East Coast naval base.

Their destination was an aircraft carrier. They had been using the radar dishes to watch for hostile forces that might find the current situation a good time to invade America. There were no known facts as to who created the plague, whether it was God-sent or merely a creation of man.

If a creation of man, then it seemed likely that war had indeed taken place and the United States was on the losing side. With no information available regarding the state of foreign countries, the Communists could be sitting pretty, just waiting for the right time to move in and take over. Or perhaps it was the radical extremists in the Middle East who had started it all with some kind of germ warfare.

Hathaway began to fume again. The towel-headed bastards had no respect for human life. Everyone knew that. They should've kept right on going in the Gulf War and wiped out the whole lot of them. They should've nuked the entire region and turned it all into a giant sand pit.

Hathaway shook the hand of the last man in line, his closest friend, Jake Peters. He'd known Jake for many years. He'd served with him, gotten drunk with him, and generally gotten in and out of trouble with him. It had been Hathaway who had first acquainted Jake with the Ku Klux Klan several years before. They had profited together and killed together. They had been insepara-ble since.

Jake was Hathaway's first choice to take along on the mission. Most everyone else was dead and that he and Jake still lived was nothing less than divine providence. This time the right side would win the war.

Hathaway turned on his right heel and spun about face, then walked three steps and turned again to face his men in military fashion.

"Dismissed!" he barked, and the men began to disperse.

"Not you, Jake."

Jake turned.

"I've got some things I want to talk to you about."

Jake walked confidently toward him, his muscles rippling beneath his tight green T-shirt. His hair, shaved tight to his scalp, made him look fresh out of boot camp. A wad of tobacco filled one side of his mouth and he spit frequently.

Hathaway lit a cigar, then inspected it as though appreciating its fine flavor. He savored the smoke for a moment before letting it escape through his nostrils. "I'm almost out of these things. Maybe we can get some more while we're out."

Jake spit, then nodded. "What'd you wanna talk to me about, Bobby?"

Hathaway turned and watched a group of men as they marched around the compound, hoping none of them had heard Jake address him so informally.

"You see those men over there?" he said, pointing. "They are oblivious to what's going on around here. They'll live or die by whatever Bates says, without question."

Jake glanced toward the marching men, feeling distain for his comrades without knowing why. But if Bobby Hathaway said so, then it must be true. "What are they oblivious to?" Jake asked.

Hathaway went eye to eye with Jake. "That we're doing nothing here. We do drills, we march, and we sit and wait. Now we're expected to go out and wait again. Sit back and watch, don't make contact. Risk our asses, mind you, but don't take action. We're no more living than those walking piles of rot out there in the Valley."

Hathaway flicked away the ashes hanging on the end of his cigar and then pushed the burning end into the palm of his hand, twisting it until it was out. He didn't so much as flinch.

"You see that?" Hathaway said. "That's the reaction of a man who's lost all sensitivity to his surroundings. A man who doesn't care anymore. The man I've become." He pocketed what was left of the cigar. "But not anymore, Jake, not anymore. From now on, we do things our way. Eventually, everyone will do things our way."

Jake spit again, leaving a brown smudge hanging from the corner of his bottom lip. Jake wasn't sure what Hathaway meant but he nodded his agreement just the same. If Bobby Hathaway said it, then it must be true.

"We'll go on this little mission," Hathaway said, "but when we get back, we'll do things our way."

*   *   *

It was nearly three-thirty in the morning before Hathaway finally attached the timer to his crude bomb. A simple relay would send an electrical impulse from the battery to the four sticks of dynamite at the chosen time and then detonate. It was beneath his skills but given the available material, it was all he could come up with on short notice. It was more than adequate for his needs.

Hathaway took a small knife and turned the screw in the back of the timer and set it for eleven that night, eighteen hours after he was scheduled to leave on his mission. He wouldn't be a likely suspect; he would be miles away when it happened. Bates would be asleep.

With a roll of duct tape, he wrapped everything tightly together and slipped it into a satchel, then cleared away the evidence by putting the leftover material into the satchel. He would wait another hour before placing the bomb.

                    *   *   *

Minutes passed like hours as Hathaway waited. He double-checked his plans as the hands of the clock inched from one minute to the next. It was a simple plan. What could go wrong? He'd be miles away when it happened.

His mind drifted. Lack of sleep had made him unsure of his own cleverness. He shook his head to clear away the cobwebs; he had to appear fresh for the day ahead. What's more, he had to be alert. It would be dangerous after they left the safety of the mountain. It would be not clever to finish this task, only to go out and get himself killed.

He had wanted to tell Jake of his plans earlier that day so they could both share in his brilliance and ingenuity but the fewer people who knew about it, the better.

Finally, the clock's hand hit the magical number: four-thirty A.M. It was time. Bates' room would be empty now.

Hathaway's adrenaline pumped as he slinked down the hall to George Bates' quarters.

9

Matt dashed through the underground street past the cafeteria, past the park bench by the underground lake, and across to Sharon Darney's lab. He was running late. There were so many things to do and so little time to do them. Jim was leaving shortly and he had to be ready.

Sharon was waiting when he burst through the door, out of breath. "You ready?" he huffed.

Sharon held up the needle. "Yes. Take off your shirt."

Matt fought to tear off his shirt and then bared his arm.

"What the hell is it, anyway?"

"It is a mega dose of antibiotics." She cleared the air from the syringe.

"What the hell good will that do? I thought there wasn't a cure for a bite from one of those things."

"There's not. Not that I know of, anyway, but it may help to have it in your system beforehand."

Matt flinched as the needle pierced his skin. After Sharon removed it, his arm began to ache and he rubbed it.

"Has Jim had his yet?"

"He got his an hour ago," she said, and trashed the empty syringe. "Does he know yet?"

"No, and I'm not going to tell him until the last minute. You know how he is; he'll try to talk me out of it if I give him the chance."

"Wear these," Sharon said and tossed two midnight blue jackets to him with the letters FEMA on the backs in yellow embroidery.

"Why?"

"Most people get bitten in the arm when they're attacked by the reanimates. If you're wearing a jacket, it will make it more difficult for their teeth to penetrate through to skin."

Matt bundled them under his arm. "Just what we need. Jackets in seventy degree weather."

"Wear them!"

*   *   *

Jim walked arm in arm with Amanda to the elevator. She was reconciled to the fact that he was going to go, no matter what. She held on to him as they stepped inside and the door closed behind them.

The elevator rose swiftly to the ground floor, leaving Amanda's queasy stomach several stories below ground. The door slid open.

Mick smiled as Jim and Amanda stepped out. At his side stood Felicia and the small golden-haired child they had come to call their own. Isabelle had been mute for almost two years, but lately she had begun to speak a little. Jim thought that the shock of losing her family and witnessing the ghastly sights she must have seen at such an early age caused her to temporarily lose that sense.

Like her newfound mother, Felicia, Isabelle had a strange gift. Sometimes they saw, or knew things, that no one else did. This gift had somehow brought them together. A year ago their intuitions had helped save them all from doom. Lately, there had been no such insight.

Mick shook Jim's hand. "Good luck. Don't take any chances. We need you here," Mick said. "If it gets too dangerous, turn around and come back."

Jim nodded. "I will."

He turned to Felicia, who held back her tears as she hugged him, waiting for that flash of insight to danger to sting her body. She almost wished for it to come so she could tell him he mustn't go, that she sensed perils in his journey, but nothing happened. Maybe it was a good thing, she thought, as she pulled away.

Jim reached out for Isabelle but she stepped away from him and hid behind Felicia. Puzzled, he took Amanda's hand and walked toward the door. Isabel fidgeted, then dashed after him. Jim stooped down and she ran into his arms and hugged him hard. He pulled away and looked into her face that shined with innocence, even though she'd been through hell in her short lifetime.

"God helps you," she whispered.

Amanda bent over and put a hand on the little girl's shoulder. "Yes, we know. God will watch over him."

Isabelle shook her head. "No-o-o," she answered, and stroked the hand Amanda had placed on her shoulder. "God helps, touches you. You have his light on you." She took a step backward and smiled. "I see it."

"Thank you, Isabelle," he said, and stood up. He waved to Mick and Felicia across the room and then gave Amanda a lingering kiss.

"Come back to me," she whispered, "or I'll come looking for you."

*   *   *

As Jim walked to where the Humvee was parked, he mentally ran through his checklist. Everything had been taken care of but what concerned him was that he might have forgotten to put something on the list.

He stopped short of the vehicle and stared at Matt, who sat in the passenger seat. Jim opened the door. "What are you doing here, Matt? I told you nobody else goes."

"You need me to go. You might need the help."

"I won't need the help. Now get out."

Matt pointed to a grab bar attached to the dash and Jim groaned when he saw that Matt had handcuffed himself to it.

"Where the hell did you get those things?"

"From the guard shack the other day."

Jim thought of walking back up the hill until Matt got hungry enough to give up but he slid behind the steering wheel instead.

"Does Mick know you're here?"

"He does. He wants me to go, too."

"I'll not be responsible for you if something happens."

"Okay," Matt said. He unlocked the handcuffs from his wrist and let them dangle from the bar.

Jim grinned. "I thought you'd had enough of those before the plague."

"Yeah, well it's sure the first time I put them on willingly," he said, grinning at the small victory.

Jim started the engine and drove up the hill and through the main gate.

𝟣𝟢

Leon was waiting by the chopper when Hal and Jack arrived at the airport. Jack went into the terminal and Hal walked up to Leon. They stared at each other, then Leon gave Hal a light tap on the arm, a silent apology that mended the rift between them.

Leon threw his gear into the back of the chopper. "Where to this morning?" he asked.

"West," Hal answered. "We're going to follow Route 17 northward for a while and see what we see. Maybe as far as Fredericksburg."

Leon was usually indifferent when it came to where they went— one place was as bad as the next—but this trip would be longer than most. Today they would be taking the chopper to its limit on one tank of fuel. Even so, his dread of the trip was less today than in the past.

Leon had finally come to view the excursions as something he had to cope with, regardless of how he felt. This was his duty, his place in this new life, his role to play.

*   *   *

As the sun rose higher, they approached Fredericksburg, a town of more than twenty thousand before the plague of flesh eaters. Now the streets and parking lots were dotted with the slow-moving figures of the walking dead in search of live prey. No one knew if they had the mental capacity to actually form thought, which they would need to conduct a search. It was more likely that they simply roamed about, mostly unaware of their surroundings, until some unfortunate soul happened along, thus triggering the instinct that motivated them.

Even from this altitude, Leon saw the utter decay of the town. Staggering, lurching living dead peppered the landscape everywhere and paper trash blew in the streets like tumbleweeds. Trees felled by storms over the past two years were still on rooftops, their branches like giant skeletal hands gripping the sides of their bearer. Broken windows and smashed doors were abundant in a sea of now-precarious dwellings.

Leon's thoughts went back to the first few days of the plague. He had doubted, as many had, the validity of the details released to the public. An unexplainable and truly strange phenomenon had taken place. The unburied dead were returning to life. It had happened so quickly that there was hardly time to let it all sink in. Most had only begun to understand how bad the situation was before it was all over.

Leon had had run-ins with many of the ghouls before finding safety on Tangier Island. Some of those run-ins had been with friends and family. Correction, the *bodies* of friends and family, not their souls. Bodies were merely the vehicles that harbored a dark and evil presence, possibly demons. Whatever they were, they were not the people he had known.

Television had been full of news reports and talk shows. Government officials and religious-oriented shows all gave their own opinions and theories on what was happening. It's a virus! It's God's doing! It's Mother Nature rebelling for mankind's destruction of the planet, they had cried. All had been blabbering idiots, he thought, while the dead had multiplied at an alarming rate.

A month, he remembered. That's about how long it took for civilization to collapse. That's how long it had taken for mankind to lose their foothold as the dominant species on Earth. Now, two years later, less than one percent of the world's population remained alive. They were outnumbered, one hundred to one.

More than likely there were others out there somewhere but they could not find them.

Anyone with any sense had gotten far away from cities and population centers. The ghouls didn't travel so wherever people were before the plague is where the ghouls are now. That's why Leon thought it was unproductive to search in the cities. Only a fool would venture there.

A warning buzzer sounded and a red light blinked on the instrument panel. The chopper's motor began to sound labored.

Jack dropped the maps he'd been studying and tapped the blinking light in a vein attempt to make it stop, his face white with trepidation.

Hal fought with the stick to keep the chopper level and beads of perspiration began to dot his forehead. He turned to Leon. "Look out the side window and tell me what you see."

Leon moved to the side window. "Black smoke, Hal. I see black smoke!"

Sweat dripped into Hal's eyes. "I've gotta set us down! Jesus, I've gotta set us down!" he said. "We're losing oil pressure!"

Leon jumped into his seat and buckled the safety straps. He moved his weapons closer and looked out the window. Hundreds of ghouls were milling about. Some were peering upward.

"There's a field ahead," Hal said. "I'm going to try to make it!"

The chopper moved forward even as it lost altitude.

Then the motor quit. The sweeping sound of the rotors filled Leon's mind as he clutched the arms of his seat. The sweeping slowed, then stopped. They floated in a deafening silence for what seemed like forever, waiting for the ultimate end of their flight.

The chopper tilted to the right and clipped a tree. The tree broke away, then slammed backward into the tail fin. Leon found himself facing downward as the chopper plummeted nose first to the ground. It was the last thing he remembered.

A cloud of pain engulfed Leon when he opened his eyes. When the chopper slammed into the ground, the force had flung him forward against the safety belts. At the very least, he had some broken ribs.

Leon hung from his straps, looking down toward the front of the chopper, which sat on its nose. Hal and Jack were crushed between the front panel and their seats.

Leon fought to release the straps that confined him. After fidgeting with the buckle, it released and he fell into the back of the cockpit seats with a thud.

Leon picked himself up from his crumpled position, his nostrils burning. The fuel tank had ruptured and fuel was flowing into the compartment, pooling around the two men trapped below him. He needed to free them from the wreckage, fast!

Leon did his best to balance himself by placing one foot on the dash panel and the other on the wrecked metal above the windshield. He faced Hal first and pulled his head away from the twisted metal in front of him. The sight made Leon pull back in revulsion. Hal's face was gone, crushed and torn away by the impact. He was dead.

Leon's breath was jagged, his face flushed. Bile rose in his throat until the acid burned in his mouth. He closed his eyes to fight the panic that threatened to consume him, then put his hands over his face to blot out what he'd just seen.

His heart rate steadied and he removed his hands and opened his eyes. The instrument panel had broken in such a way that a large metal shard had pierced Jack's chest. Dead. Leon was alone.

He stood there for a moment against the inside of the roof, dazed and confused. He tried to convince himself that he was dreaming, that none of this was real. The moment took on a surreal feeling. He watched from outside of his body but he was not emotionally involved in the terror. The surroundings became vague and out of focus.

And then the moans came.

Leon snapped back. He had forgotten about the creatures! His friends were dead and he was stranded. Lord knows how many creatures were closing in on him. How long had he been unconscious after the crash? He found his rifle and the bag of necessities lying against the back of Jack's seat.

He slung the bag over his shoulder and snatched up the rifle. Panic was returning.

A thud against the side of the downed chopper. Another thud. Moans. The unmistakable sound of hands pawing for entrance.

Leon searched for a way to escape. The chopper was wedged between two trees. Escape through the side doors was impossible. The front of the chopper was tight against the ground. His only chance was to climb back up to his seat and try to get out through the window beside it. The fumes were getting worse so he had to work fast.

Leon grabbed the safety harness and pulled himself to his seat, wrapping his legs around the back of it for a better grip. He positioned himself on the seat back and looked out the window. His heart sank. Hordes of ghouls were closing in. He would have to do battle to get past them.

He took one last look at Jack. His death was not caused by a head injury and he briefly considered putting a bullet through his brain to prevent the transformation but there was not enough time, and if the shot created a spark it could ignite the pooling fuel.

Leon leaned back and kicked at the window until it shattered onto the ground. He jumped out and two creatures closed in on him as he lay on the ground. He kicked one away and held the other at arm's length until he could bring it down to the grass beside him.

Leon sprang to his feet. The first ghoul moved in as Leon pulled his pistol from its holster. He shot it in the head and it fell where it stood. He turned and shot the second ghoul on the ground, then took off running through the field.

He spotted an opening and ran for it. Sharp pains engulfed his chest as he ran and a rib popped and moved painfully with each step.

When he reached the road, he stopped for breath and to plan his next move. The largest mob of ghouls was still behind him, near the crashed chopper, but some were moving his way with slow, plodding steps. Other walking dead took notice and moved away from their previous destinations toward Leon. Their moans and cries rose together into an eerie wail of hunger and excitement.

His mind raced. What could he do? Where could he go?

11

It was almost an hour before Jim and Matt got their first look at a ghoul in nearly a year. It wore military fatigues and was slumped over a barbed wire fence beside the road. It remained so motionless that at first it appeared to be dead.

Jim brought the Humvee to a stop fifteen feet away from where the ghoul dangled over the barbed wire. Normally he would've driven on without a second look, but this one garnered his interest. Maybe it was because the ghoul had been army before his death. Allowing a soldier who might have fought gallantly in life and then have his body used in such an obscene manner was immoral.

Maybe Jim was just curious. In any event, the area was clear and he could do that soldier a favor without much danger to Matt or himself.

They stared at the ghoul from the safety of the vehicle. Then it moved. It raised its head in short jerks and strained to gain solid footing without the aid of the fence. It staggered backward before moving toward them. It bounced off the fence, unaware that its path was impeded by the barbed wire.

The ghoul was confused. It stared at the wire barrier, unsure of how to get past it. It released an exasperated howl that gargled in its throat with what must have been the last bit of moisture remaining in its desiccated body. Its lower jaw dropped and hung open, disconnected from the upper portion in a disturbing manner. The jaw swung freely as it thrashed against the fence.

"Look at that thing," Matt said, sickened by the sight. "What the hell happened to it? It looks like it's been out here rotting like hell. I thought they weren't supposed to rot like the regular dead."

Jim opened his door and went to the back of the Humvee. He opened the gate, pulled a tire iron out, and went to the fence where the ghoul thrashed.

Jim covered his nose and mouth with a handkerchief in one hand and with the other he raised the tire iron high and brought it down hard on the creature's head. After a nauseating thud that sounded like a hammer smashing into a ripe melon, fragments of skull and brain matter spewed from the opened cavity. The creature dropped lifelessly to the ground.

Jim wiped the tire iron clean with grass and then returned it to the back of the Humvee. He was still swabbing away foul smelling bits of the creature's cranial contents when he sat in the driver's seat.

"That one wouldn't have lasted much longer anyway," Jim said.

"What do you mean?"

"I mean, that in a little while his brain would've been too severely decayed to have sustained it. It would've simply dropped dead on its own. I'm going by something Sharon Darney told me. The people who died, or were infected and died and then revived when this all first happened, have a lifespan of at least ten years, maybe more. But from the information she's gathered, she believes that one reviving now, or recently, wouldn't survive nearly as long. Their decomposition rate is much faster; they rot faster. Once the brain becomes unable to function, the creature will die. That poor soldier must've survived for quite a while before finally meeting his doom because there wasn't much left of him, assuming Sharon's hypothesis is correct."

"Damn," Matt said, looking at the dead soldier. "Hey! If they're all like that, this could be a cakewalk. I could handle twenty of those things in that condition. Beat 'em right down to the ground easy! That poor bastard looked too rotted to even bite you."

"Don't bet your life on it, Matt," Jim said.

*   *   *

Ten miles later, Jim had to stop again for a tree across the road that blocked their way. Nearby, a country ghost town that had fallen victim to the elements was half hidden in an overgrowth of vegetation. It beckoned for companionship to revive its once quaint beauty and once again become a place with white picket fences, porches with rocking chairs, and flower gardens of yellow and red.

Jim visualized the past splendor of the small community, how it might have been, of children playing ball in the narrow streets, laughing and having fun. The vision faded away in the face of the weed-filled yards and houses with peeling paint and broken windows.

Jim grabbed his rifle and made sure he had plenty of ammunition before leaving the confines of the Humvee. He motioned for Matt to do the same, then removed the chainsaw from the back of the vehicle and went to the fallen tree. He pulled the start cord and blue smoke jetted from the chainsaw in steady streams as he cut through the thick trunk. He had been ready for the possibility of downed trees that could block his path.

Matt watched for trouble, his eyes darting this way and that as Jim sliced through the tree with the expertise of a Montana woodsman. When a twelve-foot piece of the tree's trunk was removed and rolled from their path, Jim put the chainsaw back into the vehicle and brushed the sawdust from his clothes.

An unnatural calmness, empty of life, filled the country air. Even birds refused to make known their presence in the trees around them. It was never more evident to Jim that the passage of days had little meaning anymore outside the boundaries of the mountain. There was no bustling Wall Street, no air traffic in the sky, and no moving vehicles other than their own on the roads. They were in a dead world now.

Jim removed a small canteen from his belt and filled his mouth with water. He would waste no more time than needed. They still had quite a journey before they got to their destination. They'd be hard pressed to go to Tangier and if it proved to be in vain, turn around and get back to Mount Weather before dark.

Spending the night in the unprotected wild was not on the top of his list of things preferred. There was nowhere he could think of that would offer them the needed security through the night. Weapons, food, extra gas, even a small generator, were loaded into the back of the Humvee, all squeezed in around a motorcycle, but they were not equipped for a prolonged trip. These days one could not go to sleep no matter how safe and expect to wake in the same condition. Not out here. He'd learned from past experience that security was something never taken for granted.

Jim turned at the cries of anguish from behind him. Seven grotesque creatures staggered from the small village beside the road, attracted by the noise of the chainsaw. Their ragged clothes and deteriorated features were visible proof of what they were.

Matt ran to Jim's side and raised his weapon. Jim put his hand on the weapon and pushed it away. "No," he said. "We don't have the time for it. No use in wasting the ammo. We're not here to kill every one we see. Let's just move on."

Matt lowered the gun and wasted no time getting back inside the vehicle.

Jim drove through the opening he had cut out and watched in the rearview mirror as the gaggle of flesh eaters faded into the distance.

Matt hummed a tune from an old song to calm his frayed nerves. "We're gonna be okay, you know? We're gonna be okay," he reassured himself between his humming.

Jim nodded. "Yeah, we're gonna be okay."

He prayed they were right. He was sure they would encounter situations a lot worse than this one. There was still a long way to go.

12

The small convoy came to a stop in the road two miles before Culpeper, Virginia. Hathaway stepped out and spread his maps over the hood of the lead truck.

"We'll follow this road until we get to Fredericksburg. Then we'll take 95 and 64 to Norfolk. There shouldn't be too much trouble as long as we stay on the highways."

Jake nodded as Hathaway refolded the maps.

Hathaway felt confident as he glanced at his watch. By this time tomorrow, Bates would be dealt with and command would logically fall to him. It shouldn't have come to this. He should've been given the post in the first place but now it was out of his hands. The plan had been set into motion.

He would ride back into camp in a few days and accept his new position. He would finally have the power he so deserved, small though it was. Power over less than a thousand people wouldn't have meant much before the plague, but now it would mean so much more.

An army one thousand strong could go out and effectively take whatever they wanted. There would be alcoves of other survivors who would be dominated and added to his numbers, the undesirables weeded out in the process. Bates was right about one thing: They should be prepared for the possibility that foreign nations might move in and take over.

He didn't see this as an immediate threat but as soon as the plague was over it was something they would have to be prepared for. It would be a race to see who could get organized first.

"Sir?" a voice said. "Sir?"

Hathaway turned to find Donald Covington, a fresh-faced boy of twenty-two, a kid who looked up to him as a role model. His hands shook as he waved a quick salute.

"What is it?" Hathaway asked.

"There are some of them coming in from the west, down by a farmhouse. Looks to be about eight or ten."

Hathaway's expression hardened. "There's *what* coming, boy?"

The boy fidgeted. "Monsters, sir. Ghouls."

"The next time you have something to report, make sure you clarify what you're reporting. To be efficient, we need facts, hard accurate facts. Battles are lost because of poor communication. Do you understand?"

"Yes, sir."

"Good!" Hathaway beamed, his voice suddenly cheerful. "Now, how far away are they?"

"A couple hundred yards."

"Then there's no reason to worry just yet. It'll take them ten or fifteen minutes to get here, as slow as they move. Make sure we keep a good lookout. If any get too close, shoot the goddamned things in the head and be done with it."

"Yes, sir." The boy gave another quick salute and disappeared around the truck.

Hathaway smirked at the young lad's nervousness. He was the least experienced in the group, brought along, basically, to groom as Hathaway saw fit. He was little more than an errand boy but he'd learn.

Hathaway walked away from the front of the lead truck and into everyone's view.

"Listen up!" he ordered and everyone moved closer. "I stopped us here before we enter Culpeper for a reason. This will be the first time we will pierce a formerly populated area. We will surely encounter the undead in larger numbers than any of you have seen in a while. I expect everyone to keep their wits about them and behave in a manner befitting what you are, trained soldiers. We will proceed through town without stopping unless it is absolutely necessary, and continue on until we reach Fredericksburg."

Hathaway glanced toward the pack of ungainly creatures slowly approaching through the field. "Move out."

The small convoy of trucks roared to life and moved on.

13

Leon took off in a foot race against the horde of walking dead that closed in on him from all directions. Groups of decomposing creatures clutched at him as he ran past, gasping for air. They were too slow to catch him as he dashed by. The morning breeze carried their cries in waves of high-pitched wails that assaulted his ears to the point of madness. He blocked them from his mind as he ran.

His predicament was grave. He was smack dab in the middle of Fredericksburg, with several miles between himself and the Interstate highway running south. To reach home, that was his best bet. If he could find a working automobile it would make his situation less perilous.

Leon ran until exhaustion overtook him. He found a place to momentarily hide, a truck that had come to rest on its side. Careful not to let any of the creatures see him, he slipped out of sight behind the truck. His breathing became more even and he sought to devise a plan.

He was unfamiliar with the town in which he found himself stranded. He knew the general direction of the Interstate from seeing it through the window of the chopper. With trash, trees, and wrecked cars littering the roads, it would be difficult to reach it, even with motorized transportation. He tried to clear the blanketing haze that had suddenly formed around his thoughts.

"A car," he whispered. He pounded his clinched fist into an open hand. "Focus, focus!"

When he got into a crouched position to peek out from behind the wreck, he was blindsided by a heavy blow. He reeled backward, falling into the grass by the roadside. His head throbbed and his ears rang with a deafening intensity. A large, shadowy figure grabbed his boot and pulled. Leon was yanked from the grass and heaved back onto the road as the ghoul continued to drag him.

Leon reached for the wrecked truck as he was pulled past it but his grasp was broken by the seven-foot specter currently in control. It walked sluggishly, legs bent at the knees, shoulders slumped as it dragged its feet step by plodding step, all the while pulling Leon, who thrashed and twisted against its hold on him.

The huge ghoul still retained a lot of its strength. Usually they were weak, attacking in packs to make up for their decrepit and decomposing bodies, but this giant handled Leon with ease.

Leon's fingernails dug into the cracked asphalt as he dangled at the end of the big ghoul's grasp like the quarry at the end of a woodsman's hunt. Why wasn't it attacking? he wondered. Was it carrying him away to feed without interruption from others? No, he thought, they weren't smart enough to figure out something like that.

Leon heard the cries of others. He raised his head. He was not being dragged off to some hidden location so the big ghoul could feed alone, he was being taken into a waiting crowd of them. It was going to share him!

Leon thrashed at his captor again. He fought with all his strength. He kicked at the hand that held him but the ghoul continued walking, unaffected by the blows. On Leon's third kick, the giant released its grip and Leon moved, crablike, backward from it, then clamored to his feet.

The ghoul turned and lurched forward, but Leon had already moved beyond his reach. Its maw hung open and a milky slime dripped from it onto the ground as it howled in frustration at its failure. It flailed its arms about like a child throwing a temper tantrum. The others, who had been waiting patiently, began to writhe and wail in unison with the big ghoul and quickened their pace toward him.

Leon turned quickly and once again found himself on the run. His main objective remained to find a working vehicle.

The first prospect proved to be useless when he discovered no key in the ignition. He moved to the next one, a silver sedan with a sunroof, and leaped inside. It had a key, but the battery lacked enough charge to turn the engine.

Leon pounded the steering wheel and jumped out. Several creatures exited the open doorways of buildings lining the street. More topped the crest in the road behind him. He would have no time for rest. No time to try to hotwire any of the cars without keys. It was vital that he keep moving or he'd find himself quickly surrounded, with no escape.

Keeping an even pace, he checked each and every vehicle as he jogged down the streets of Fredericksburg toward the Interstate. All of them either had no keys or wouldn't start after two years of sitting idle.

The ghoulish crowd following Leon grew larger by the minute. For every hundred feet he jogged through the streets, a few more creatures joined in the chase.

Leon did his best to keep silent, unlike his pursuers who made enough noise in their agitated state to literally wake the dead.

Ghouls began to appear ahead of him. If he was to make it out of the city alive, he would have to endure a sustained run to lose the following crowd. It would not give him the time to check more vehicles, but there was no other choice for now. He could not shoot his way out; there were simply too many.

Leon increased his pace to a moderate run. The slow-moving horde of zombies quickly fell behind. Once he lost them from view, he changed direction and turned down a side street. He kept the same pace through two more intersections and then turned south again onto a four-lane road.

He suddenly found himself in the commercial sprawl of Fredericksburg. Historic buildings had lined the streets previously but now new structures clogged every square inch of the four-lane highway on which he now stood—strip malls, fast food joints, gas stations, convenience stores.

For the time being, all was quiet. Leon turned to face every direction several times before feeling secure enough to settle down on the curb beside the thruway.

He scanned the area for abandoned cars. A green van rested precariously against a telephone pole in front of an office building, the front wheels three feet off the ground, the front end crushed into a V shape that wrapped around the pole like a hotdog bun.

A pickup at the gas pumps of a service station was probably abandoned when its user found the station closed and his truck out of gas. He'd check it anyway, but not before he had a short rest on the curb.

His chances of reaching home were slim to none. He began to think he'd have been better off dying in the crash with his friends. At least their deaths were quick and painless. It was a preferred option to what might be in store for him.

Leon tilted his head back and fell, exhausted, into a patch of grass behind him. He gazed at the pale blue sky. It would be so easy to fall asleep. Just closing his eyes would do it.

Through the soft but steady gust of wind he heard a faint sound. Slight as it was, it was familiar to him. The cries of the undead. The mobs were getting closer.

PART

II

Un-caged Hate

14

"Our best bet is to follow that road through town and get on the Interstate headed south," Jim said. He lowered the binoculars and handed them to Matt.

Matt looked over the scene below. They had taken a small detour from their path to the top of a hill to gain a better perspective of what lay ahead. Up to this point, their trip had been mainly uneventful. They had stayed on back roads, away from towns, whenever possible. This would be the most dangerous leg of their journey until they reached the coast.

Matt scanned the area from left to right with the binoculars. He almost missed the small finger of flame and black smoke barely visible behind a stand of trees in the distance. He refocused the lens. It was a mile or so north of the direction they were headed.

"I've got something here, Jim," Matt said, and handed the binoculars back to him. "There's smoke down there but I can't make out what's causing it."

Jim studied the situation through the binoculars. "It could be caused by lightning. Looks like maybe a tree was struck or something."

"Do we check it out?"

"Absolutely," Jim replied.

The Humvee came to a stop beside a large field on the outskirts of town. At its far edge, a burning mass was wedged between several rows of trees. The trees, and even the grass around the burning object, were ablaze and would block them from getting too close.

Jim shifted to four-wheel drive and barreled into the field, ignoring the rolls and dips of the terrain as the Humvee plowed its way through with ease. They got as close as thirty feet before the burning grass forced him to come to a halt.

The two men wasted no time exiting the Humvee, weapons in hand. Silhouettes of creatures lumbered about in the distance. The moving shapes were featureless and dark but nonetheless identifiable but too far away to be an immediate danger.

Jim and Matt watched the object burn without speaking. They knew what it meant...there were other survivors! The helicopter before them had recently crashed, very recently, in fact. Even if no one survived the crash, it had to come from somewhere and that's where the others would be.

"What now?" Matt asked.

Jim gave a quick glance to the approaching figures still a safe distance away. "Nothing changes. We do what we came to do. We move on."

"Yeah, but what about this?" Matt inquired, pointing to the wreck with the barrel of his gun. "Shouldn't we try to find out where it came from? I mean, we did come looking for survivors and it would seem that this is pretty good proof that there are survivors. We can't just leave now without knowing."

"And how would you suggest we find the answers to your questions, Matt? Shall we go over there and ask some of those friendly folk on their way to greet us right now? Maybe they will know. Hell, maybe one or more of them were in this thing when it crashed. I'm sure that..."

Jim's voice trailed off. He had actually done something he'd only seen on television or in the movies. He had given himself an idea in the middle of chewing someone out, sort of like McHale of *McHale's Navy*, or the Professor on *Gilligan's Island*. When they had rattled on how impossible their friends' ideas were, they realized that somewhere inside those far-out plans was the masterpiece of an idea, though Jim doubted his idea would be a masterpiece. Still, it was worth a shot.

Jim pawed through the gear in the back of the vehicle until he found what he had been looking for: a climbing rope. "Get in, Matt! I've got an idea."

Jim worked with the rope for a moment, then threw it between the seats and drove the Humvee straight at the approaching mob of ghouls.

"What the hell are you doing?" Matt yelled. "This is the wrong way, man! We want to go that way!" Matt pointed toward the road they had left in order to enter the field, his eyes wild with fear.

"Just calm down, Matt. I'm not going to get too close. Lock your door."

Matt pushed the lock down, hard. "Hell, man, we are already too close!"

Jim slowed as he approached the army of walking corpses and began driving between them. Bloodied fists and severed limbs thumped and pounded at the Humvee. Rotted faces pressed toward the reinforced windows, their eyes glazed with a milky film.

Matt sank down in his seat.

"I'm looking for something in particular," Jim said. "Pay attention!"

Matt sat up higher.

"I'm looking for a fresh kill. Someone who looks like they haven't been dead too long. Keep your eyes peeled."

Matt did his best to do as Jim requested but it was difficult to look at the ghouls up close. He wanted to shut his eyes until it was over. Worst case scenarios filled his thoughts. What if the vehicle broke down? What if they got stuck in the bumpy field? He couldn't shake the dread.

Then he saw it.

"There!" Matt pointed.

One of the creatures had been burned beyond recognition. His smoldering clothes hung in scorched strands from his blackened body. He staggered along the outer edges of the pack.

Jim steered toward it.

Once he got near the chosen ghoul, Jim pulled a safe distance ahead of the pack and stopped. Rope in hand, he jumped out. He loosened the knot he had made in the rope and started twirling it high over his head. When a large circle had formed, he tossed it at the selected ghoul. The rope landed below its shoulders and Jim pulled the hoop tighter around the ghoul's arms. He wrapped the other end of the rope around his door handle and got back into the driver's seat. Tires spitting dirt and dust, he drove away from the pack, dragging the ghoul along behind.

After he had driven a safe distance, he stopped the vehicle and grabbed his rifle. Jim aimed for the head, squeezed the trigger, and the creature was dead.

"Keep a look out while I check it out," he told Matt.

Matt got out and leaned against the door, his rifle propped on his thigh, and watched as the mob inched closer. They could only afford to stay for a few minutes before the mob got too close. More creatures were closing in from the opposite direction. They had attracted quite a lot of unwanted attention.

Matt glanced at Jim, who was rummaging through the dead man's pockets. "Hurry up, man!" Matt yelled, his voice cracking. "We're gonna have company real soon."

Jim stood and walked away from the smoldering creature.

"Find anything?"

"Nothing. Everything on him was too badly burned." Jim sighed. "Maybe he was on that chopper, maybe he wasn't. He could've gotten too close after the crash and then caught on fire in the burning grass. There was something in his inner jacket pocket that looked like a map or something, but I couldn't make anything out. It just crumbled in my hand. We'd better move on before they get any closer."

"We've done all we can do here," Matt said, noticing Jim's mood. "There's no use in feeling guilty."

"I don't feel guilty," Jim said. "Disappointed but not guilty."

"Yeah, me, too. It would've been nice to find someone already. It would've saved us the trip to Tangier."

"No, it wouldn't have saved us the trip to Tangier," Jim said. "Even if we had found someone here, we'd still go to Tangier. That's where the signal came from. But it would've been a nice bonus to find others here. I'm hoping there are a lot more people out here than we thought. In any event, it's time to go," he said, eyeing the approaching mob.

Jim couldn't help but think that, had they arrived sooner, they may have been able to save one or more of the occupants of the chopper. He knew it wasn't his fault but from the beginning of the plague it always seemed to be too little, too late. He hoped things would change once they found their way to Tangier Island.

Matt opened the map of Fredericksburg he had taken from the Mount Weather complex and traced the route Jim had decided to take. Matt advised him what streets to take for the safest passage through the city to the Interstate.

"Turn here," he said, just in time for Jim to make a hard turn, tires screaming on the paved street.

Another near miss when Matt yelled, "LEFT HERE!"

Jim made another quick turn onto a larger road, then another quick swerve to miss a large crowd of ghouls clustered together, unseen, until the Humvee was practically on top of them.

Jim sped through the crowd and drove on before finding a spot to pull over to the side of the road. His hands gripped the steering wheel and his jaw muscle twitched.

"Damn it, Matt! Will you please give me a little more warning on where to go than before we're in the middle of the intersection?"

Matt held his hands up, the lighter palms toward Jim. "Sorry, sorry! I'm doing my best. Maybe if you slow down a bit..."

Matt's words trailed off as three camouflage-painted trucks with mounted machine guns came to a halt around their vehicle, blocking their path. Armed men in fatigues assumed positions around the trucks and trained their weapons on them.

Jim and Matt, stunned at this turn of events, sat perfectly still. One move could send rapid-fire bullets blazing into the Humvee.

A man stepped forward and stood in front of them. He looked beyond Jim and Matt to the creatures a half mile or so down the road, then he focused his attention on Jim and Matt.

He was a strong-looking man, bulked up in his upper body, probably mid-to late-thirties, with short brownish red hair and a thin mustache that ended at the corners of his mouth. For a moment he simply glared, as though contemplating his next decision.

"Get out," he ordered. "Slowly."

Jim and Matt moved in even steps to the front of the Humvee.

"I'm Lieutenant Robert Hathaway. I am in charge of this unit of the Virginia Freedom Fighters. Who are you?"

Matt drew a breath to speak but Jim placed a hand on his chest and he stopped.

Hathaway walked closer. "I won't waste time with you," he sneered and cast a quick glance toward the advancing horde. "Who sent you?"

Jim and Matt remained silent.

Hathaway moved in closer to Matt, their noses two inches apart. Hathaway sniffed, then wrinkled his nose. "You stink, boy," he taunted. "Didn't your mamma teach you to take a bath?"

Matt felt his anger rise but he remained silent, trying to gauge the situation.

Hathaway stepped over to face Jim. "What are you, some kinda nigger lover? Are you with our nigger-lovin' government?"

"I know who you are, mister," Jim growled through clenched teeth. "I know your kind. You're a disease, like those walking piles of filth back there. You should've been wiped out with the rest of the garbage in this world."

Hathaway snickered. "Disease. Filth. That's pretty good. That's pretty damned good." He stepped away and snapped his finger at one of his subordinates and pointed to Matt. Before Jim could react, the other man placed a well-aimed bullet into Matt's heart. Matt slumped to the ground, a large pool of blood forming under him.

Jim howled and lunged at Hathaway, who slammed the butt of his pistol into Jim's skull. The blow knocked Jim from his feet and nearly rendered him unconscious. By the time he regained his wits, he was on his knees, held by two militia soldiers.

"You son of a bitch," Jim cursed as he fought to remain awake. "I'll kill you for that."

Hathaway grabbed him by the hair and tilted his face upward to meet his hardened gaze. The pain from the blow to the head and the fact that his hair was being pulled from that very spot sent him in and out of blackness.

"Now, you tell me where you're from," Hathaway barked. "That vehicle you're driving is government issue. Where's your home base?"

Jim spit in Hathaway's face. It dripped from his cheek until he wiped it away with his sleeve.

Again the butt of the pistol came, and so did the blackness.

15

When Jim came to, he was bound with rope and lying face down in the back of one of the trucks that moved swiftly and smoothly. His mouth and lips were dry and peppered with debris from the bottom of the truck bed. His head ached from the pistol whipping and his hands were tied tightly together beneath him.

He tried to clear his head of painful cobwebs before giving any outward indication of regaining consciousness. The memory of Matt's cold-blooded murder replayed over and over in his mind.

Jim twisted his hands back and forth, testing the bonds, but to no avail. After several tries, he surrendered to his predicament for the time being, then rolled over onto his back and sat up. He pushed himself into a corner of the truck bed with his feet.

A single militia soldier sat guard on one of the wheel wells. As Jim situated himself for a better view of his predicament, the soldier trained his weapon on him.

The barrel of the mounted machine gun bolted to the center of the truck bed swayed slightly as the vehicle roared down the highway. It moved with the motion of the truck, then came to a stop, its muzzle automatically aiming at Jim as though some unseen force had directed it to do so.

The soldier grinned.

From the location of the sun, Jim figured they were moving south, the direction he wanted to go but not the way he wanted to get there. He knew his captors. Not personally, but he had heard of them.

Six years before, several black churches and colleges had been set ablaze. The Virginia Freedom Fighters were the prime suspects but no one was ever brought to trial. The evidence had been thrown out because of an illegal search and seizure. The Freedom Fighters were little more than a militarized Ku Klux Klan, their beliefs founded in white supremacy and anti-government rhetoric.

Believing that the U.S. government was becoming a dictatorship bent on controlling every aspect of American people's lives, this particular organization gave militias a bad name.

Jim eyed the machine gun pointing at him. If he could break free from his bindings, he would have a chance to escape. Other trucks like the one he was held captive in traveled ahead of them. There were none behind. Three other men rode in the cab, separated only by the rear window. For the time being they paid no attention to the goings on in the back.

Jim wrestled with the ropes on his wrist.

"You get those off and I'll have to shoot ya," the soldier said, watching him closely.

Jim stopped his struggle. "You're going to shoot me anyway, aren't you?"

"That's not up to me," he snickered. "Unless you make me have to. Then I'll put a bullet in your brain. Don't want ya gettin' back up now, do we?"

Jim looked at the sun again. His best guess put the time at about two o'clock. He had been unconscious for at least two hours.

"Where are we going?"

"You'll see when we get there."

"You afraid to tell me?"

The soldier roared with laughter, then cocked his head. "Now why the hell should I be afraid of you? You someone to be afraid of?"

Jim lowered his gaze. "Nope, I guess I'm just along for the ride," he said, trying his best to prevent the hatred he was feeling from showing in his voice.

"That's what I thought. You didn't seem like much back there. You or your nigger friend."

Jim's jaw twitched with anger. He fought the urge to explode onto the man, tied hands and all.

"His name was Matt. He was a better man then you will ever be." Jim stared through the hair hanging over his eyes to catch the man's reaction.

"He's a dead man," the soldier said. "And so will you be if you don't shut that filthy mouth of yours."

Jim lowered his gaze and purposely allowed the hard knot of hatred to rise in him as he reclined in the corner of the truck bed. He had felt red-hot anger at various times in his life but never before had he experienced the swell of malignant emotion that now threatened to overcome him. Use it, he thought, control it.

"You could all be dead men real soon," he whispered. "The whole damned lot of you, and that won't be a bad thing."

16

This wasn't working out, Leon thought as he stepped onto the Interstate. He was still a long way from home, without the benefit of motorized transportation. At least he had left the hordes of creatures behind. He was now alone on a long stretch of highway leading south that would take several days to walk to the coast. The thought of closing his eyes for sleep terrified him. He would surely wake to meet his fate at the hands of rotting corpses.

What were the odds of that happening? Each week they took their lives into their own unprepared hands by getting into that chopper and flying around searching in vain, all the while making half-assed repairs and safety checks. None of them were experienced enough to ensure a safe trip each and every time. Hal could fly the chopper but he knew only enough about the mechanics to fix the most obvious problems. It was a bad idea with good intentions. That was the trouble with good intentions.

This was certainly the road to hell, two dead and another hopelessly stranded, probably soon to join them.

His boot heels clicked on the asphalt as he walked, even though he tried his best to walk quietly. In his mind, any noise was too much and the tapping sound with each step seemed to amplify around him in hammering, mammoth thumps. He moved to the side of the road and walked in the grass.

Occasionally, Leon could make out buildings through the trees that lined each side of the sprawling highway. It would only take one of those ghouls loitering in the distance to take notice of him and all the nearby creatures would swarm.

He had been walking for what seemed like hours, at times catching glimpses of creatures wandering around exit ramps and under bridges. Most took no notice of him as he quietly crept by.

Now, squatting by the road, he eyed a car in the middle of the Interstate ahead. A lone figure stood at its side, staring into the direction of the evening sun. Too far to determine if it was a ghoul or living person, Leon took no chances as he watched, motionless and low to the ground.

The only weapons Leon had were his pistol and rifle. Using either to destroy the creature, if it was one, would bring others to his location from all around. But he had to do something because it stood in his way. He could simply run by it but it would tag along and that would attract others. Besides, he needed to check out that car.

Leon went to the other side of the road and down the embankment between the lanes running in the opposite direction. It offered him better cover and at the same time it put him in a better position to come up from behind, unnoticed.

He moved up the gully, carefully guiding each step to prevent discovery. Halfway there, he stopped to contemplate his course of action. He needed another weapon, something that didn't make as much noise as a gun, something solid for smashing in the creature's skull.

Leon searched the ground around him. He picked up several rocks but all were too small to be of any use. Then he caught a glimmer of light reflecting off an object fifty feet in the gully ahead. He crawled on all fours to it. It was an iron pipe about three feet long and crooked in the middle.

Leon reached out and pulled it to him. Holding it close to his chest, he shimmied up the embankment between the lanes and behind the figure standing by the car. At the top of the embankment, he studied it for signs of life. The clothes were ragged and covered with filth. It leaned awkwardly over the roof of the car, its head tilted up.

He raised the pipe and in three running steps Leon was close enough to strike a fatal blow to its brain. He swung hard and the pipe struck home. The creature twirled around as its body collapsed to the ground. The head flew away and bounced, rat-a-tat-tat, down the road.

Leon jumped away, surprised by the ease of his attack and by what he now realized was a mannequin, a plastic clothing store dummy. Someone had wired it to the roof of the car, for what purpose, he couldn't imagine, but when he hit it, the wire that had been wrapped around its neck broke and it fell to the ground.

He let loose a sigh of relief but bewilderment lingered as he stared down at the dummy on the ground. "Bizarre," he whispered.

Leon jumped into the driver's seat, happy to see keys in the ignition. He feared another disappointment if it didn't start. "Come on, come on," he cooed, then turned the key.

The engine sputtered to life and Leon pumped the gas pedal because the motor wanted to quit. It finally steadied into an even thrum and Leon howled with excitement. He gleefully pounded the steering wheel at this turn of good fortune.

He had found a way home.

17

The imposing aircraft carrier towered above every other ship in the port. Over a thousand feet from bow to stern, other ships paled in comparison.

A thick haze hung over the bay, contrasting the clarity of the vessels close to shore against the miasma that surrounded the giant carrier almost a mile out in the bay. It was a vessel of might and absolute power yet it had been powerless to prevent the total collapse of humanity. A multi-million dollar joke left to one day rust and sink to the bottom.

Jim turned his face away from the great ship and back to his immediate predicament.

They moved slowly now that they had entered Newport News. The ever-narrowing street was littered with abandoned cars and other debris. Jim watched as they passed less-than-capable ghouls who crawled or staggered from alleys and doorways. They were now mostly rotting piles of stinking flesh due to the elements and passage of time.

For a few moments the massive carrier fell from view as the caravan of trucks wound their way down the forgotten street toward the bay through the old section of town. It appeared again a few minutes later, even more impressive as they negotiated the road leading into the harbor. Larger than life, it gleamed in the evening sun. Its weighty presence commanded respect and awe from all who beheld its majesty. *U.S.S. Nimitz* it proudly proclaimed.

Jim found his footing in the moving vehicle and stood up behind the cab. His wrists were raw from the bindings he yearned to rip free.

They were almost there. A few hundred yards and they'd be along the shore. In spite of his situation, he felt a spike of excitement. The ship mesmerized him. It was such a magnificent creation that he found it hard to divert his eyes.

"Sit down or I'll knock you down!" his captor bellowed.

Jim turned and glared angrily but did as he was told. "What are we doing here?"

The man moved forward. "We're saving the world, or what's left of it, anyway."

"Really?" Jim said. "How's that?"

The man didn't answer. His attention was focused on the harbor.

"By killing innocent people?" Jim asked. "Is that how you'll save the world? What kind of insanity are you people living out here?"

The militiaman delivered a vicious kick to Jim's stomach, sending him sprawling in the bottom of the truck bed. The force of the blow sent the air from Jim's lungs.

"Insanity? You want insanity? How's six thousand years of war for insanity?" He kicked Jim again. "People living in fear every day of what's to come next. How about working your ass off for every little portion of shit that's dished out for you while others get it handed to them so they can sit on their lazy asses and collect welfare, then spend our hard-earned money buying crack and heroin. How about fucking dead people walking? How's that for insanity?" Drool hung from the man's lower lip. "You just lay there and keep quiet. I don't need to explain myself to you. You just shut the fuck up!"

Jim gulped oxygen back into his lungs, then settled back into his corner. His determination hardened and his hatred for these people grew darker, a feeling he was not accustomed to. It was not in his nature to feel so much hatred for anything or anyone. It would be easy to lose control and in doing so, lose rationality. It would be his downfall. If he was to escape, he had to keep his wits about him.

The trucks stopped and militiamen spilled from them, taking protective positions around the caravan. Each aimed their weapons in a way that covered a full three hundred and sixty degree swathe.

As Hathaway barked orders, several of the men boarded a small yacht anchored close to where they were parked. The yacht was a Languard Nelson 113, about forty feet long, with an aft cabin. Both the flag of the United States and the Confederacy waved in the breeze.

The men disappeared below deck.

Jim watched, cataloguing his surroundings, until the guard forced him from the back of the truck, pushing him toward the yacht and Hathaway.

Hathaway watched as the men carried out his orders without question. His eyes gleamed, drunk with the fix of power he possessed. And, like a junkie, he craved more.

The boat's diesel motors growled in unison as the men finished their tasks of prepping it for the trip. Jim watched as, one by one, the men who had taken positions around them moved close to the boat and once again took up a defensive posture.

Ghouls began moving closer from every direction but the men refrained from firing their weapons. They were well trained. It would be a waste of ammo to fire on them unless they were in immediate danger. Others would soon replace them.

Hathaway pushed Jim toward the boat. "Get on!" he barked.

Jim climbed aboard. "Keep your wits," he muttered to himself as he stood on deck. Hathaway was the last to come aboard, flanked by Jake, his second in command.

A simple nod of Hathaway's head and the boat began to move. Once it was away from the shore, it turned around and headed in the direction of the *Nimitz*. They were going to the aircraft carrier.

Jim looked at Hathaway, who returned the look with a smug grin. He was indeed in power but was he the leading figure of this outlaw group? How many more were willing to carry out the dastardly deeds that these few were disposed to do?

Jim had to find out.

18

Sharon Darney marveled at the sight. For only the second time in two years she had caught a glimpse of the culprit. Black and featureless, it darted back and forth on the screen, unsure where to go now that it was separated from its host.

There was nowhere for it to hide, nowhere to escape her study. Trapped between the microscope slides and exposed, it still remained very active. It was the same creature that two years before had offered the last gift. This microbe would not escape. She would learn from it this time. She would find out why the dead rose.

The tiny organism's host, a reanimated corpse of a man in his thirties, was strapped to an examination table separated from the main room of Sharon's laboratory by Plexiglas walls. The reanimate had been in her custody for the full two years, except for her brief stay with the other survivors at the prison. He was the only surviving corpse upon their reoccupation of the Mount Weather Underground and presented her with another puzzle to unravel.

After war had been waged between the two opposing factions, more than a hundred bodies had littered the corridors throughout the facility. Before she could make her escape, those bodies had become undead corpses in search of human prey.

Normally, they could have expected longevity of ten or more years but that had not been the case. Only months later, the ghouls were once again motionless and inactive. It had made their return to the complex easier but had created another perplexing riddle to solve. Why did every corpse in the underground cease to function except her original specimen still strapped to the table?

Unlike the others, he had been captured up top and brought below for study. The others had been killed below ground and then had revived but their existence had ended shortly thereafter. They had simply dropped dead. Now that she had another piece of the puzzle trapped on the glass slide, she would find out more.

The logical place to begin would be to match the organism to something already cataloged. They had tried this before, with no success. If she could find a close similarity in another organism, she might have a point of reference, somewhere to begin.

Sharon considered the image of the tiny life form on the computer screen. Dark and unremarkable, it resembled nothing she had ever seen. She would go through the records again. The computer banks had held information on every microbe, germ, and disease known to man. She would go through them one by one until she had covered them all.

*   *   *

Felicia sipped her tea at the kitchen table. Oddly enough, the drink had flavor. That was odd because Felicia knew she was dreaming. There should be no sensation of flavor in dreams. She could also smell the honeysuckle that grew heavy against the back yard fence, entwining the pickets so thickly that it formed a privacy barrier between her grandmother's house and the one next door.

The sight of the honeysuckle in full bloom through the kitchen window brought to mind memories of her childhood, of afternoons running about and greedily sucking the nectar from the flowering thicket one tiny drop at a time.

Ever since her last night at the prison, her sleep had been devoid of the pleasant dreams that had carried her away from a dead world to the company of her beloved grandmother. In those dreams, her grandmother had warned her of the impending doom that was to fall upon their sanctuary. She had also warned her of "the wolf."

The wolf had arrived in the form of a deranged preacher with thoughts of godhood and a band of devoted followers intent on destroying them all.

That had been their last night at the prison. That was the night the wolf and his followers met their fate at the hands of thousands of rotting corpses. The night that Felicia's side lost half of their numbers. Felicia was nearly killed and she had concluded that her near-death experience had brought about the end of her "gift."

That night, less than seventy survivors escaped their prison stronghold and found their way to the place they were now, a seven-story hole in the ground with all the conveniences of home, an underground military complex constructed in anticipation of a nuclear war or other national emergency.

It offered a safe haven, a world without sunlight and warm summer breezes. As safe as it was, it sucked the life from Felicia a little more each day by depriving her of the barest essentials, like real sunlight that warmed the face and body and the power of spirit that had given her.

She was depressed. If not for Mick, she was sure her sanity would've been lost long ago.

Felicia took another sip of tea and studied her dream surroundings. Usually her grandmother was there to greet her but today she was alone. It was daytime in her dream but surely it was nighttime in her real world.

In her real world, she was nestled close to Mick, his arm wrapped tightly around her, holding her fear in check during a late evening nap. Mick's presence offered a sense of security but the nagging reality of the dead world above them was ever present, like waves crashing against the beach, ever eroding her grasp on sanity.

Perhaps the dream had come to her again to ease her pain, a gift from her grandmother who felt her building anguish. It was a warming thought and Felicia took comfort in it as she drank her tea.

*   *   *

Amanda awoke on the floor of her kitchen where she had cried herself to sleep with grief over her dead husband and lost dreams. Today was the day. She would have to make her escape today before too many of the creatures converged on her house. Today she would still have a chance.

She groped about in the semi-darkness, throwing essentials into her backpack and making a mental checklist. Be sure to take all the shotgun shells, and this time remember the damned safety. Right, right. The first thing she had to do was end his suffering.

Amanda slipped on her jacket and backpack and grabbed the gun. Her heart was pounding as she readied herself to do what had to be done. She turned the deadbolt as quietly as she could, hearing the muffled shuffling on the other side of the door. She turned the lock on the doorknob, swung the door inward, stepped back, and raised the shotgun.

The sunlight blinded her and silhouetted the dark figure of her dead husband in the doorway. He took a stumbling step toward her and she saw the dead visage and milky eyes of Jim Workman.

Amanda choked the rising scream in her throat and the strangling sound that emerged from her echoed in the empty lobby as she sat bolt upright in the easy chair she had stationed herself in to await Jim's return. She sucked in gulps of air and then leaned over and vomited into the wastebasket.

Amanda paced the floor, her arms folded. She held them tightly to her to keep away the feeling that she would literally explode with worry. Since Jim had left her, feelings of helplessness had returned until she thought she would burst at the seams. Sleep offered no respite.

She cursed Jim under her breath. It was inconsiderate of him to cause her to worry so. It was uncaring of him to go off and leave her alone like this. "Uncaring, inconsiderate asshole!" she said.

She regretted the small outburst as soon as it left her lips.

What if something had happened? That was an awful thing to say. She swore to herself then and there that she would never allow it again. The next time, she would go where he goes, do what he does, and stay by his side. Never again would she be the mindful little woman who stays behind to wait and worry.

19

Jim Workman watched as the fading light of the day filtered through the bars of the ship's brig. The sound of metal tumblers turning in the lock brought his mind into focus.

Two men stood before him. One of them was a scruffy giant of six-foot-eight with a crooked nose and missing teeth. He grinned at Jim with a jack-o'-lantern smile with his weapon trained on him.

The other, smaller man was clean cut and presented himself with standard military discipline. He stood straight, one arm at his side, the other on the pistol grip in his holster.

"Lieutenant Hathaway wants to see you," the smaller man said. "Stand up and keep your arms to your side, sir. Walk ahead of us and don't make any quick moves."

Jim stood up, careful not to startle the unkempt giant into squeezing the trigger, and walked through the door into the corridor ahead of the two men.

Jim kept an even pace as he walked down the narrow, darkened hallway. The small man walked ahead of him, the large oaf followed behind.

In Jim's mind, he envisioned the Captain Kirk deception of bending over in make-believe pain, turning on the oaf behind and taking his weapon, then killing them both. Even if the outlandish feat was successful, there was no place else to go. Escape from the ship would be very difficult. No, there was no need for such a desperate measure just yet. If they were going to kill him, chances are they would have done so already. Obviously, they wanted information first. He continued down the corridor trying to think ahead, waiting for his opportunity.

In a few minutes, Jim found himself standing on the bridge of the mighty ship', a spacious room surrounded by windows. Hathaway stood by the one overlooking the flight deck, peering into the near night darkness.

The oafish giant pushed Jim into a chair.

"Funny, isn't it?" Hathaway said, his attention still focused outside. "One ship like this could quite possibly conquer the world right now." He turned to Jim. "You see, I doubt there's an organized army on Earth right now in possession of such a thing. We have enough aircraft to lay waste to anyone who opposes us. We can equip them with nukes and destroy entire cities. Of course, those cities are already graveyards, infested with those murderous sons of bitches, but my point's made."

Hathaway smiled, then moved to face Jim. "Where's your home base?" he asked pleasantly. "What company are you with?"

"Company? I have no company. I'm unemployed, like most everyone now." Jim turned on a deceptive smile.

"What's your outfit? That's what I mean," Hathaway said. "Don't play games with me."

"I'm not playing, not with you. We were alone. We were loners. We had no home base, no outfit, and no company. We lived from day to day, hand to mouth. We were on a search for food when you found us."

Hathaway moved to a console across the room, picked something up, and then returned to Jim. "I know that to be a lie," he said, "because I have this." He shook the map they had been using to plot their way to Tangier Island.

Jim swallowed hard. The map could lead them to Mount Weather.

"We got this from the vehicle you were driving. It has a travel route traced in yellow." Hathaway unfolded the map and pointed to a particular point. "We found you here, in Fredericksburg. Where were you traveling to when we found you, or were you just out for a ride about town?"

Jim showed no emotion. "I've never seen that map before. Where'd you say you got it again?"

Annoyance began to show in Hathaway's voice. "We got it from the Humvee you two were driving. Now I'll repeat the question: Where is your home base?"

Jim remained silent.

Hathaway exhaled loudly. "The route traced has two ending points. One to the north on Route Seven, about twenty miles north of Leesburg, Virginia. The other point ends just north of here at the coast, a place called Smith's Point. We've been picking up a little air traffic in that area." Hathaway pointed to the spot near Tangier Island. "Is that where you're from?"

"I told you, I'm not from there. I've never seen that map before and I have no home base. It must've been in the Humvee when we found it."

Hathaway folded the map. "You'll tell us what we want to know and you'll tell us now."

The large oaf who had been standing close by handed his weapon to Hathaway and rolled up his sleeves as he walked to where Jim sat. He smiled again, exposing a toothless grin, then backhanded Jim across the face.

The blow sent Jim and the chair he was sitting in crashing to the floor. Jim staggered to his feet as the giant moved in for another strike. Jim met him first with a kick to his groin, a kick that hardly fazed the giant. A quiet moan escaped with his breath and then he swung.

Jim ducked and he missed. Another blow made contact with the side of Jim's head. He crashed to the floor and the giant stopped. Jim's head throbbed in pain.

Hathaway looked down at him. "Where's your base?"

Jim spit as he lay face down on the cold metal floor. His spit was red with blood. "No base."

The giant grabbed Jim from the back, lifted him to his feet, and swung at his face.

Blood spewed from Jim's nose as he crumpled toward the floor again, stopped by the giant who held him up long enough to slam several hard punches into his chest and sides.

Jim dropped motionless to the floor, barely conscious of anything except the cold metal floor and the blood that now flowed into his eyes. The air had been forced from his lungs and he was on the verge of passing out.

"Last chance, hero."

Hathaway's voice seemed far away to Jim.

"Where's your base? Where are you from? I swear to God, I will kill you and every one of your friends if you don't answer me. If you don't think I can find them on my own, you are wrong. For your friends' sake, you had better tell me something now!"

Jim was too dazed to answer even if he wanted to. It wouldn't have made any difference because nothing they could do to him would make him tell. The startled look on Matt's face as he realized his fate flashed through Jim's mind. Nothing they could do to him.

The giant began kicking him as he lay on the floor. Kick after kick came until Jim lost consciousness. The giant picked Jim up again and slammed a fist into his face before Hathaway ordered him to stop.

Hathaway put a boot against Jim's shoulder and rolled him onto his back. Jim's eyes were open and unfocused. His face was covered in blood. Hathaway leaned down and tried to get a pulse from Jim's wrist. There was none.

"You've killed him! Jesus Christ, I told you not to do that," Hathaway said.

The oaf dropped his head in shame. Not for killing the man but because he had failed to follow Hathaway's order. That was priority number one. Pleasing the lieutenant.

Hathaway kicked Jim's chair and it skidded across the floor. "I needed him for information. You were supposed to keep him alive until I had it!"

The rage left Hathaway as quickly as it came and he walked back to the window and stared out at the deepening twilight. "Take him outside and throw him over. The fish have to eat, too."

2 0

Leon lay on the front seat of the car he had commandeered, too afraid to raise his head. The night was pitch black, without even the moon to offer light. He was parked by the harbor at Smith's Point on the mainland.

Smith's Point was where people landed when leaving Tangier Island by water. Several boats were anchored there, and a few more at Tangier, so there would always be a way home from the mainland.

Sleep did not come easily this night. Leon wished he would've gotten there before nightfall. He could've grabbed one of the boats and been on his way. But without light, he could not see and without sight, he was not going to budge. He'd simply have to stay still and wait out the night.

From time to time he heard footsteps close by. He held his breath as they passed, afraid to even breathe. The eerie wails of the walking dead did little to comfort him. Some close, others distant, they reminded him of different things. There were some who sounded like crying infants. Some like a whale's song. One sounded like a screech owl, high and shrill. Still others sounded like wounded animals. All were lonely sounds, calls of desperation and need. He listened, motionless.

At any time, he expected a thump on one of the car's windows and clawing hands trying to gain entrance. If that happened, he would be forced to move the car to a safer location. When he had arrived at the harbor, there had been no ghouls in sight. It seemed safe at the time but since then, several ghouls had shown up. They always did. It didn't matter where you went, they eventually found you.

Many people he had spoken with believed that the ghouls possessed some kind of sixth sense, a kind of radar. Certainly tonight it seemed to be so. They passed close to him with increased frequency but so far none had spotted him.

"Dumb bastards," he whispered. If that was true and they had that psychic ability, they probably were too stupid to realize what they were looking for unless they actually spotted you. Stupid was a good thing. Stupid was great. They can keep on being stupid, he thought.

Leon's eyes grew heavy. They closed several times without his permission but he quickly opened them again. Lying on the seat was too comfortable. He was physically drained from the day's events. He had survived a helicopter crash, been chased by zombies, and had walked for miles before finally finding this car. He had lost two close friends. He wanted to sleep. He wanted to close his eyes and dream good dreams.

But that would be a mistake, possibly a fatal one. Turning over in his sleep could make the car move ever so slightly. The slightest movement would be enough to show his position.

He was also known to snore, a window rattler, actually. Ghouls would swarm to the car from all around. They would break through the windows before he had a chance to escape.

To top it off, he was hungry. His stomach growled at the mere thought of food. He held his hands over his stomach in an attempt to quiet it. He wondered if they could hear it. Who knew? Maybe they had the hearing of a cat and the eyes of an eagle.

Leon was afraid but he was very tired. His eyes closed again, but only for a second.

21

The sudden impact of Jim's body hitting the water brought life back into his body and his eyes opened wide. In the few seconds before he sank too far beneath the surface of the cold water, he was able to gain his senses enough to realize where he was and what had happened. He was still disoriented enough so that it took him a moment to figure out which way was up so he could swim to the surface.

His head and shoulders broke the surface and Jim sucked air. Treading water caused intense pain in his extremities; he'd literally been beaten near death. It would be difficult to stay afloat and almost impossible to swim to shore, which was not visible in the moonless night.

He could guess which direction the shore was and start swimming, but if he swam the wrong way, out to sea, he wouldn't survive, not in his condition. He needed to be certain.

Jim searched for a clue of which way to go. Only the outline of the carrier and the light from the deck and windows stood out against the dark background. There were no city lights, no shoreline to see, but he could see the carrier. He could even see which way it faced. Jim searched his memory to remember how it was faced from shore when they had arrived. Aft faced the shore. He was sure of it.

He began to swim.

He stopped many times because the pain was so intense but he made progress. He could barely make the shoreline out but it was there and it was getting closer.

Jim struggled until he was finally wading in the bay surf. Once he cleared the water, he collapsed onto the sandy shore. His arms and legs felt like throbbing rubber.

A light rain splashed his face and Jim opened his mouth to let the clean droplets quench his parched throat. The soothing sound of the rain melted some of the pain he was experiencing.

Then his memory returned. He had forgotten about the plague and the danger he faced on the shore, away from the militia on the ship. He was without a weapon and injured. He would surely have unwelcome company soon.

Jim lurched to his feet and the pain raced through his body, threatening to send him back down to the sand. He braced himself with his hands on his knees until he gained enough strength to continue. The cold water of the bay had at least staunched the bleeding cuts and gashes. For all he knew, he could be bleeding internally. Every step he took was a labor.

The rain continued, harder now, and he wiped it from his eyes and limped his way to where the trucks were parked. The rain was good. It covered the noise he made. Hopefully, the creatures, if around, wouldn't notice him. He was confident some were around but in the darkness it was impossible to see them.

The silhouettes of the trucks were just ahead. He'd been lucky so far; he'd gone unnoticed. Just a few more feet and he'd be safe. He thought of Amanda. She would be worrying herself sick by now. It saddened him to think about it. If his suspicions about Tangier were wrong, he would not put her through it again. If there had been no problems, he would've returned to Mount Weather tonight.

Jim reached the first truck and fumbled in the dark to find the driver's door handle. The door opened and the interior light flashed on, blinding him for his eyes were unaccustomed to light.

His sight focused and he saw his .44 laying on the seat where his captors had left it when they had taken it from him earlier that day.

As he reached for it, movement to his left caught his attention. He turned.

A foot away, a decaying specter of humanity. The creature's face showed substantial decomposition. It opened its mouth and moaned pitifully, then grabbed Jim by the throat.

Jim reacted with a fist to the thing's head and it fell awkwardly backward. Jim made a move toward the fallen ghoul to finish it off, then thought better of it. He was too badly injured to do battle. He jumped into the truck and locked the doors.

The truck light turned off once the door was shut and once again Jim fumbled in the dark for the keys. If there were none it was quite possible that he was finished. In his condition he would not be able to resist an all-out attack from more than just a few of the creatures.

The creature he had knocked to the ground was on his feet again, pawing at the truck window. Jim's hand swiped the side of the steering column and the keys jingled in the ignition.

The tension in his chest lessened and he smiled.

22

An hour later, Jim Workman had cleared the city limits and was well on his way up Route 64, moving north. The militia commander had wanted to know his starting point on the map Jim had used to trace his journey to Tangier Island. That meant that the militia was not stationed on Tangier or Hathaway would have known which starting point was the correct one.

The Island was still Jim's destination but without a map to point the way he would become lost soon. Another map was needed to keep him on the right path.

He passed a road sign that said "Williamsburg 12 miles." He would stop there to find a map.

*   *   *

It was after midnight when Jim took the Williamsburg exit that looped around and up onto another road. The night was still except for two deer that grazed by the road's edge, then darted into the woods when the truck's headlights unsettled them. At least the plague had not infected anything but man. It was not the end of everything, just of civilization.

Jim brought the truck to a stop and checked his surroundings. He had driven into the parking lot of Busch Gardens amusement park. The silhouette of one of the roller coasters was directly ahead, its arching tracks blending into the dark sky. The park was dim and uninviting, a sinister looking thing, under the circumstances.

Who knew what evil dwelled there, hidden in the shadows? Possibly there were crowds of ghoulish children attracted by past memories of pleasure, beckoned by the promise of comfort, maybe even an interlude from their fractured, strange new existence. That was something those things did. They clung to things familiar or places that had given them happiness. Those were the places to avoid.

At the far end of the parking lot, a convenience store was positioned so departing park guests could spend their unused vacation cash on the way out.

He drove toward it.

Jim stood by the truck, an ear to the wind, and listened. The rain had stopped so he had to make sure it was safe before continuing into the building.

The wind was devoid of the voices of the dead; no moans or cries from tortured souls, just a gentle breeze.

Jim grabbed his weapon from the seat and walked to the store, the headlights showing him the way.

The store was untouched. Most places had been looted and vandalized during the plague's early outbreak but this one had been spared that turmoil. Jim pulled at the door but it was locked.

Next to the door was a smoker's outpost, a receptacle that stood about three feet high and was shaped like a genie bottle. The long slender neck was good for gripping and the round weighted bottom was perfect for smashing. Jim swung it at the door and shattered the glass, then tossed it aside. His body ached as he scanned the area for trouble.

The store was dark except for the area in front lit by the headlights. Jim found a flashlight by the register and tore it from its package, then did the same with a pack of batteries. He scanned the shelves for maps to help him on his journey.

He stopped at a rack by the front window. He found a state map and a Rand McNally Road Atlas. He grabbed both, then hesitated as the light crossed a stack of yellowed newspapers with the headline, "Dead Continue to Rise and Multiply." The date was September 10, two years before.

On the road again, Jim roared north, certain the militia would attempt to find his "home base." They'd probably start at Tangier, then move north from there. They might even find the compound at Mount Weather. Though it was secure from the ghouls, an organized army would have no problem breaking in.

From what he'd witnessed, no person of color would have a chance with these men. They were not an ordinary militia but a splinter group with depraved plans and no conscience. He had to warn both the island, assuming there were survivors there, and his own people.

Jim drove faster.

*   *   *

Leon opened his eyes. The sun was not up yet but a faint glow filled the eastern sky. He had fallen asleep, something he promised himself not to do. The mistake had done him no harm. He was unmolested and he had gained a much-needed rest. A few minutes and it would be light enough to make a move for the boat.

Leon moved to the front seat for a better look and to gather his weapons. The area was clear of creatures. The ones who moved by him through the night had moved off, unaware of his presence.

The sky grew lighter, blending from a pale orange in the east to a shade of purple in the west. It was enough to illuminate Leon's surroundings.

Leon stepped out of the car and stretched. He was both surprised and pleased that his injuries in the chopper crash were not as painful as he had expected. He breathed in the salt air of the bay and walked toward the boat.

He stopped before getting there and turned as a green army personnel truck drove into the harbor and stopped by his car. A tall battered man with dark hair stepped out.

As the two men measured each other, the same thought passed through each man's mind: Was this going to be trouble?

23

Felicia and Mick sat with Amanda and Izzy in the cafeteria, eating a tasteless but filling breakfast. Amanda picked at her food with fading interest. Worry had quelled her appetite.

Izzy piled grits in the center of her plate, then poured syrup around it. She furrowed her brow, unhappy with its appearance. Discontent painted her small face.

Felicia watched Amanda pick at her food. "You're going to worry yourself to death," she scolded. "He'll be back."

Izzy placed a half-finished string of beads on the table beside her plate, then fished a small bag of M&Ms from her pocket. She poured them into her hand and separated them by color.

With a huff, Amanda dropped her fork and looked at Felicia. "They should've been back last night," she said.

"That only means that they're late, not dead. If they found someone there, they probably stayed an extra day to get some rest before the return trip."

Izzy took one of her piles of candy and placed the pieces on her grits, taking special care in their placement.

"He wouldn't do that," Amanda said. "He knows how much I worry."

Izzy finished her work of art and showed her pleasure in the finished project by clapping her hands.

"What's that, Izzy?" Felicia asked, her attention drawn away from Amanda by the child's outburst. "Are you playing with your food?"

Izzy nodded and smiled. "It's an island," she said in a child's carefree voice.

Amanda turned her attention to Izzy's creation.

"Why are all the green candies on top?" Felicia asked.

"All the people," she said, pointing.

She now had everyone's attention.

Felicia noticed one of the pieces of candy was red. It was placed in the center of the others. "How about that red one? What's that?"

Izzy's smile widened. "That's Jim. He's going to help the others."

"Oh, I see," Felicia said. "Where's Matt? I don't see him."

Izzy's smile faded. She fell silent as she removed the pieces of candy from the plate and pocketed the string of beads. "Not there."

"Where is he, Izzy?" Felicia asked, cocking her head at Izzy's troubled expression.

Izzy put the candy on the table and dropped her head and moaned. "Tummy feels funny now. Can I go rest?"

Felicia nodded and Izzy left the table, pale and drawn.

A portent of doom hung in Izzy's wake. A sense of dread was suddenly palpable.

For the remainder of the meal the three adults remained quiet.

*   *   *

Sharon Darney prepared the slide for the addition of blood cells to the organism contained there. If what she suspected were true, she would quickly see the results. If her calculations were correct, it would take no more than thirty minutes for the changes to take place.

The specimen on the slide was rare, indeed. A virus of sorts, it could survive on its own without the aid of a human host. What puzzled her most was that only a fraction of the virus needed to inflict the damage necessary to cause death had been found. That explained why no one had found it before the world fell apart. They simply didn't have the time.

Sharon doubted that more than one million individual organisms existed in a body, living or dead. That meant there were ten organisms per million human cells. It was unlikely that the organism itself could be responsible. More likely, it was a carrier of some kind or, more accurately, a small factory living in the body unnoticed until death. Only then did it become active.

But that left another puzzle. Why did a single bite infect a living person and cause death? Even in reanimated subjects, the numbers remained the same. Their numbers were too low to cause death. It also didn't explain the reanimation of the body after death, or the desire to consume human flesh.

Sharon took the blood and added it to the slide containing the microbe, then placed the slide into the electron microscope for viewing. At first she saw no changes. The black organism failed to attack the blood she had added. It was alive, there was no doubting that. It shook and quivered on the slide but nothing more. She was beginning to think that her hypothesis was wrong.

Then it happened. As the living blood cells began to die, the black cell sprang into action. The cells that had died first were the first ones to be assaulted.

The black cell began to produce smaller organisms resembling mitochondrias and lysosomes that penetrated the cell walls, replacing their counterparts that inhabited the dead cells.

Then something even stranger happened. The dead cells began to show signs of activity. With lightning speed, they each produced one single organism. It was different than the mitochondrias and lysosomes created by the black virus-like organism. To her amazement they looked like chloroplasts, that part of a plant cell responsible for photosynthesis, of creating energy from sunlight. They in turn attacked the living cells.

The chloroplasts penetrated the living cell membranes with ease when the cells should have rejected their advances. It meant that the cells were fooled into thinking they were supposed to be there.

The previously living cells began to die once the chloroplast-like organism became part of them. They in turn created an organism of their own to infect other living cells. A chain reaction had occurred. Reproduction was swift and precise. In only seconds, every blood cell had been attacked, changed, died and reanimated.

Sharon had witnessed something that possibly no other researcher had ever discovered. The answers were there all along. They had simply not looked long enough to find them.

24

Jim was the first to make a move. This man was not part of the militia. He was black and that was a death sentence with the bunch he and Matt had encountered.

The man's posture was not threatening. He simply stood by one of the boats, looking absolutely shocked to see another warm-blooded living soul.

Jim approached the man cautiously, his hands out from his body as he went, palms up in a non-aggressive posture. The man looked shaken and the last thing Jim wanted to do was provoke a defensive action that could lead to an unwanted battle. In his present battered state it would certainly be a short one.

Jim stopped several feet in front of him. Extending his hand and nodding in an easy friendly drawl he said, "Jim Workman. Sure is good to see a friendly face out here."

Leon did not make a move to accept the proffered hand. He took a moment to size up this stranger who was slightly taller than himself and more muscular and well fed. He was not a drifter. His face was strong but judging from the myriad of cuts and bruises, a recent encounter had not been a friendly one.

Leon recognized the haunted, anguished eyes many plague survivors had. He relaxed but a fragment of suspicion lingered.

"I'm Leon."

"I'm trying to get to Tangier Island," Jim said, pointing to the bay.

Leon didn't recall seeing this man before but then there were a lot of people on the islands. Maybe he was from one of the others. He had met most of them, but not all. But this man would have stuck out in his memory.

"Are you? What island are you from?"

"I'm not," Jim said. "I'm from inland."

Leon was immediately wary. He was obviously lying. There were no survivors inland; there were too many creatures there. He'd seen with his own eyes, on countless occasions, the desolation of the mainland.

"We've searched there many times and found no one," Leon said. "How is it that you managed to survive this thing for so long and what brings you here now?"

The fact that Leon had said *we searched the mainland*, and not *I searched the mainland* did not escape Jim's notice. This man was not alone and Jim was not about to reveal anything about the mountain or the other survivors until he knew more. He had to be sure it was safe first.

"I had a good hiding place," Jim said. "About a year ago I received a radio signal from Tangier. I wasn't able to respond to it but eventually I knew I would have to come here to see for myself. To tell you the truth, I didn't think I'd find anyone still around."

Leon smiled, his distrust fading. "Well, you found us," he said, and finally extended his hand for Jim to shake. "There's a lot of us on the islands. We moved there when this shit first started. Its safe and about as normal as things can be right now, I guess. You're welcome to tag along with me if you like."

Jim nodded and followed Leon to one of the boats anchored nearby.

Leon placed a wooden plank between the boat and the dock and they boarded the small craft. The deck was darkened with mildew and mold grew around the cabin's doorway and in every visible crack and crevice. It was obvious that it had not been used or maintained much over the last couple of years.

Jim looked for any sign of trouble. He was surprised that they had been able to stand out in the open, unmolested for this long. He was not anxious to tempt fate.

A lone ghoul lurched about on the deck of a sailboat fifty yards to the north. The boom, sails, and rigging shredded by past storms, the creature awkwardly maneuvered between the tangled cables, then squatted on the deck, where it remained motionless, content for the time being.

Leon worked hurriedly. He checked below deck for leakage before removing the covers to the engine compartment to check for deteriorated wiring and fuel lines. When he was satisfied that everything was as it should be, he primed the motor with fuel and took the seat at the controls.

Jim continued to keep a vigilant eye on their surroundings.

The motor moaned as Leon tested the worthiness of the batteries. Over and over it turned, first slowly, then faster, then slow, labored gasps again. The creature on the other boat stood and took notice of them. It began to howl in what could only be described as a call to arms.

The motor continued to crank but strained to start. From the morning shadows trudged more of the foul demons, aware of their prey by the sudden noise and the sailor-zombie's calls.

Ghouls in various stages of decay poured through the gates just up the hill from the harbor, their bodies hideously mangled, driven by a common desire. Within seconds they were converging on the two desperate survivors.

Jim removed the steel cable looped around a cleat in the dock. He kicked the wooden plank away and it dropped into the water. Only a few feet from the dock, they needed to get further away before the dead got close enough to board.

Jim gripped the rail that rimmed the edge of the boat and then kicked at the dock, nudging the boat another foot away, but the aft bumped the bow of a sailboat anchored beside them.

Jim jumped onto the deck of the sailboat, which rode lower in the water than the big cruiser, skidding across the deck of the sailboat as he landed. The masts were split and the rigging was torn and strewn across the deck of the small vessel.

With a few hard jerks, Jim broke off two pieces of the splintered masts and threw them onto the deck of the cruiser. He pulled himself back onto cruiser's deck, panting and flushed from the strain on his battered body.

"First things first!" he shouted at Leon. "Help me out here!" He handed Leon one of the broken masts as he moved past him.

Leon sprang from his seat and followed Jim's lead, using the broken mast as leverage to shove away from the dock. The men heaved and pushed the boat more than twelve feet from shore, out of the reach of the creatures, some of whom teetered precariously on the edge of the dock. They lurched and wobbled like giant, decaying, puss-covered Weebles.

"Drop the anchor before the tide drags us right back to them!" Jim shouted.

Leon ran to the winch and released it, letting the steel cable with the attached anchor drop into the water. Jim pulled his pole in just as the first wave of creatures reached the edge of the dock.

He watched as they reached out toward him, hovering at the dock's edge. In their zeal to reach their quarry, the mob surged forward. A mangled creature in moldering khakis and a shredded navy blazer, the entire right side of his face ripped away, toppled off the edge of the dock and disappeared into the murky water.

The mob drew back in unison, wary of the water. "They can't get over here," Jim said. "They can't swim. I think they're afraid of the water."

"Yeah, I know, but what do we do now?"

"Do you have any side cutters or anything that will cut a battery cable?"

"There's a toolbox over there. I'll look."

Leon removed the top tray from the toolbox and found what Jim wanted underneath. They looked like heavy-duty pliers with a cutting edge on one side of the jaws. They were rusty but useable. Leon tossed them to Jim, who placed them in his pocket.

"Stay here," he shouted, and dove into the water. His battered body ached as he paddled.

Leon watched as Jim swam to a powerboat anchored several piers over. The creatures also watched. Some stumbled down the dock toward the boat Jim had boarded.

Jim worked fast to cut the batteries free, leaving as much of the cables intact as possible by loosening the wing nuts that held them in place. In less than a minute he had the two batteries from the other boat resting on the deck.

He found a floating life ring and ripped the lid from a broken cooler. He placed the ring in the water, put the cooler lid on top of it, and carefully placed the batteries on the plastic lid. Jim eased into the water beside the makeshift raft and pulled it with him as he swam.

When Jim reached the boat, Leon pulled the batteries aboard, then reached down to help Jim climb over the edge. As Leon gripped Jim's slippery hand to pull him up, he felt a sudden hard jerk and nearly lost his tenuous hold on him.

"What the—" Jim's expression registered shock. "Shit! Pull, man! Pull!"

Jim struggled to help Leon hoist his weight over the side of the boat. As he clung to the railing to keep from being pulled back into the water, Leon leaned over the side of the boat and grabbed the back of Jim's jeans to pull his body out of the water and onto the deck.

Jim felt the drag of the extra weight on his legs. "What is it? Get it off!"

The panic in Jim's voice pushed Leon into an adrenal burst of energy. He pulled Jim over the side, along with the hideous blue-coated zombie who had fallen off the dock. He clung to Jim's leg, gurgling bay water and gnashing its teeth.

Leon grabbed the broken mast pole and brought it down squarely on the top of the creature's head. The ghoul lost its grip on Jim and slid back over the side of the boat and disappeared into the bay.

Jim, breathing heavily and trying to regain his senses, lay in a wet heap on the deck.

"You okay, man?" Leon asked, offering his hand to help Jim up.

"Yeah. We'll chalk that up to a learning experience. They can't swim but they don't drown either. Thanks, man. I wasn't ready for that one."

"No problem. There aren't many of us left. We gotta stick together, right?"

"Right," Jim replied, but his eyes reflected the deeper and more troubling knowledge that not all survivors were going to stick together. Some had their own agendas.

Jim went to work cutting away some of the coating to expose the bare wire on the cables attached to the batteries. He loosened the connecters to the boat's batteries enough to force the newly-exposed wire into them, then tightened the terminals. He now had the power of four batteries connected to the boat.

"If these have any charge left in them, it should be enough to start now," Jim said.

"And if it doesn't?"

"Then we have a long swim ahead of us, and we've just seen that that might offer more problems than we can deal with."

Leon slid back into the seat. He'd been through this in his search for transportation after the chopper crashed. If the motor didn't start this time, they were in trouble. They were cornered by the monsters.

Leon turned the key and pressed his thumb on the black starter button. The motor turned again, this time with much more force. It popped and sputtered, teasing them with bursts of ignition before finally roaring to life.

"Yeah!" Leon whooped. He fired the engine's RPMs as Jim winched the anchor onto the deck.

One of the creatures on the dock made a desperate attempt to reach them and fell into the water, sinking to the bottom as the boat raced away.

25

Sharon Darney left the elevator and broke the thoughtful silence Amanda was enjoying. She sat up from her reclined position in the padded chair by the window and forced a smile.

Amanda had barely left her station in the lobby since Jim's departure. They were in the ground level room often visited by Felicia when she became depressed from the lack of sunlight in the underground.

The room was large, with floor-to-ceiling windows on one of its walls that brought in the beauty of manicured lawns and flower-beds now overgrown and thick with weeds from years of neglect. Still, it was a refreshing change since it allowed the sunlight to pour in and brighten one's mood. It was simply called The Sunroom by the inhabitants of Mount Weather.

Sharon walked to the windows, her white lab coat trailing behind her as went. At the windows she turned her face upward and let the heat of the sun warm it before turning to face Amanda.

Amanda's eyes were bloodshot and lined with dark circles from lack of sleep. Her slight smile now gone. She fell back into the chair again and resumed her disheartened posture.

Concerned, Sharon said, "You're not supposed to be up here alone, you know. What if something happened?"

"I don't care."

"Mick would be mad if he knew."

Amanda walked to the window and stared out at nothing in par-ticular. "Mick can kiss my ass. I'm a big girl. I can take care of myself. If I wanted to be around other people right now, I would've invited someone up here with me."

Amanda's gaze settled on the waist-high weeds as they gently bent beneath the late morning breeze. She imagined what the breeze might feel like if it were blowing through her hair and inhaled deeply, expecting to smell the summer fragrances so close but only dry re-circulated air filled her lungs.

"You're worried about Jim. We all know that, but that's no reason to turn away from the rest of us. We're worried, too."

Amanda softened her mood. She had drawn inward, even from Felicia. She was mad at Jim; she hadn't wanted him to go on this mission. It was far too dangerous and he had been insensitive to go in spite of her objections.

"He'll be back, Amanda," Sharon said. "Jim's a smart guy. He knows not to take chances."

"He took an unmitigated chance by going out there, so don't tell me he won't take chances. Sometimes I wonder how smart he really is, taking these foolhardy chances."

Sharon's lips parted to respond with more words of assurance but her expression suddenly changed to one of alarm. At her indrawn gasp, Amanda followed her gaze, turning toward the window as a gray-faced ghoul smashed against it. Shocked, she stumbled away to a safer distance.

The ghoul patted the window with its creased hands and pulled its face along the glass. The action left a slimy trail across the window as fluid oozed from its open maw.

Sharon moved closer to study the creature. "Go get Mick, and tell him to bring some help."

Amanda broke free of her stupor and raced to the elevator, disappearing into the underground.

*   *   *

Mick charged from the elevator with a sawn-off shotgun, Griz and Felicia close on his heels. Griz was a burly man with an unkempt beard and a .357 holstered around his large waist. He followed Mick closely, more for the safety in numbers than the desire for a fight. In spite of his rough-and-tumble appearance, Griz was a gentle soul. He would fight if he had to but it was not his nature. But once the need arose he was in for a penny or a pound.

Amanda and Felicia cautiously eased in behind them but stopped short of approaching the windows.

Mick advanced to where Sharon was watching the creature.

Sharon sighed. "Well, I guess the question's been answered as to whether there are still reanimates out there."

Mick nodded, his eyes studying the danger outside. "We pretty much figured they were."

"Shoot him, Mick!" Felicia cried, her eyes wide with terror. "Shoot him before he breaks in here!"

"Don't worry, he can't get in here. That glass is two inches thick. It would take more than one of those things to get through it."

Sharon touched Mick's shoulder. "No, don't shoot it," she whispered. "Capture it."

Mick jerked away from her touch. "Capture it? What in God's name for? You have a specimen downstairs already and I've got to tell you, there's a lot of people who would just as soon that one was shot, too, including me. I'm not crazy about having any of those things down there where we live."

"That one is cut up. I've dissected it. And, besides, I need a fresh one."

Amanda wrinkled her nose. "It doesn't look too fresh to me. I agree; shoot the ugly bastard."

"No. I need one I can work with and to compare with the other one. I need more than one specimen."

Mick's face tightened. "No!"

"Damn it, Mick, if I don't have what I need to conduct my experiments, I can't guarantee I'll ever find answers."

"Answers? How the hell will finding answers help us now? The world has gone to shit. There's no one left to help out there and now you want to risk our health and lives to catch that thing so you can keep busy?"

Sharon walked to the window. "Do you ever want to go back out there?" She pointed outside. "How about future generations? If we can't find a solution, there won't *be* any future generations. If we manage to get through this without humanity getting completely wiped out, we need to know what to do if it ever happens again. We need to know so we can prevent it. We need to know because the next time…Well, let's hope there is no next time."

Sharon sighed heavily. "I need that one to ensure that it doesn't happen again."

Mick turned to Griz. "You up for it?" he asked against his better judgment.

Griz shrugged. It wasn't his first choice. "Yeah, I'll help ya, but I ain't gonna get bit. If there's a chance that's gonna happen, I'll shoot it," he groused, his heavy voice booming louder than he'd intended.

"Fair enough. Heard that, didn't you, Sharon? If things don't go right, we destroy the thing and send it on to hell where it belongs."

Sharon nodded. "Fair enough."

Mick paced the floor, trying to form a plan. He understood that Sharon's motives were genuine, he just didn't see the point. This would be the last time he took such a risk for the sake of science.

Unable to formulate a foolproof plan, he turned to Griz. "Go downstairs and get a roll of duct tape from the maintenance room. Do it quickly."

He wondered if there were more of them outside and how this one had gotten inside the fenced-in complex. If they were fortunate, it was a loner.

Griz returned minutes later with the tape. Anxiety mounting, he clenched his jaw until his teeth ground together. He hated those things. He hated the looks of them. He hated how they smelled and the sounds they made. He swallowed hard and fought back his apprehension of the task at hand.

Griz offered the tape to Mick, who waved his hand in such a way that Griz understood he was to keep it. In his mind Mick's plan began to form. They would use it to restrain the creature. It was a simple plan but effective. He had always believed that duct tape could be used to remedy any situation. He had first learned that little tidbit more than fifteen years before, while working stage crew for a rock band. They had used rolls of the stuff every weekend to tape everything from wires to midrange speaker cabinets to prevent them from vibrating off the bass bins when the music got so loud that the thump-thump-thump of the bass drum pounded in your chest with a force strong enough to almost take you off your feet. Duct tape was worth its weight in gold to the long hairs.

Mick eyed Sharon. "Once we go through that door, you close it and lock it behind us." Mick and Griz walked to the door at the far end of the room, just left of the windows. "Watch us through the glass and don't open it again until I give you the signal, okay?"

Sharon nodded.

Felicia gnawed at her fingernails. "Be careful, Mick. Don't let it get you," she warned between panic attacks.

Mick forced a smile and gave her a lighthearted wink.

Sharon typed the code into the keypad to unlock the heavy steel door and closed it again after the men went through. She moved to the window with Amanda and Felicia to watch the scene unfold.

Mick ran toward the creature and delivered a sound kick to its midsection. The force propelled it backward and off its feet. Mick slammed it over onto its stomach and planted a knee in the middle of its back, pinning it firmly to the ground.

Griz took the tape and wrapped it several times around the creature's ankles binding its legs tightly together. He did the same with the wrists, careful to pull the sleeves of its jumpsuit down over the decomposing skin before wrapping the tape tightly around them as Mick held them behind the creature's back.

Keeping the ghoul pinned, Mick reached into his back pocket, retrieving a neatly-folded bandana. He handed it to Griz.

"Wrap this around its face and then use the tape," he said. Mick then rose from his position and grabbed a handful of the creature's mangy hair.

The creature moaned pitifully as Mick planted one foot on its upper back and jerked its head backward to give Griz the needed room to wrap the cloth and the tape around its head and mouth.

When that was done, the two men stepped away and watched as the creature squirmed on the ground, unable to break free from the bindings. Mick scanned the grounds for more of the creatures who may have gone unnoticed before giving Sharon the signal to open the door.

With Griz's help, he carried the ghoul inside and placed it on the floor in the middle of the room. Felicia and Amanda backed away but Sharon stooped to examine it more closely.

"All right," she said, rising. "Take it to my lab."

"You got a table or something to strap this thing to?" Mick asked. "It has to be confined, you know."

"Of course I do! You don't think I'm going to let it just run free, do you?"

26

Tangier Island came into view and Jim strained his eyes to make out the details as best he could. He had waited quite a while for this moment and his excitement mounted.

They were moving in on the west side of the island. As the boat moved closer, piers and stilted buildings appeared through the morning haze. Small boats rocked gently as the tide licked the shoreline. A man took a moment to wave to them as he prepared for his daily fishing trip into the bay. Another man kissed a woman who held a baby, then stepped into his boat.

Jim smiled, reveling in the illusion of a normal life without the walking dead horror of the mainland. The smile remained, tugging at the corners of his mouth before his thoughts suddenly returned to Amanda, Matt, and the militia.

Leon turned the wheel and the boat followed the shoreline. People were attending to their morning business. Some rode bicycles, others carried buckets of water. The island was alive and life went on. The sight gave Jim an overwhelming desire to get back to the Mount Weather Underground as fast as he could and bring Amanda and the others here to enjoy it with him.

But there was too much to do. He couldn't let the urgency of the moment get washed away by what he was seeing. Danger still existed for his people, and for these people.

As they approached the pier, Leon throttled back and slowed to a coast, letting the waves carry them up against the wooden posts until they were in position to secure the boat. Jim stepped up onto the pier's planked walkway.

For the first time in two years he was not looking over his shoulder for an attack from behind. There were no walking piles of rot on the island, just living, breathing people going about their lives. The morning sun felt good on his face, not alien, not foreboding, just good in a normal kind of way. At this moment, Jim was on vacation from the dead world.

Leon finished tying the boat and Jim offered a hand to help him up onto the walkway beside him.

Leon sighed heavily. His two friends were dead and now he had to explain that to the others. He glanced at Jim, who stared straight ahead, a smile gracing his face. He had the look of a prisoner just handed his freedom after many years of confinement.

"You've been out in that shit for a long time, haven't you?" Leon asked. "Nice to have some freedom back, isn't it?"

Jim nodded. "From the start. I've seen a lot of people die. Good people. Friends."

"We all have," Leon said, thinking of his lost comrades. He walked toward the settlement with Jim. "But there's none of that here. When people die here, it's from natural causes and we're ready for it."

Jim allowed himself the luxury of feeling secure for the moment, though he felt guilty because he knew that Amanda was worrying herself sick by now.

He noticed a single landing strip about two hundred yards away. A small airport with one hanger made him stop. Hope of an easy way home flooded him. "Is there any flyable aircraft in that hanger?"

Leon eyed it with a heavy heart for his lost friends. "Yes, there's a plane in the hanger. We never used it. The chopper was best suited for our purposes."

"You have a helicopter?"

Leon diverted his eyes away from the airport. "Not anymore. We crashed yesterday. I was the only survivor."

"Was that *your* bird burning in Fredericksburg yesterday?"

Leon nodded.

"What happened?"

"We lost oil pressure and went down. My two friends were killed on impact. I climbed out and found my way back to the spot where I met you."

"I'm sorry about your friends."

Leon grimaced. "Yeah, me, too. They were good people."

"I understand. It's hard losing people you care for." He patted Leon on the back. "Can I take a look at that plane?"

"Sure. You fly?"

"I did back in my military days, but I haven't done much lately."

"Yeah, I figured you for military. Air Force?"

"Navy Seals."

Leon raised an eyebrow, impressed. "Yep, I should have guessed. You look the type," he said, walking toward the hangar. "I didn't know Seals flew."

"I didn't say I flew in the Seals, although the Navy has great pilots. I just said I haven't flown since my military days."

Leon nodded. This guy guarded every word he said. Leon wondered what he wasn't saying.

Leon slid open the heavy hanger door and daylight flooded inside. Jim walked to the small single engine plane parked in the center of the hangar and ran a hand down the fuselage, as though caressing a woman. "Cessna 150M. 1970s. Probably 1975."

Jim moved to the wingtips. "It has a bit of hanger rash here on the tips. No big deal. It also looks like the tips have had some repairs done to them. Has anyone been flying this thing since the plague?"

Leon walked closer. "Yeah, one of the men killed in the crash. Hal would take it up from time to time just to keep it loose. He said it would freeze up if he didn't. I figured he just wanted to do it for the fun of it."

"Probably a little bit of both, I imagine," Jim said. "I'd like to take it up for a quick spin myself before I leave, just to check it out."

"Leave? What do you mean, leave? Where would you go?"

Jim turned. "I'm afraid I haven't been totally truthful with you. You see, I lost a good friend myself yesterday."

Leon's interest peaked. "Go on."

"I've traveled from northern Virginia. Besides myself, there are about sixty other survivors located in an underground military complex."

"Military?"

"No. Like everything else, the place fell apart before we arrived. The personnel stationed there turned on each other and destroyed themselves. I like to think that we had a little divine intervention in finding our way there." A vision of Izzy's angelic face flashed through his mind. "We've been there over a year now. Like I told you, I received a radio signal from Tangier about a year ago. That part is true. I was on my way here when I met up with you but my trip was interrupted before that and my friend was killed."

"By those ghoulies?"

"No. We were met in Fredericksburg by a militia, a particular nasty one at that. They killed him."

"*They* killed him? Why?"

Jim looked evenly at Leon. "Because of the color of his skin."

"Jesus! Where are they now?"

"They took me to an aircraft carrier down at the port in Norfolk. They have at their disposal a lot of firepower, including jet planes armed with nukes. They thought they killed me but I escaped. Now I'm worried they'll find my people and yours. They found a map I had used to lay out my route. If they follow it, it will lead them right to this island, or to the Mount Weather Underground. Either way, it's bad news."

Leon scratched the top of his head. "Son of a—! We have to do something! Do you think there's a chance they'll use those jets to nuke us?"

Jim considered it. "I doubt it. I think they'll be more interested in forcing their way of thinking on you, subduing you more than destroying you. Your people, I mean. You're a black man. There's no place in their world for you. You, they'll kill."

Leon swallowed hard. "You'd think that way of thinking would be gone now, wouldn't you?" He shook his head ruefully.

"Not as long as men like that survive. As long as they exist, so will their way of thinking."

27

Hathaway studied Jim's map while he drank his morning coffee. He sat at a small table attached to the floor by a single pole screwed into the metal floor of the bridge. It overlooked the flight deck and he glanced up from the map from time to time to watch as several men tried to make two of the A6 bombers flight ready.

The men scurried about replacing fuel, checking lines for wear, and resetting the onboard computers. Two years of being idle had caused many of the aircraft computers to shutdown.

Many of the militia's members had served in the regular military, some of them in the Navy. They were accustomed to this type of work; it was second nature to them. But very few of them knew how to pilot a jet aircraft.

Hathaway traced his finger along the yellow line, studying every inch for a clue to where Jim was from or where he was going. He traced the line to its southern-most point, which ended at a place called Smith's Point. The area was too close to Washington, D.C., and its suburbs to be safe for human habitation. The ghoul population would be thick there.

More than likely he was from the northern point. He began his journey from somewhere at the north end of the line, but where? It could be anywhere.

Hathaway reclined in his seat and took another sip of coffee. He wrestled with that thought until Jake stepped onto the bridge and broke his concentration. Hathaway folded the map and stuffed it into his pocket.

Jake hadn't come to the bridge for any reason in particular. The manner in which he wandered around the room, then finally settled in front of the windows, gave the impression that he was simply bored.

Hathaway left his seat and stood next to Jake, watching the men work below. Jake stared down, his jaw flexing with a wad of tobacco. Hathaway waited for Jake to speak first. When he didn't, he said, "We'll be heading back soon. Tomorrow, maybe."

What he really wanted to tell Jake was of his clever plan and the bomb, that soon he would be in complete charge. But not just quite yet.

"There's not much else we can do here," Hathaway said. "This ship is a floating pile of junk. We'll never get those engines back online. About all it's good for is its radar capabilities."

Hathaway fell silent and turned his attention back to the men on the flight deck. "And they think they are really doing something down there. All they really are is a bunch of squids! Nothing more than deck grunts. There's not a single man in the bunch who can fly one of those A6 bombers. It'll take months to get to the point where any of them will be of real use to me."

Hathaway turned away from the window. "No worries, though. I've got other things to take care of first."

Jake stopped chewing and turned. A brown smudge of tobacco hung from the right corner of his lip. "What do you mean? I thought we had decided not to find out who's been flying around down here."

Hathaway picked up his coffee cup and downed the last of it. He had another plan, one that would reveal the origin of Jim, but he would not divulge that information just yet. It was better to keep it to himself. "Nothing to concern yourself with."

"You wouldn't be trying to cut me out of any good action now, would you?" Jake asked.

Hathaway smiled and walked away, leaving Jake alone by the window.

Of all the men chosen for this trip, Robert Hathaway trusted Jake more than any of the others. Jake wasn't the sharpest knife in the drawer but right now that's what Hathaway needed. Jake could not be used in his plan to find the origin of Jim. It was important to know where he had come from. The man was smart and disciplined. He held his secret, even to his death. He was well trained, a soldier.

There was no doubt that he was a soldier, one with a big secret. That made him dangerous. There was more than just the one man, Hathaway was sure of it. He was protecting others. How many, he didn't know. If the carrier was in working order his worries would be negligible, but that would not happen anytime soon. Maybe never.

The *Nimitz* was nuclear powered but the reactors were in a state of disrepair. If he were to command an invasion, he would have to depend on old-fashioned manpower in order to be successful.

Hathaway thought of using Marty Gibson for his secret mission. Marty was smart but sometimes he went off half-cocked. He had used Marty to guard Jim until they got to the carrier. Marty would surely slip up. No, it had to be someone smart and disciplined.

Christopher Smith would possibly do the job to satisfaction. He was a little young but he was a fine soldier. He had only known him for the two years of the plague and that left a little to be desired when it came to trusting him or knowing his limits, but he was the best available choice. He would have a meeting with him first, tell him what he needed to know, and equip him with necessities for his mission.

Hathaway, comfortable with his choice, walked to the flight deck to oversee the work he had ordered the men to carry out. He gave pause to consider how his plan back at the base was unfolding. He had not received any signals yet and he wondered if something had gone wrong. He should've heard something by now. His radio worked. It would pick up the signal from camp, even at this distance.

He brushed the troubled thoughts away and went about his tasks. Chris Smith was first on the list.

Hathaway found Chris in a lifeboat just over the port side with a larger-than-usual fishing rod swinging from his grip. He tossed it out into the bay and waited for a bite, unaware that he was being watched.

Hathaway grabbed one of the lines attached to the boat and swung a rope ladder close enough for a good grab. He was over halfway down the seventy-foot drop to the boat before Chris realized he had company. He reeled in the fishing line and cast it out in a different direction as Hathaway finished his descent.

"You know what the best thing is about getting stuck with the job of watching over this ship?" A smile lightened Chris' face as he spoke.

Hathaway thought for a second, then shook his head.

"Well, I'll tell ya," Chris said. "Fresh seafood, that's what. Crabs, blues, all here for the taking. Just cast a line or a net."

Hathaway smiled. "I'm glad you enjoyed your stay."

Chris stopped in the middle of casting his line. "Enjoyed? You make it sound like I'm going somewhere."

"You are. I've got something I need you to do. Something you need to keep to yourself."

28

"The men who were with you when the chopper crashed, did they have families?" Jim asked.

Leon nodded. "Yeah, Hal did. He has a wife here. How do I tell her that he's dead? Like everyone else here, she's already lost so much."

"How about you, Leon? Did any of your family make it?"

Leon stared off into the distance. He drew a deep breath into his lungs and released it before he spoke. "I don't know. I was in Virginia Beach with my lady when this shit first started. She didn't make it." He rubbed his temples as though remembering hurt his head. "She was gut-shot by some crazy bastard who had lost his mind and was shooting up the streets. He must've killed fourteen or fifteen people before the cops shot him in the face."

Jim noted the weary expression on Leon's face, as though he were trying to draw the strength to go on with his story from some inner well that had nearly run dry.

"She got back up. They had already covered her body and were about to put her in the back of the ambulance when she started moving again. She just sat right up and took a big bite out of one of the medics."

Leon sucked in the corners his mouth. His brow was deeply furrowed. "Hell, I didn't know what to do so I wrapped my arms around her from behind to get her under control. I tried talking her down. I thought that she had just lost it after getting shot. Shock or something. I kept telling her, 'Stop, baby, you're hurt. Stop so they can help you.'"

A tear escaped the corner of his eye and ran along the side of his nose. "But she was like a wild animal. They finally got her strapped in and took her to the hospital. It took them two days to pronounce her dead." Leon sniffed. His dark brown eyes stared at the dirt at his feet. "She was dead from the git-go. By the time I finally got my shit together, it was too late to travel home."

"Where's home?

"Pigeon Forge, Tennessee, four hundred miles to the west. My damned car got stolen so I was pretty much stuck. I tried to call home but there was no answer. You ever been to Pigeon Forge?"

"No, can't say that I have."

"It's one giant vacation strip. Like the beach boardwalk without the sand and ocean. People roll in there by the thousands every week. It's wall-to-wall people and bumper-to-bumper traffic. They all come to see the Smokey Mountains and Dollywood. I'll bet this thing turned that place into hell on Earth. I can just imagine how those people panicked. Bunch of damned, dumb-ass tourists. If my family had any sense, they climbed to the top of one of those mountains to wait this out. I know Pop, though. He probably broke out the ol' shotgun and stuck around." Leon sighed heavily. "I hope not."

When Leon stepped through the door at Julio's bar, a broad smile stretched across the little Mexican's face. He dropped his cleaning rag and, his arms in the air, ran toward Leon. "Leon! Leon!" he shouted in his usual animated way. "Where the hell have you been, man? We have so much been worried about you. We thought you may been dead, man."

Being the bearer of bad news showed plainly on Leon's dark face but he said nothing.

"Where is Hal and Jack? Not with you?"

"No, Julio, they're not. The chopper crashed." His next words were hard to speak. "They're...dead."

Julio slumped. "Oh, that's very bad, very bad. They were good men, Leon. They were heroes. They save lots of people and bring them to this island. I liked them very much."

Leon nodded somberly. "They liked you, too, Julio."

Julio patted Leon on the back. "You are okay, though, right?"

"Yes, I'm okay." He turned toward Jim. "Julio, this is my new friend, Jim. He's another survivor of our lost world."

Julio took Jim's hand and shook it fervently. "Come, my friends, you have a drink on the house."

Julio steered Leon and Jim toward the bar. It was eleven in the morning, too early for any of the islanders to find their way to Julio's.

Jim glanced around the empty room as he and Leon took a seat at the bar. It was dimly lit, with high tables lining the walls. The bar was centrally located, with several small tables surrounding it. There was a jukebox against the wall by the door and sports memorabilia lined the walls, mostly Washington Redskin Pendants and Capitals hockey sticks.

Jim's perusal of the room was broken when Julio returned to the bar with two glasses of wine. Leon nodded his appreciation to Julio and drank the wine in one long gulp, as though he were drawing strength from a magical nectar to shore him up for the tasks that were still ahead of him.

Jim waved his away.

"Have a drink, Jim," Leon said, smacking his lips at the tangy taste. "Julio makes some good apple wine."

Jim smiled. "It clouds my thinking. I need to stay focused. Maybe later."

Jim watched as Leon drained his glass.

"Well," Leon said, wiping the last drop of wine from his mouth, "I guess I should go tell Hal's wife the awful truth. Then we'll get you settled in here. I've got to go check on Milly first."

Jim stood up and pushed his stool close under the bar. "Who's Milly?"

"Milly is my Golden Retriever. She's been locked up in my house since I left yesterday morning. She's gotta be getting' pretty hungry by now."

"Okay, but after that I need to get back to Mount Weather. There will be some people pretty worried about me by now. Besides, I have my own bad news to pass on to the others."

"Don't you think you should stick around for a while first? I mean, get settled in and plan your trip back?"

"No, there's no need. I'm going to fly back in that plane down in the hanger. That is, if no one here has any objections."

"You're welcome to use it. No one here will be needing it. No one here can fly the damned thing. It'll just sit there and rust if you don't. Are you sure it's safe?"

Jim smiled thinly. "I haven't seen any flying zombies so it's safer than traveling on the ground."

Jim followed Leon through the small town until they arrived at his home. The ground was less sandy there and some of the lawns had grass growing in sporadic areas. The trees lining the street, mostly apple trees, grew thick. The ground around them was covered in grass. Obviously, the soil in this area had been brought in to accommodate their growth. It differed drastically from the sandy, rocky shore several blocks away.

Leon opened the front door and Milly met him head on, nearly taking him off his feet. She lunged against his chest and licked at his chin, happy to see her master.

Leon grabbed the side of her face and wrestled with her, uttering silly nonsense like one would to an infant. "Whatcha doin', girl? Did you miss your Papa?"

Milly jumped down and dashed across the yard. Leon watched until she got to the street. When she didn't stop, he pulled out a small brass whistle on a chain around his neck. He put the whistle in his mouth and blew. Jim heard nothing but Milly stopped dead in her tracks and sat down.

Leon smiled. "Works like a charm," he said, laughing. He held the whistle up. "It's a dog whistle. We can't hear it but she does."

"You've got her trained pretty well, don't you?"

Leon swelled with pride for his pet. "She's a good girl. I've had her since she was a pup. She wasn't much more than that when this shit started. She's been with me ever since. She keeps me company and she senses things that people miss. She alerted me to trouble several times when we first came to this island. It wasn't completely safe at that time. If one of those damned zombies came close, she knew. She hates them. She barks like hell."

"An animal like that is good to have around. Especially now."

Leon smiled and looked at Milly, who was sitting patiently, waiting for her next command. "She's my best bud. She'd be good to have around anytime."

29

The possibility that his planned coup had failed wasn't what bothered Robert Hathaway. It was the fact that he had not been able to determine who Jim was and where he had come from. He would, of course, deny any involvement in the bombing but Jim had obviously been military and if a splinter faction of the United States Military remained, they could be real trouble. They'd be organized and they would have had functional weaponry to survive the plague. They would ruin his plans of righting the wrongs of the world. They wouldn't subscribe to his way of thinking.

He had thought that Jim had died on the carrier but now he wasn't sure. When they left the carrier to return to the mountain base, one of the trucks was missing. He had been careless and left the keys in the ignition. There hadn't been the threat of theft, since there were no known survivors in the area. If Jim had survived the beating, he might have reached the shore and taken the truck. That possibility greatly disconcerted him.

The caravan entered Fredericksburg and Hathaway ordered them to stop. He would do one more thing in an attempt to find the origin of Jim.

The Humvee was exactly where they had left it the day before. The black man he had ordered shot was not. That was to be expected. It was no accident that he was shot in the chest. A headshot was too good for his kind. It was better to let him walk around

132

like the rest of those foul-smelling monsters. Besides, it gave them the opportunity to shoot him again, adding to their amusement.

They came to a stop beside the Humvee and the soldiers poured from their trucks to take positions around the perimeter as zombies flooded from doorways and alleys to fill the streets around them. This time, Hathaway gave the order to shoot. There were too many close by to save ammunition this time.

Shots rang out in steady bursts and the smell of gunpowder filled the air. Creatures half decayed but still mobile and very motivated began to fall as their heads exploded. More came to replace those who had fallen. The streets were becoming thick with walking death. Their stench filled the air and mixed with the smell of sulfur. It was the smell of war and of death.

Hathaway ran to the vehicle and started rummaging through it. He didn't have much time. The protected perimeter became smaller by the second. The ghouls were getting closer and too many to effectively exterminate.

Donald Covington, the young boy Hathaway had been personally instructing, was the first to be overwhelmed. He had waited too long to retreat to a safer, closer location. Several ghouls closed in on him and took him to the ground. His clothes were ripped from his body, exposing the boy's pink flesh.

Uncaring ghouls tore into him and quickly disemboweled the screaming youth. One fiend pulled the entrails out of the boy's stomach cavity and another moved in to feast on them. The horror of the situation was difficult for even the most hardened of the militia members, knowing that their comrade was still alive and aware of what was happening to him. His cries of agony finally ceased as the creatures continued their grisly feast.

Hathaway returned his attention to the glove compartment in his frenzied search but he found nothing to help him. Perturbed, he scattered the papers he did find on the floor. The registration was simply issued to the U.S. Government, nothing more.

He searched under the seats. Flares, chains, and a fire extinguisher were the only items there. He gritted his teeth, angry at his failure.

Hathaway moved to the back and opened the gate. Another man went to the ground and cried out as he was besieged by the hungry horde. The perimeter was collapsing.

A single motorcycle took up the bulk of the space in the back of the Humvee. A tool box and chainsaw to its left, a small generator to its right. Hathaway searched the tool box but its contents shed no new light to the mystery.

Deflated, he leaned against the rear gate and stared into the vehicle. Two jackets lying behind the motorcycle caught his attention. As Hathaway reached past the bike and threw the jackets to the side, a flash of gold lettering caught his eye. He pulled one of them out of the vehicle and studied the embroidery on the back. He fingered the raised lettering. "Yes!" It was the information he needed. "FEMA!"

30

Hal's wife, Anne, took the news better than Leon had expected. Death had become part of daily life for all the survivors. Hal had put his life on the line nearly every day since the beginning of this nightmare. She could already feel the hole left in her life by his death. She knew this day would one day come and the sadness was overwhelming.

She listened quietly as Leon explained what had happened. Head down, she stared at the wooden planks on the front porch. When he was finished, she nodded and closed the door.

Jim, waiting by the curb, had found what he was hoping for: other survivors. For nearly a year he had been obsessed with leaving Mount Weather to find other survivors, but the only thing he could think of now was getting home again to Amanda. He had endangered their safety by leaving. He feared the militia would find them and the thought of his family and friends at the mercy of those animals chilled his blood. He had to get back there. Now.

Jim and Leon walked to the hanger where the Cessna was stored. Jim stared at the machine and hoped it was up to the trip.

"You say that Hal kept it in good flying condition?" Jim asked.

"He did the best he could. She'll fly. How long she'll fly, I couldn't tell you."

Leon walked to the front of the plane and dug his fingernails into the peeling paint on the nose. Milly followed close behind, her tail wagging happily. Jim watched Leon, who had something on his mind. First he patted the nose of the plane, then rubbed his hand across the propeller before inspecting the stability of the wings. His feet shuffled with indecision.

"You know, you can come with me if you like," Jim offered, sensing what might be on Leon's mind.

Startled, Leon met Jim's gaze. "No, I don't think I could do that. Not after yesterday. I never did like going out there in that mess."

"It's all right, Leon," Jim said. "Don't feel pressured into doing something you're not comfortable doing. I'm fine to do this alone. I just thought you might want to go along."

Leon smiled briefly at the notion but deep down he was unsure of his feelings. It was the same as with Hal and Jack. He dreaded the thought of going on those rescue missions but in the end he always did. Well, not this time. This one he'd sit out.

"I appreciate the offer but no thanks. Maybe next time. You will be back, won't you?"

"Yes," Jim said. "I'll be back.

Jim gave the plane a once over, checking the fluids and fuel. The trip was more than one hundred miles. He didn't want to find himself in a forced landing halfway between the island and home. A small landing strip at the southern end of Mount Weather was long enough to handle small jets. The Cessna would have no trouble landing there.

The trip would take less than two hours. Soon he would be back in Amanda's arms, easing the anxiety she must be feeling by now. He thought of Matt, who should have stayed put. God knows, he had tried to stop him but no one could have predicted the events that unfolded. Once again, danger was finding its way to them, to their sanctuary.

Jim opened the cockpit door and crawled into the pilot's seat. Though it had been a while, it would be easy to fly this plane.

He wiped the dust from the gauges and started the engine. It roared to life with little effort. It had been well maintained. He increased the RPMs until it thrummed evenly, without sputters. His stomach began to churn with the pain of hunger. He hadn't eaten since leaving home. Home, he thought. Unbeknownst to him, the Mount Weather Underground had become home. He was anxious to return to Amanda. She is what made it home.

Jim slid open the large doors to the hanger and sunlight streamed in. Leon ran toward them, out of breath, a black satchel slung over his shoulder. Milly, always the good dog, ran at his side, her tail wagging happily.

Jim smiled when he saw them. "You sure?"

Leon eyed the plane, its motor purring rhythmically in the hanger. "I'm sure."

31

He watched intently, unaware of anything except Sharon's move-ments at the far end of the room. He was upright but bound at the feet. The invisible barrier could only be touched with outstretched fingertips. He yearned to be close to her, to touch her. The empti-ness hurt, a craving that could not be extinguished.

He pulled in vain at the restraints, then lunged at the invisible barrier he could barely reach. Dejected, he moved back to the wall.

The other one was still with her. It was of no interest to him but he could not look at it without feelings of anger. When she gave her attention to the other one, a feeling of contempt flooded his being. It would be good to push that one away until it was out of sight but bound to the wall as he was, it could not be reached. The other one was not standing upright, nor was it even moving much.

He couldn't remember much about what had brought him to this place. Was he searching? He felt as though he had been, and still was. He was different than the one on the other side of the invisible barrier. He had known this before but he just now remembered it again.

He looked at her longingly. A kind of lust filled his misfiring brain and drool began to flow over his lower lip and slide down his chin. If he could only touch her, taste her. A desire for what she pos-sessed enveloped him. It pulled relentlessly at his fragmented thoughts, a void to fill up, a craving unfulfilled until it consumed his entire being. If he could touch her and become one with her he would become complete, satisfied.

Sharon finished her work at the desk and moved to the door to the left of the Plexiglas wall. She watched the specimen as it tried to get out of its bindings, a confused expression on its face, unable to compute a solution to his dilemma. It watched her between feeble attempts to break free, a pitiful glance from time to time to make sure she was still there.

Mick and Griz would be here shortly to dispose of the reanimate who had been in the lab for the past two years. It was no longer of any use to her. Its decomposition rate had accelerated recently and it was literally falling apart.

Bound to the examination table, its lower jaw had disconnected from the upper. The creature's mouth hung open and the odor had become rancid, even for one of the specimens.

· The new specimen wanted nothing to do with the older, more decomposed specimen on the table. It shuffled about as far away from it as its bindings would allow and did not seem to even want to look at it. It often looked at her with longing in its eyes, arms outstretched as though beckoning her to come closer. A pleading cry rose from its dried and decomposing throat in quick, jagged gasps that faded away more quickly than those of a living person.

Sharon moved to the workstation and filled a small syringe with a clear liquid just as Mick and Griz entered the room. Mick walked to the Plexiglas wall and stared at the creature lashing out from the darkened corner.

"I thought I told you to leave that damned thing tied to a table," he said.

Sharon picked up three facemasks, handed one to each of the men, and wrapped the other around her own neck by its elastic band. "I've been handling these things for over two years, Mick. I think I know what to do and what not to do. One thing I do know: don't handle them without gloves."

She tossed two pair of yellow rubber gloves to them and motioned for them to put them on.

"Well, still, it would've been nice if you had called me for some help. If he'd gotten away from you…"

"Your point's made, Mick," Sharon said. "Next time I'll call you and you can come watch. Now put those masks on or you'll wish you had when I open that door so we can get him out of there."

Mick slipped the mask over his mouth and nose. Griz followed his lead.

Sharon unlocked the door and entered the room, then moved behind the head of the creature that had been lying on the table for two years. Its body, in a coma-like state, had remained still for several days. From time to time, the fingers of the left hand twitched, the only sign that a life force still inhabited the reanimated corpse.

The bound creature in the corner lunged and Griz jumped back in reflex. Mick stepped forward, as though to do hand-to-hand combat with it.

"Don't worry," Sharon said, her hand on Griz's chest, "he can't get loose and he can't reach us from there so calm down." She tossed Mick a hard look and he relaxed but he kept a vigilant eye on the ghoul just in case.

Mick watched as Sharon drove a needle into the base of the ghoul's skull and injected clear liquid into it. "What are you doing?"

Sharon threw the empty syringe into a nearby wastebasket and straightened her mask. "It's an old trick that Doctor Brine taught me before he died. Rather than shooting them or sawing their heads off to put them down, he would inject acid into the base of the skull. Their blood flow ceases with death but the nervous system remains very active. The acid will work its way in and around the brain and destroy the nerves that keep the body going. This one will die now." She looked thoughtfully at it. "It would've died soon anyway."

"I thought you said these things would last for ten years. Has that changed?" Mick asked.

"When I said that, the hypothesis seemed to be the correct one. However, lately I've been seeing something different. At least from this one, but it could be because I've been dissecting it. That may have shortened its lifespan."

Mick checked the creature's bindings and then flipped down the levers on the table legs, freeing the wheels for movement, and rolled it into the open area of the lab. He parked it before closing the door and locking it. He pulled the mask over the top of his head and flung it into a nearby wastebasket. He sucked in the fresher air of the lab.

"You can just take that thing up top and bury it somewhere," Sharon said.

"Any place in particular?"

"Any place you want."

Mick shrugged. "I still don't see how keeping these things down here is helping us."

Sharon smiled. "You'll see real soon, Mick. I've gotten quite a bit of information from these specimens."

"Anything you want to share?"

"In time. Tomorrow, maybe. I want to go through my findings one last time before I tell everyone what I've learned."

*   *   *

Secrecy was key. If Mick or any of the others knew, they would stop her. She had considered the possibility that she could be jumping the gun, so to speak, but she couldn't stay and wait. Not one minute longer. Besides, she would only go for the day.

Amanda stepped out of the elevator and into the knee-high grass near the now-abandoned security gate. Many of the survivors crept to the surface from time to time, in spite of Mick's warnings. His caution bordered on paranoia, as though merely sticking their heads into the sunlight would bring a world of trouble down upon them.

She shielded her eyes from the glare of the midday sun. After spending so much time underground, her eyes had become unaccustomed to the outdoor brilliance. It hurt to look upward. It was unnatural, she thought, living this way.

Her hair was tied back into a ponytail that had grown nearly halfway down her back over the past two years.

The cumbersome backpack she carried weighed heavily on her. She shifted it to her left shoulder and took a moment to don a pair of sunglasses to shield her eyes from the sun's rays.

The backpack was filled with the essentials she would need for her short journey. Two police .45s were holstered to her waist, one on each side. She carried a sawn-off double-barreled shotgun in her right hand, though she had no idea what kind of weapon it was. She had brought along the shells that were stored with it.

Amanda skulked across the lawn and down the hill toward the warehouse. From there she would get a vehicle for her trip. Without the map Jim had used to plot out his route, she would have to guess which way he had gone. She remembered that he was planning to take Route 7 to 17 until he got to Fredericksburg. From there she wasn't sure, but he would've taken the safest course. The wide-open Interstate heading south seemed logical.

The bay doors on the front of the warehouse were twenty feet high. There was no way to open them from the outside so she entered through the rusty, squeaking door to the left. Once inside, she saw the reasoning behind the large doors: Tanks were parked neatly in a line down the center of the building. Cranes, two of them, no three! One was barely visible at the far end of the dimly-lit room.

Amanda removed the sunglasses.

Farther down, barely visible, were what looked like rocket launchers. Two of them had rockets loaded, ready to be sent to targets.

Her eyes quickly adjusted to the dark room as she looked for a means to travel. There were a few of the wide, squatty looking Humvees like Jim had used parked near the wall but they looked awkward to drive and hard to handle. She shied away from them in favor of a green brush truck. The size of a regular pickup, it had tool chests that ran the length of the bed on both sides.

Amanda jumped inside and found an empty ignition switch. She sighed at the thought of tracking down the keys. She flipped down the sun visor and the keys fell into her lap.

32

Jim pulled back on the wheel and the plane eased upward. It felt good to be flying again. As the small plane went higher, the aspects of piloting came flooding back to him. He was beginning to feel in tune with the plane. The island shrank beneath them and he turned to the northwest.

Milly was lying between the seats, front paws outstretched, her head resting on them. She had quickly fallen into a light sleep.

Leon watched as Tangier faded away behind them. He'd not known Jim for long but the man had a way of gaining trust and loyalty. There was something about him that was noble and honest. He was a born leader. He was leading now and Leon didn't mind following, not as long as he was following a man like Jim.

He'd never been in the military and had wondered how so many men could go into battle without blinking an eye. They could blindly charge up a hill to take the high point, knowing full well the difficulties and perils. He knew now; they had a good leader. A man they trusted with their lives. Jim was such a man.

The plane swooped lower. The sudden move woke Milly and she sat up.

Leon watched as ghouls dotted the landscape below. "Jesus," he said, "it just doesn't get better, does it?"

Jim leveled the plane out at three hundred feet and flew northwest. "Can you tell where we are?"

"Yeah. Colonial Beach. We flew over this place several times in search of survivors."

"I need to get to Fredericksburg to find my way back. Without the benefit of using a map, I'm going to have to fly by sight to get home."

"If you want to go to Fredericksburg, you'd better turn this thing more to the west or you'll miss it. It's not that far."

The left side of the plane dipped and Jim took it a bit higher.

"Wiped out, man," Leon said. "We've been wiped out. There's not a living soul down there, just the walking dead. God really had it in for us, didn't He?"

Jim mused over Leon's question. "Someone did."

They flew westward, toward Fredericksburg.

33

The caravan of trucks topped the ridge two miles from camp. Gray smoke blended between the thick trees of the mountain, the smoldering odor heavy in the air.

Hathaway leaned forward in his seat. His scheme must've gone as planned. The smoke was obviously from the explosion. He made a motion with his hand and Jake accelerated the truck's speed.

Hathaway's eyes widened. He had not anticipated this. Most of the encampment had burned to the ground and many fires still smoldered. Women and children huddled in the center of the camp. Around the perimeter, militiamen watched the surrounding woods and the road leading south. Others pulled bodies and goods from the burned structures. The ground was littered with the dead. Some were their own people, others were not.

The trucks had barely come to a stop when Hathaway leaped out and ran into the center of the catastrophe. He turned around, taking in every detail of the calamity. His shoulders slumped at the realization of the numbers lost, of the disastrous outcome.

He turned toward George Bates' office. It was completely destroyed, as were several surrounding buildings. His lips parted. "Jesus," was all he could manage.

He studied the ground and the bodies lying there. Many were their own men, many more were definitely not. Some were mutilated and partially decomposed. They were zombies! Those damned rotten sons of bitches had found them.

"Goddamn it!" he screamed, and kicked the head of the corpse that lay at his feet.

Jake stumbled his way through the carnage to stand at Hathaway's side. He stood in stunned disbelief, unable to utter a word.

"It's gone!" Hathaway cried. "It's all gone!" His rage burned. "WHO DID THIS!"

A tall dark-haired man in his thirties with close-set eyes and a scar that ran from his left eye to the bottom of his ear turned toward Hathaway and walked toward him with deliberate steps. The man was Ben Colby.

Seeing him, Hathaway seethed with contempt. Colby, the stupid prick, Hathaway thought. He thinks he knows it all. Yes, sir, he thinks he's in charge. He thinks he has all the answers. But he doesn't know shit. Damage control, he thought. I can still pull this thing together. I can handle it.

Hathaway watched as Colby walked up to him. Colby dropped his rifle to his side and stuck the butt in the blackened soil. Hathaway gritted his teeth at Colby's total disregard for the weapon's care.

"I'll tell you what happened," Colby said, his eyes narrowing as he spit the words at Hathaway. "Someone set a bomb in Bates' building. You wouldn't have any idea who did that now, would you?"

"As likely to have been you as anyone," Hathaway countered and pushed him aside. He took several steps forward, away from Colby, to scan and assess the situation.

Colby followed. "The propane gas tanks outside the building next to Bates' office went up minutes after the initial blast. The explosion set half the camp on fire. By this time many of our people were outside. The gas sent a jet of flames right into the crowd. You should've been here to hear the screaming. Women and children burned like human torches and they died in agony. They died a slow death. There were just too many to help in all the confusion, my wife included. No, sir, it wasn't me. I didn't do it."

Hathaway walked away again, Colby close on his heels.

"And that's not all," Colby said. "Oh, no, there's more. Most of the ones who died from the blast came back. You know, it's funny. You'd think that after dealing with this for so long we would've expected that and would have been ready, but we weren't. Most of us were still in shock when they started to walk around again. My wife? I had to shoot her in the head. I had to. It was hard, but I did it. Then I shot another."

Colby's fury grew as he continued. "Before long it became a little easier to shoot the people I've known for the last two years. After all, it's really not them anymore, is it?"

Hathaway closed his eyes and his mind to his responsibility for this disaster. It had no bearing on the outcome but he couldn't look at Colby.

"And it wasn't just *our* people coming back that we had to worry about. Bart Shockley shot Phil Stanton's wife in the head, so Phil shot Bart. She had gotten up after she had burned to death and was determined to take a bite out of ol' Bart. Phil went completely loco after that and started shooting up the place. We had to end up shooting the poor bastard in the head."

"There's more than our people on the ground here," Hathaway barked.

"Yeah," Colby said balefully. He wanted to get under Hathaway's skin. "We finally got things under control. Got the fires stopped and began to clean up the mess. We were physically and mentally exhausted. We'd lost half our people. Many were in mourning. We didn't know."

"Know what?"

"That others were about to find us. They must've heard the explosions and saw the smoke from the valley below. They came in the night. Took us by complete surprise. We lost a lot of people here this week."

Hathaway tried to get an estimate of how many had survived. It was hard to tell but it was bad. "This place isn't safe anymore," he said.

"Well, you're in charge, big shot," Colby said. "For now, anyway."

Hathaway, vexed by what remained of his conscience, strode away. Jake followed, leaving Colby to finish his tirade with raised voice.

"You're the one with a plan, aren't you? You figure out what we're going to do, where we're going to go."

34

Steam roiled from under the hood of the brush truck as Amanda entered Fredericksburg. The sweet smell of antifreeze filled the cab and her heart pounded. The temperature gauge was pegged to the right. She was in trouble. The truck was beginning to miss and sputter.

Amanda glided to the side of the road, turned off the motor, and made a safety check of her surroundings. She had tried to bypass the inner part of the city. She was on the dual lanes that would take her to the Interstate running south but she somehow had missed her mark and ended up in an area thick with structures. It was not a safe place to be. There were creatures around and some had taken notice of her when she stopped. They were slow but it still left her with very little time to work.

As swiftly as possible, she popped the hood and ran to the front of the truck. When she lifted the hood up, steam billowed into her face and antifreeze fumes took her breath away.

The radiator hose had a large tear in its side. She didn't know much about auto mechanics but she knew enough to know that it wouldn't go far without water.

It would be useless to look for water here. There was no electricity to power the water supply. There were no creeks nearby, either. Luckily, she had brought some water with her.

Amanda ran to the cab and pulled out a gallon jug of water and unscrewed the cap. From the floorboard she grabbed an old rag and went back to the front of the truck. She glanced toward the creatures still approaching. More were visible now than a moment ago.

She set the bottle down and wrapped the rag around her hand to unscrew the radiator cap. It came off without the expected spew of pressure. The gapping hole in the upper hose had already released it.

She quickly poured in the contents of the bottle. With the last of it came a popping sound somewhere in the bottom of the engine compartment. Amanda looked down to see that the modest amount of water she had put in had leaked out onto the asphalt under the truck. She had poured the cold water in too fast. The sudden temperature change had cracked the block. She cursed and threw the bottle aside.

Amanda slid into the seat and tried to start the truck again. It wouldn't get her far, but anywhere was better than where she was.

The motor barely cranked. It sounded labored and dry. Then it quit doing anything at all. One quick pound on the steering wheel and she gathered her things and jumped back into the street.

Creatures were closing in from all directions. She tossed the backpack over her shoulder, grabbed the shotgun, and ran south down the dual lanes in an effort to clear the closing crowds. She ran until she didn't think she could run anymore, but still she pushed on. She ran for nearly another mile, until she saw something that caused her to skid to a stop.

Up ahead was the Humvee Jim and Matt had used. Indecision wracked her entire being. Uttering a brief prayer, she trotted toward the truck. Fear of what she might find caused her heart to clutch in her chest.

The rear door was open. The motorcycle was still loaded in the back. It *was* their vehicle. Her spirits sank.

Minutes passed. Amanda lost track of how long she stood there, staring at the truck, trying to think of the ways Jim could have survived. She was taken completely by surprise when she felt a hard tug on her backpack. She turned around with a startled scream.

A gray-faced man growled at her and reached a claw-like hand toward her face. She shoved him away and, like an old western gunfighter, drew one of the .45s strapped to her side and shot it in the head.

Another ghoul reached for her as she slipped to the side to avoid its grasp. It moaned when its stump of an arm missed. She pulled the trigger and most of its head disappeared in a cloud of flying gore.

Amanda stumbled backward, falling against the side of the Humvee before regaining her balance. The street was quickly filling with the lurching undead. They reeled and swayed toward her in their usual mindless manner, clutching and moaning as they came.

Something had gotten them stirred up recently. It takes time for this many to come together in one place, in these numbers. Jim and Matt must have had an encounter here.

She turned back the way she had come but it was filled with disfigured corpses. Horrid creatures, putrid, disfigured, disgusting remnants of a lost civilization, the sight of them was maddening to her. She swallowed the urge to scream for fear that once she started, she would never be able to stop. This is no time for hysterics, she thought. Jim and Matt may still be close by.

The opposite direction was not as populated, not as risky. She could possibly fight her way through it. She ran in that direction as fast as her tiring legs would carry her. Adrenaline coursed through her body, her blood pounded in her ears. She tried to think clearly.

What is that sound? A motor? Yes. It's the sound of a motor. A plane!

*   *   *

Jim brought the plane down as he passed over Fredericksburg. He wanted to look around where they had left the Humvee. Matt was still down there somewhere. He was hoping his body would still be crumpled on the ground in front of the Humvee. Matt was a good man and didn't deserve to be walking around like those things. If he wasn't there, Jim owed it to him to come back one day and remedy the problem.

He swooped down in the area he thought the Humvee should be. There was an unusually large crowd of creatures, many more than one would expect. He passed over them at two hundred feet. They appeared to be gathering for something.

Leon watched as they made the pass. He had seen this kind of gathering in the early days. It usually meant that they had found living prey and that he would have to watch someone die at the hands of hungry ghouls. They rarely got to the ground in time to save them.

Jim turned the plane around to make another pass.

Amanda watched the plane as it turned. She started waving her arms and shouting at it. Three creatures moved in quickly to cover her and bore her to the ground under their weight. Two undead corpses were directly on top of her and the third fought for an opening.

She held a ghoul under the neck with her left arm to prevent it from biting her. The other ghoul dropped down with its gapping maw, its rotted, swollen tongue lolled out at her as its grossly disfigured face came closer.

As it neared, Amanda forced the tip of the pistol into the creature's mouth. Fearing infection, she closed her mouth and eyes and pulled the trigger. Most of the brain matter exploded out the back of the skull but some of it spewed from its mouth to splatter over Amanda's face. She kept her mouth shut. Even the creature's blood, once introduced into her body, could contaminate her.

She pushed the limp body to the side, the pistol still hanging from its mouth.

The third creature saw this as an opportunity to get closer. Amanda quickly squirmed away from the creature she was holding with her left arm. Her sudden move caused it to fall face first to the asphalt. The other one, on its knees, reached for her but she had already gotten to her feet. She gave it a swift kick in the face and it fell backward. She wiped the blood from her face and rushed to an open spot. Again she waved her arms at the plane as it approached.

Jim swooped down closer this time, much lower than the last pass. He saw arms waving as he approached. The plane swished past close enough to blow the hair on her head. "Jesus!" he screamed. "It's Amanda!"

Leon looked down at the woman on the ground as they passed. "What? You know her? How could that be?"

"We've gotta put this thing down, fast!"

Jim came back again. He could see Amanda below, moving erratically to keep from being surrounded. He brought the plane back around and lowered the flaps to decrease speed. The street was straight and long enough but it was filled with the undead. He had no choice.

"You'd better brace yourself, Leon. This is not going to be an easy landing."

There was no time for Leon to voice an objection. The plane bounced against the street several times before coming down to stay. But it was coming in way too hot.

Amanda saw it rushing toward her and dove to get out of the way. The plane slammed into a pack of the walking dead as it skidded down the street. One creature made direct contact with the spinning propeller. It exploded into a thousand pieces as blood and body parts splattered the plane and the windshield.

One of the propeller blades broke off and slammed though the windshield between Jim and Leon and lodged in the ceiling behind them. The right wing crashed into another crowd of them and tore off. Bouncing down the street beside them, it splintered into several pieces. The plane skidded sideways as zombies bounced off its side, tossing them into the air.

The tail crashed into the Humvee and ripped away with a loud crash. The plane spun around several times before it came to a stop. There was no time to waste.

"You all right, Leon?" Jim yelled.

Leon raised his head up off the dash and rubbed it. "Yeah," he said. His head throbbed. He'd be counting himself lucky to get away with just a concussion.

A creature pounded on Jim's door. He pushed it open and kicked the fiend away. He drew his weapon and promptly blew its head off. It stood headless for a moment before dropping to the ground.

Jim jumped from the cockpit with Leon and Milly right behind him and raced toward Amanda.

Amanda had scrambled to safety down a narrow side street and watched the scene unfold as the plane came down. She couldn't believe her eyes when she saw Jim get out of the plane. She must be dreaming. He couldn't have possibly been in that plane, at this moment.

She started to walk to him. Her walk became a jog, which became an all-out run. She crashed into him without slowing and wrapped her arms around him.

Jim allowed himself a moment of release as he kissed her head, then her upturned face before she pushed him away.

"I've got some of their blood on me. Don't kiss me. You could get infected."

"We've got to get out of here," he said.

Amanda glanced at Leon and realized with a jolt that it wasn't Matt.

Jim looked to see where the Humvee was. The impact of the plane had flattened two of its tires and slammed it into a telephone pole. Hundreds of creatures filled the street around it.

Amanda pointed and said, "This way."

Jim realized that the only way out was the narrow side street that was more like an alley than a street.

He led the way and the three of them ran into the entrance of the darkened alley. Leon turned when he heard Milly barking behind them. She had stopped and was standing her ground against the approaching army of undead. Many of the creatures were already within a few feet of the dog.

Creatures reached for her. Milly sidestepped and snapped at the ones closest to her, snarling with bared teeth. She backed away and the horde of monsters followed her. They crowded around her, momentarily distracted from the three humans in the alley.

Leon pulled the dog whistle from under his shirt and blew hard. In unison, the creatures turned their attention to the fugitives in the alley and away from the dog. Leon looked suspiciously at the whistle between his fingers and then back to Milly, who continued to hold her ground.

He blew on it again. This time Milly came running but the whistle had a definite effect on the creatures. They began to wail and fling their arms about wildly. They crowded into the alley stumbling over each other as though they were being driven.

"Let's get out of here, now!" Jim yelled, taking Amanda by the arm. The three of them ran down the alley toward the sharp left turn at its end.

Jim was the first one to turn the corner. He stopped and stared. Amanda and Leon turned the corner. All three stared at a dead end less than twenty yards away.

The alley, sandwiched between two buildings, had turned to the left about three hundred feet in and came to a dead end where the building on the right L'd in to meet the building on the left. There was nowhere for them to go.

The creatures continued to rush toward them.

"Get out your guns!" Jim shouted.

Leon patted his pockets. "Mine's in the plane! Shit!" Amanda tossed the shotgun to Leon and realized that she had no other weapon in hand. She pulled the remaining pistol from its holster. She slung off the backpack and pulled out the box of shells, tossing them to Leon.

"We can't do this! There are too many!" Amanda screamed.

"We've got no choice," Jim answered, and soothed her with a hand on her shoulder. "Just shoot out a hole for us to run through," he said. "You can do it."

He looked back at Leon, who had moved all the way to the dead end, searching for a way to climb up the walls.

Jim knew there was no escape there. He had already looked. Leon quickly realized it for himself and ran back.

The creatures were closer, about two hundred feet away now. They needed something more to get through the advancing wall of undead. It would be nearly impossible to make it through by simply shooting some of them; they didn't have nearly enough ammunition.

Milly sat next to Leon. She had quit barking but a steady snarl reverberated through her bared teeth. "Does she sick 'em?" Jim asked.

"What?"

"Will she go after them if you tell her to? It may give us the extra time to get through."

Leon looked thoughtfully at Milly. "Yeah, she'll—" His eyes widened in surprise. "Sweet Jesus!" he screamed and pushed Milly to one side.

Jim looked down. Milly had been sitting on a manhole cover! Leon fell to his knees and stuck his fingertips into the indentation in the lid and pulled. The lid refused to yield. Jim bent down and both men pulled at the cover. It still refused to give way.

"No, this can't be happening," Leon said at this quirk of fate. Right at their feet was their means of escape but they had no tools to use it.

Jim searched the alley around them for something to pry open the lid. Milly began to growl louder and Amanda had to grab her by the collar to keep her at bay.

"Give me the shotgun!" Jim commanded.

Leon handed him the sawn-off. Jim stuck the end of the barrel into the notch and pried. The lid lifted enough for Leon to get a grip under the rim and pull. "Just lay it to one side of the hole," Jim instructed. "We'll need to put it back on from inside to keep them out." Jim reached over and grabbed Amanda's pack. "You first."

Amanda didn't move.

"Now, sweetheart! We'll follow."

Amanda shoved Milly toward Jim and sat down beside the hole, her legs dangling into it. She leaned forward to the ladder on the inside and crawled down into the blackness.

Jim motioned for Leon to do the same. After Leon went down the hole, Jim handed Milly to him and shot two of the closest ghouls before slinging Amanda's pack over his shoulder and climbing in himself. He reached up, then and strained to pull the lid back into place. It slammed down just as one creature's fingers reached in under it. The creature, not knowing any better, pulled his fingers out and the lid popped into place. Jim heard them banging on it as he descended.

Once at the bottom, they were in total darkness. A trickle of moving water swished around their feet. They held their breath, waiting to hear a noise, a movement of any kind other than their own.

Amanda spoke first. "The flashlight...it's in the bag."

Jim fumbled in the darkness until he found the zipper and opened the bag. He plunged his hand inside until he felt the cylindrical shape of the flashlight. He pulled it out and clicked it on.

The sewer drain was about six feet wide and twice that high. The ledges along each side were a little more than a foot wide and two feet above where the water trickled past.

They stood on the ledge, listening to the commotion above. Jim got a bearing on their direction as best he could and worked to formulate a plan of action.

They would go north.

35

"Amanda's gone!" Felicia proclaimed as she bounded into the room.

Mick laid the generator part on the table and looked up at her. "What are you talking about?"

"I can't find her anywhere. I've looked all over. She's gone."

"She can't be. Where would she go?"

Felicia bit her lower lip. "I don't know. We've got to look for her."

"She's around somewhere. Where did you look?"

"Everywhere. Down here, anyway. I didn't think she'd go back up top after our last encounter there." She was almost unable to breathe when an unimaginable thought struck her. "Mick, what if she went looking for Jim?"

"She wouldn't do that. She knows better. Jim hasn't been gone that long. There's no reason for her to worry so much yet. It would be lunacy for her to go out there alone. I can't believe that."

"I *can* believe it. You don't know how desperate she's been the last day or so to know if he's safe."

"He's only been gone for two days. There's no reason for her to flip out yet."

"He told her he would be back the night he left. When that came and went, she started worrying and she was mad as hell. I have to tell you, I'm worried, too. It's not like him to promise one thing and do another. Something's wrong. I feel it."

Mick came and stood in front of her and looked deep into worried eyes that were swimming with unshed tears.

She reached up to caress his cheek and absently stroked his mustache. Her premonitions were returning. If Mick had learned one thing, it was not to second-guess her when she was like this.

"Okay, I'll go look up top," he said. "She's around here somewhere." He drew her close to him.

Felicia was a worrier, but her worries were usually well founded. Unlike Amanda, who was more independent, Felicia needed comfort and love. She soaked it up like a dry sponge. He had always thought that her closeness with Izzy was more than the psychic link they had. She needed love and she needed to express love to others. The young child was perfect medicine for her in a dying world.

Mick squeezed her hand before walking away. "Go find Griz and tell him to meet me in the armory. He can go up top with me."

*   *   *

The sky was overcast and clouds blew swiftly past as a spring wind gusted over the mountain. Mick and Griz started their search at the main gatehouse. If she had left the property, there could be clues there.

The two men stood in front of the gatehouse. Mick looked into the dark room through the small glazed window by the door. It was hard to see clearly but it looked clear. He opened the door wide. Everything was as it should be. Nothing seemed disturbed or out of place since the last time he was there.

Printouts and fax papers still littered the floor. When the surface division went belly up, the officer on duty had abandoned his post in an apparent hurry.

When Mick stepped inside, bullets rolled around like loose marbles under his feet. Griz held the door open while Mick made a cursory search of the room but he found no clues.

"I don't know why I'm doing this," Mick muttered. "She's down there somewhere." He spiked a finger toward at the ground.

Mick closed the door and walked to the main gate. The gate didn't swing open, it slid on a track to the right to allow entrance to, or exit from, the compound. A heavy chain and lock kept it from doing so when they were in lockdown, what they had been in since they'd been there.

The only exception was when Jim left and the gate was locked again behind him. Mick jerked on the heavy chain without thinking. The lock fell open. Without a word, he ran to the guard shack. There were two known keys to the gate. Jim had one with him and the other was kept in the top drawer of the desk in the shack.

Mick yanked open the drawer and found nothing. He rubbed his forehead to ward off an approaching headache. Amanda knew about the key. She was one of the few people who did know.

"What's wrong?" Griz asked.

"We've got problems."

36

Jim led the way as Amanda, Leon, and Milly followed. The sewer smelled horrible but not in the way one would expect a sewer to smell. It wasn't the smell of human feces and urine. It was more akin to an old mildewed coat and rat droppings. It was overpowering and the smell of ammonia burned their nostrils.

They forged ahead, feeling their way through the dark tunnel lit only by the small flashlight. Jim stopped and turned to Amanda and Leon. "Shhhh!" He held his finger up to his mouth. They stood motionless, listening.

The rustling sound came again. Jim shined the light upward. Several rats watched them from a pipe overhead. They hunched down, their long snouts bent over the pipe, whiskers twitching.

Jim shined the light on the walls around them. "How far do you think we've come?" he whispered.

"I don't know," Amanda said.

"About a half a mile or so," Leon whispered.

"Yeah, that would be my guess, too," Jim said.

"What's wrong, Jim?" Amanda asked, moving closer to him.

Leon did the same but faced the direction behind them. He stared nervously into the darkness.

"We need to find a way out of here as soon as we can," Jim said. "This may not be a good place to be."

"Worse than up there?" Leon asked, peering into the dark void. Another sound startled him and he jumped. "There's not more of those things down here, are there?"

Jim flashed the light in that direction. "I don't think it's zombies." He glided the light back and forth over the sewer walls and ceiling.

Amanda grew more nervous. "Jim, what's wrong?" she demanded.

"Rats!" He hissed.

Then they heard it. The sound was like that of an approaching wave, the thrumming of hundreds of running little feet, like someone thrumming their fingers on a bass drum. Anxious and hungry, screeching, "Screech! Squeak!"

The rhythmic sound grew louder behind them as it grew closer.

"Ah, man!" Leon groaned. "What's the deal with everything wanting to eat us?"

Jim grabbed Amanda by the hand and yelled, "RUN!"

He pulled Amanda along behind him as he ran through the sewer tunnel. Leon stayed close behind, tugging at Milly's collar whenever she stopped to growl at the threat in the darkness behind them.

He could hear the running rats in the darkness, even over the sound of their own stumbling footsteps. He shook off visions of thousands of them chewing at him, covering his body until he collapsed in the tunnel to be left behind, bleeding, and slowly dying as they filled their little bellies on his flesh.

How he hated rats! Rats, mice, squirrels—they were all sharp-toothed, nasty little rodents full of lice and crawly things. No, no, no! he thought to himself as he ran. No, no, no!

They made a turn in the darkness and Leon felt a small thud as a rat fell onto his shoulder from the pipe above. A piercing pain when it bit him. He slapped it away, dashing it to the floor. He ran faster. He didn't think it was possible to run any faster, but he did. He ran so fast that he slammed into the backs of Jim and Amanda, who had come to a sudden stop. The impact almost knocked all three of them to the floor.

"There!" Jim pointed to the ceiling. A ladder hung on the wall that led to a manhole. "When we get up there. Be prepared for anything. We don't know how many of those things will be hanging around, so be ready to run again."

Leon breathed heavily. He wasn't sure if he could go another step, much less run again should they need to. The sound of the rats had faded. Maybe they had outrun them.

"I can't do it. I can't take another step," Leon gasped.

Jim shined the light in the direction they had come. There were no rats so they were safe for the moment. "Okay, we'll wait here for a second and catch our breath. But we can't stay long."

Amanda supported herself with her hands on her knees to regain strength for another possible sprint. "Why are they chasing us? Rats don't eat people."

"They do if they're hungry enough," Jim said, watching the tunnel behind them. "And I'd say they're pretty hungry. There's been nothing for them to eat, no garbage left by people for two years. There hasn't even been sewage for them to pick through."

"That's disgusting!" Leon said, repulsed. "One of those foul things bit me on the shoulder." He rubbed at it. "You don't think they're zombie rats, do you? That's not why they're chasing us, is it? Because if it is, there ain't no antibiotic that's going to cure me."

Jim shook his head. "No, they're just rats. Hungry rats."

"Well, just the same, it would be my luck to get the bubonic plague from those dirty little bastards."

Leon's tirade was broken by the soft pattering of the scurrying rats somewhere down the tunnel as they continued their chase. In his mind's eye he saw them, fur matted to mangy hides, crowding the tunnel six deep on their quest for food, their whiskers twitching in anticipation of a meal. Squeak, squeak!

Leon flexed his jaw, grinding his teeth at the thought.

Jim handed the flashlight to Amanda and climbed up the ladder. He looked back at her. "If the rats get too close, climb this ladder behind me and get off the floor as far as you can."

"You bet," Amanda said.

Jim shoved his shoulder under the manhole lid and pushed. It was tight, just like the other one after two years of neglect, but after a few thrusts, it broke free and popped out of the hole. He did his best to lay the lid quietly to the side.

He stuck his head out and turned around so he could see in all directions. To his surprise, there were no creatures in sight. He had come up on a side street, a residential area. It was a pleasant-looking neighborhood in spite of the unkempt yards and peeling paint.

He peered back into the hole and hushed them with a finger to his mouth. "Come on," he whispered, waving them up with a hand.

Amanda came up first and Jim helped her out. Leon climbed out next, after pushing Milly through, and collapsed on the asphalt beside Jim. They stayed silent. No one wanted to attract unwanted attention. Below, the rats noisily made their way to where the three of them had been standing moments ago.

Jim put the lid back on the manhole. "We need a car."

"Good luck with that," Leon said. "I had a hell of a time finding one that would start. All the batteries are dead."

"Did you look in any of the garages of the houses you passed?"

"No, I didn't. I didn't have much time to take that sort of a detour. I had a ton of zombies on my ass every step of the way."

"Well, that's where you'll find a car that starts. It will have been kept from the elements. Some of them should have good batteries." Jim turned to Amanda. "Why are you here? Has something happened at Mount Weather?"

A rueful smile raised one corner of her mouth. "No. I came looking for you. I was worried."

"There was no reason to be worried. You risked your life and, as you can see, I'm fine."

Amanda's relief was tempered with irritation. "I won't let you do this to me again, Jim. I'm not going to wait behind while you go on some insane, dangerous mission to save the world. I won't."

"Okay," he sighed. She was so headstrong.

Amanda smiled, determined that she would break him of his headstrong ways.

They rested there while Jim scanned the area. It had been a nice neighborhood and many of the houses had attached garages. Some of them were likely to have cars in them. If only one would start.

"We'd better get started," Jim said. "Have you eaten, Amanda?" His need to protect and take care of this woman was getting the best of him.

I've got food," she said, rummaging through her backpack. "Where's Matt, Jim?"

The question took him by surprise. In all the turmoil of crash landing the plane, fighting off the zombies, and running from a teeming army of voracious rodents, he had pushed it aside. He wasn't prepared to explain everything in detail yet.

"He's gone, Amanda. Some men killed him because of who he was."

"What do you mean?" she asked, handing a sandwich to each of them. She broke hers in half and gave half to Milly.

Jim pulled her to her feet. "I'll explain it all later. Right now we need to get out of here."

Amanda felt the loss. Time should be set aside to mourn but that was a luxury they could not afford.

She looked at Leon, who had been running by her side through this living nightmare. He had a similar masculine look as Matt but he was leaner, less muscular. Not as tall, either. Leon was less than six feet tall. Matt was at least six-one, and Leon's skin was darker.

"I'm Leon," he said with a slight smile.

Amanda tried to smile back but found it difficult so she simply nodded.

"We'll try there first," Jim said, pointing to a large brick home with a three-car garage. "We've gotta get out of the city before dark." He watched the sun disappear behind a line of trees in the west. "If we get stuck here after dark with no means of transportation…"

The house was still in good condition. No windows were broken and the doors were all in one piece. Jim walked across the wraparound porch and jiggled the knob on the front door. He turned to Amanda and Leon. "It's locked."

He tried a window. When it failed to open, he walked out of sight to the rear of the house. Amanda and Leon waited anxiously at the end of the sidewalk.

In a few moments they heard the locks being turned on the front door. It opened to reveal Jim standing on the other side. They hurriedly moved inside, out of sight.

The foyer was large, with hardwood floors and a giant chandelier that hung from a cathedral ceiling. It opened into a formal living room with a centrally-located fireplace that was open on two sides. Bookshelves covered two walls and a thick layer of dust covered the furnishings and floor. The air was damp, with a musty, stale odor and a hint of spoiled meat.

Jim went to the fireplace, pulled a poker from the caddy, then pulled Amanda and Leon to the center of the room. "Stay here," he told them and walked away.

"What's wrong, Jim?" Amanda whispered. "Why do you need that poker?"

Jim pointed to the floor. "Footprints. Not ours."

In the settled dust were footprints that led to a closed door at the end of the room. Jim crept toward it.

"Use your gun, Jim," Amanda suggested, looking dubiously at the iron poker.

Leon laid a restraining hand on her shoulder. "It would be too loud and attract unwanted attention. Just be calm. He'll be okay."

Jim opened the door and drew the poker back to strike. It was an empty closet. He relaxed his grip, puzzled. He studied the footprints again. They went to the closet but they stopped there. The dust was disturbed in front of the door, as though someone had collapsed on the floor.

He saw a blood stain on the door trim close to the knob and near the floor. To his right, the dust was scuffed off the floor in two tracks, as though the person no longer lifted their feet to walk. The scuffs went through an arched doorway and into the kitchen.

Jim followed the trail but found nothing. No more tracks were visible on the ceramic floor.

The door in the kitchen would certainly lead to the garage on the side of the house. He sensed danger somewhere. The footprints looked fresh in the dust, maybe as recent as the last month. Whatever made them was possibly still there.

Using hand motions, Jim cautioned the others to stay where they were before he opened the door. If something came at him, he would need room to deal with the danger.

Jim drew a deep breath, pulled open the door, and came face to face with it. Amanda gasped in sudden surprise. Milly exploded into a rage of barks and growls.

Grossly decomposed, it fell forward onto him. Jim pushed it away and it fell against the opened door, then slid to the floor. Its skin was very wrinkled and dark, a man but not hulking. It moved at a snail's pace in an attempt to regain its footing. The ghoul wore jeans, but no shirt.

Unlike any of the others Jim had seen, this one was purple from waist to the neck on its left side. It had probably been lying on its side for a period of time and blood had pooled there. It functioned poorly, even for one of the creatures.

Jim looked into the garage for more before turning to the pitiful specimen on the floor. It reached out for his shoe and Jim kicked its fingerless hand away before driving the poker into its left eye.

Amanda turned her head and closed her eyes as Jim pushed it onto its belly, face down.

"We have a minivan," Jim said with a crooked smile. "And if it starts, we have a ride home."

Leon moved closer. "A minivan sounds good to me. As long as it moves, I don't care what it is."

Jim opened the door and checked for keys. There were none. He checked the visor and the console between the seats. There were no keys to be found. He turned to Leon. "Go check the house for keys. Be careful. There may be more of them in there somewhere."

As Leon jumped all three of the stairs leading from the garage to the kitchen, Milly tagged along. When Amanda attempted to follow, Jim yelled, "No! Stay here. He can handle it."

Jim opened the hood of the van and pulled the two caps off the top of the battery. The acid level looked okay. He replaced the caps and noticed a small generator under a table on the back wall. He began to rummage through the garage for a charger. If the battery was dead, that could be a lifesaver.

He found none.

It was nearly dark when Leon returned to the garage. "No keys, man. I looked everywhere but I can hotwire it if you need me to."

Jim grabbed some tools that were lying on the table and crawled under the dash without answering.

"I guess he can do it," Leon said to Amanda.

Jim pounded the steering column several times until the casing broke free. With a screwdriver and hammer, he removed the locking pin that prevented the steering wheel from moving before going to work on the wiring. After a few moments, he raised his head and gave a thumbs-up to Amanda and Leon.

Jim touched the two wires together. They sparked and the motor cranked. It dragged on, agonizing turn after agonizing turn before he let the wires fall apart and climbed into the seat. He reclined and closed his eyes. They were in trouble.

A loud bang on the garage door made him leap from the van. "They're here!"

Another crash against the door. Amanda backed away from the center of the garage to the back wall. "We've got to do something, now!" Leon shrieked, panic washing over him.

Jim frantically searched the room for anything that could help them.

Darkness smothered them as the last rays of light began to disappear. "The light! The flashlight!" he yelled to Amanda.

Amanda pulled the flashlight from her bag and handed it to Jim as another crash shook the garage door, then another and another. Inside the house, glass shattered onto the floor and Milly began to bark again.

Jim pressed the button with his thumb and the flashlight's beam split the darkness. He shined it around until it met Leon's face. "Lock that door." He shined the light over to the door between the kitchen and the garage.

"What good will that do? It locks from the kitchen side!"

"Yeah, but those things don't know that. It may take them a while to figure it out. It might give us the time we need."

"The time we need for what?" Leon cried. "Praying?"

"To get out of here! DO IT!"

Leon had barely locked and closed the door when a thud rattled it. He had been too close to one of them when he stuck his hand around the door to lock it. He backed away when the realization dawned on him.

Jim pulled the generator from under the table and checked it for fuel. It was half full but the gas smelled stale. Hoping it would be good enough to start, he replaced the cap and slid it closer to the van.

"Get me something to plug into this if it starts," he told no one in particular. "I need to drain some of the power this thing makes or it'll blow the battery."

Jim grabbed an extension cord from the table and clipped one end off with a knife, then cut the rubber coating from around the wires, exposing them.

Leon found a yellow light stand with two square lights attached on top and dragged it to where Jim squatted, rigging the cord. He looked at Amanda and Leon, who stood over him. Amanda held the flashlight for him and the fear in both of their eyes was obvious. "God help us," he said as the pounding around them intensified.

He pulled the start cord hard three times. Nothing. Then a thought occurred to him. He took the flashlight and shined the light around the sides of the generator, looking for a choke. He found it, and a small prime button. He pushed in on the button several times until he was confident the fuel had circulated thoroughly and pulled the choke and cranked it again. It sputtered, then fizzled out.

It was the sign of life he was looking for, and a ray of hope.

He pulled the cord again and the generator sputtered to life. The crowd on the other side of the garage door had grown larger and their relentless hammering had buckled one side inward. Several arms thrust through the opening in an attempt to grab anyone near. It wouldn't be long before the whole door came down. The creatures sensed that and intensified their attack.

Jim plugged in the yellow lights and the room lit up. The ghouls discolored faces could now be seen pressed against the garage door windows. There were many more than they had thought.

Jim picked up the extension cord and plugged the good end into the generator. "Leon, get in and touch those two wires together under the dash. I'll use this to give it the extra juice it needs. Amanda, you get in the back of the van and lock the doors."

Amanda opened her mouth. "Jim—"

He cut her off with, "I'll get in, too, as soon as it starts."

Amanda grabbed Milly and reluctantly did as she was told.

Leon twisted the wires together and the engine cranked slowly. On the other side of the door leading to the kitchen, one of the zombies fumbled around the knob. The pressure of his hand moved the lock to the open position.

Jim touched the wire to the battery terminal just as the kitchen door came open and ghouls staggered into the garage.

Sparks flew. The battery began to smoke but the engine turned faster.

The creatures moved toward Jim. Excited by the presence of living flesh, they quickened their pace. The van engine roared to life and the battery exploded, sending hot acid spewing toward Jim's face. He turned and most of it splattered across the side of his head but some got into his eyes.

In his blindness he felt the cold grip of one of the creatures as it grabbed his throat. Like lightning, he sent an uppercut to where he thought its chin would be. The attack cut empty air.

The creature struggled to control its prey enough to attack on its own. Jim tried to open his eyes but the pain from the burning acid intensified. Another ghoul bit at his shoulder but pulled away with a hunk of cloth from Jim's shirt.

Realizing the peril he faced, Jim forced his eyes open long enough to see through cloudy and teary eyes. Three creatures tugged at him as he thrashed and kicked at them. He slung the one at his throat to the floor and made a dash for the van, jumping in on the passenger side. "Gun it, Leon! Crash though the garage door and run right over them!" he shouted as he wiped at his eyes.

Leon revved the engine and slammed the gearshift into reverse. The wheels squealed as the van roared backward and smashed into the garage door, which collapsed into a V-shape around the van and bounced violently over the bodies of the reanimated corpses outside. The neighborhood had become populated with hundreds of ghouls who bounced off the van as it sped backward toward the road at the end of the driveway.

Leon didn't ease up on the gas pedal when he slammed the gearshift into drive and sped away, leaving the hungry mob behind.

Amanda took a bottle of water from her backpack and handed it to Jim. He flushed his eyes as best he could as Amanda and Milly settled down in the back seat.

As long as the motor didn't stop running, they would be okay. The alternator would keep the van going but if it stopped running for any reason, it would not start up again.

Leon drove on, weaving the van around ghouls drawn by the commotion. "What now?" he asked, his voice cracking with fear.

Jim did his best to see into the darkness beyond the headlights. "Seventeen. Find Route Seventeen. That'll take us home."

PART

III

Plans of Power

37

Chris Smith eased the boat closer to the shoreline and dropped anchor a couple of hundred yards off Smith's Point. He would take time to refuel and get some rest in the safety of the bay before morning.

The red gas can was heavy as he pulled it from its resting place behind where he was seated. He set it down in front of him and looked across the water into the night. His presence had not gone unnoticed by the indigenous population of Smith's Point. They moaned and howled in the darkness. Some cackled like hyenas while others yelped. It was a strange mix of chilling sounds.

Chris was not sure of anything anymore. His comrades were not exactly the type of people he would normally pal around with but survival was unlikely without them. The militia had saved his life a year ago and for that he was grateful. They had fed him and kept him safe ever since but he did not subscribe to their way of thinking. They were elitists, born and bred to be shining examples of the white race. At least that's what they believed. To each his own, he thought. Anyway, what did it matter now? Like it or not, they were all he had left.

The gas flowed into the tank with a *glunk-glunk* when Chris held the can over the opening. When the can was empty, he twisted the cap back into place.

He still wasn't sure what he was supposed to do. Maybe he was to be a spy of some sort. Hathaway was always so secretive and had given him little information to go on. He was to come to Smith's

Point and check things out first. He was to look for living people and report back his findings to Hathaway on the radio he'd been given.

If he found no one alive at Smith's Point, he was to go across the bay to a string of islands and search there. At no time was he to tell anyone who he was or from where he had come. He was just a survivor out looking for food in the middle of this godforsaken mess.

He didn't like it but he had no choice. It was true that they had saved his life but they would have no qualms about taking it away should he prove himself a liability.

Chris threw the can into the back of the boat and leaned back for some sleep. He closed his eyes and listened to the ghoul-song echoing from shore. The sounds reverberated through his mind as he slept and made for some very disturbing dreams.

38

It was ten at night when the minivan arrived at the Mount Weather security gate. Jim stepped out of the van and listened intently to the night. Chirping crickets were music to his ears. There were no footsteps or cries from lurching ghouls to bristle the hair on the back of his neck. It was a calm, cool country night on top of a mountain, away from the rotted remains of civilization.

Jim helped Amanda out of the van. He took the gate key from her when she held it out to him and he ran his fingers through her long dark hair.

"The chain's not locked," she said.

He offered her a warm smile. Even if she had not caught the subtle message, it was a silent promise to never leave her again.

Amanda and Leon followed Jim as he walked to the gate and punched in the code on the keypad. He entered each number: eighteen, fifteen, thirteen, five, eighteen, fifteen. Each time he pressed ENTER before going to the next number.

A soft chime rang inside the guardhouse. The lock clicked and the gate opened.

Mick was walking to his room to meet Felicia when he noticed the blinking red light over the intersection of halls leading away from the main thoroughfare. He stopped and stared at it, then bolted down the hall to Griz's quarters. He pounded on the door until the burly man appeared.

"Something's on the compound grounds," Mick said. "The red light is blinking."

"Jim?" Griz stepped back into his room and returned with two M16 rifles.

"God, I hope so," Mick said. "Or Amanda."

Jim entered the second code to open the door into the lobby area that Felicia found so therapeutic. His hand found the light switch on the wall and the room glowed with florescence. He closed the door once Leon, Amanda, and the dog were safely inside. "Home sweet home," he said with a smile. He motioned them ahead toward the elevator.

Five, two, six was the three-digit code to the elevator and Jim entered it without thought. The door slid open with a swish.

They had found the security codes soon after they had settled in Mount Weather. It had taken some doing but eventually they had been able to break many of the codes to get information from the complex's computer systems.

The elevator began its rapid descent and Leon's knees buckled. By the time he regained his wits and balance, the door opened and they were on the main level of the underground, more than three hundred feet below the surface. They stood face to face with Mick and Griz, who had their weapons raised and ready.

Mick quickly lowered his weapon and grinned at the welcoming sight of Jim and Amanda. "Jim! Thank God it's you!"

Jim nodded wearily.

Mick's eyes blazed when he looked at Amanda. "Damn you, girl! You scared the hell out of me, tearing out of here like you did. I thought—" He stopped mid-sentence as his eyes settled on Leon. "Where's Matt?

39

Chris awoke with a start at dawn. He watched a seagull perched on the front edge of the boat until it took flight, then wiped the crust from his eyes and sat up.

The shore was visible now in the morning mist and it was unsettling to see what had been making the chilling sounds during the night.

A group of nearly one hundred creatures wailed and flailed their arms along the water's edge. Each time the waves crashed to shore, they backed away. When the water receded, they moved en masse back to the water's edge. It was a surreal water dance dictated by the rhythm of the sea.

Chris watched them for a while before taking the map from his pocket.

Tangier, the southern most of a string of small islands in the bay, was the closest island to Smith's Point. Smith's Point was a departure point to the islands and part of the mainland. There were just too many walking dead there for anyone to survive.

Then again, any of the islands would be a sound choice to put down roots. Once cleared of the ungodly inhabitants, its isolation would provide a safe and pleasant existence.

Chris refolded the map and put it back into his shirt pocket. He watched the creatures on shore for a while longer and decided that he would not investigate Smith's Point.

It took about thirty minutes to reach Tangier. The fog surrounding the shoreline was much thicker than the mainland.

Chris leaned forward and squinted his eyes to identify a movement he saw through the haze. A man raised his arm behind his head and then thrust it forward. After a while, he repeated the action. He was fishing. Chris could make out the rod as he drew closer.

Chris eased the engine to idle and slowly chugged along the coastline, leaving the man behind. He didn't want to become known just yet. He had provisions in the boat to dispose of first. The radio might raise suspicions. He would come ashore at a place that would afford him his privacy to stash his equipment. He had to make contact with Hathaway soon.

By then he should be settled in and would know his next course of action.

40

Leon joined Jim, Amanda, Mick, and Felicia for breakfast in the main cafeteria at dawn. They were quiet as they nibbled at the tasteless rations. The excitement of Jim and Amanda returning safely was subdued by the news of Matt's death.

Leon was amazed at his new surroundings. The Mount Weather Underground was an engineering marvel. It was safe, if drab, with most of the walls painted a dull gray. The concrete floors were already wreaking havoc on his legs and feet. The cafeteria was brighter but it reminded him of the schools he'd attended in his youth.

Most of the sleeping quarters were more of the same: Rows of bunk beds lined large rooms with metal lockers for personal belongings. Only the hierarchy's quarters, meant for the President and his staff, were pleasing but they were limited in number.

Mick pushed the powdered eggs on his plate into a tight pile, then scattered them again before finally pushing the plate aside. "Cardboard," he complained.

The others looked up from their plates.

"This crap tastes like cardboard," Mick said.

Jim swallowed his eggs. "What do you expect? It's probably two years old. All of the food is."

"I'm sick of it," Mick grumped. "I'm sick of this place, too. Sick of the isolation. What's out there, Jim? How bad is it?"

Jim put his fork down and pushed his own plate away. "I thought you were ready to wait this thing out here. Wasn't that your thinking only days ago?"

Mick shrugged.

"It's bad," Jim told him. "It's as bad as it's ever been. Those things are everywhere. To be cornered means death."

"You said there were people on the islands," Mick said, and shot a glance to Leon. "It's safe *there*, isn't it?"

"Yeah, it's safe, and there are a lot of people there. If you mean to suggest that we move there, I'd love to, but I'm not sure how all the extra mouths to feed would impact their food supply."

"It's an island, for Christ's sake!" Mick said. "We can fish. Besides, our food here won't last forever. You said that yourself. And what if that militia finds us?"

Jim looked to Leon for input.

"I think it would be fine," said Leon, taking the hint. "I don't think sixty people will make much of a difference on how much we get to eat. Like Mick said, you can fish. And we have plenty of fruit trees. Where the soil permits, we grow gardens." He grinned wryly. "Fresh tomatoes," he teased.

"Oh my god!" Felicia cried. "Fresh tomatoes?"

Still grinning, he said, "Apples, too."

Mick couldn't help but smile at the possibilities. Fresh food, sunlight…It was the chance for a normal life again. "Can we do it safely?"

Everyone stared at him.

"Can we make the move safely?" Mick repeated. "Get out of this hole and have a life?"

Jim pondered Mick's question. It wasn't as though he hadn't already given it some thought. "With time to prepare, I think we can. We have the weapons again. The warehouse up top has plenty of armored vehicles. Everything we need is here to make a move. There's only one problem.

"When we get to Smith's Point, we need to have a way to get everyone quickly across to the islands. The boats anchored there are small and we don't know how many of them will actually move.

The ones that do may not hold all of us and we can't afford to hang around there for very long."

Leon ate the last morsel on his plate. "We have many boats on the islands," he said, still chewing. "If we send a party out ahead of the main group, we can get them over to The Point and be ready. Not a big deal."

"It is a big deal," Jim said. "It's a big move. We need to think this thing through first. And we should talk this over with everyone. Let them decide for themselves. Some of them may not want to go."

Sharon Darney approached their table. She opened her lab coat so the long tails would hang comfortably at her sides and pulled up a seat beside Amanda. She smiled at the others, who only stared at her.

"Did I miss something?" Sharon asked.

Jim stood and gathered his tray for disposal. "Nothing much. Just some talk about the possibility of moving to the islands."

"The islands?" An eyebrow shot up in surprise. "When?"

"We don't know. Soon maybe. We'll see. I'm going to call a meeting with everyone tomorrow night to discuss it."

"That sounds good," Sharon said. "I have so much to tell you all. I can do it then."

"What, Sharon?" Jim asked.

Sharon's eyes twinkled mischievously. "Everything."

41

Felicia tugged at the juicy red apple until it broke free from the branch and brought it to her mouth for a bite. Just as she was about to bite into it, a familiar voice from behind said, "There you go again. Are you back on that vegetarian kick?"

Stunned, Felicia dropped the apple and turned around. "Where have you been?" she cried and threw her arms around her brother.

"Easy, easy," he said. "You're choking me."

"Where have you been?" she asked again, and pulled away.

Her brother smiled and his sky blue eyes twinkled with laughter in the morning sun. "You know."

"No, I don't know."

"I couldn't just run up here. I had things to do first.

"That doesn't make a bit of sense," Felicia said. "Of course you could. It's so pretty here."

Felicia twirled around in a circle, her arms outstretched. She smiled and tilted her face to the sun. After several turns she slowed to a stop. "Where is 'here'?" she asked, realizing that she was in a strange place.

He took her by the hand. "Come on, I'll show you."

He pulled her up the hill and through the trees into the clearing where their grandmother's house stood and Felicia realized where she was. She was dreaming again. It was surprisingly comforting. She had missed the dreams.

"You see now?" he said, pointing.

Felicia nodded and followed him inside.

Once inside, she turned to her brother but he was gone. She called him but he did not answer.

Felicia ran through the house, searching for him but he was nowhere to be found. She stopped in the living room and watched the flames in the fireplace lick the sides of the logs placed evenly there in rows of three.

"Keeps 'em out real good," a voice behind her said.

Felicia turned. "Grandma! Where did you come from?"

"I came from the kitchen, child."

Felicia looked back at the fire. "Keeps who out, Grandma?"

"The wolves, child. Can't let them in. They'll ruin everything. They'll get into the pantry and eat all the supplies. Hateful animals, they are. No compassion, you know."

"I know, Grandma, but we got rid of the wolf already. He didn't fool us."

Isabelle Smith turned and hobbled back to the kitchen. "One of many, child. You know that. I told you before. Don't you remember?"

"Yes, I remember," Felicia said, following her. "My brother was here just a minute ago but he's gone now. Where did he go?"

Isabelle poured two cups of tea and placed one in front of Felicia. "He didn't go anywhere, child. You brought him here and you sent him away."

Felicia took a sip of the tea. It was good, sweetened just the way she liked it. "Then where did I send him?"

"He has his cross to bear, just as Jesus had His, child. You've come a long way and fought many battles but the time's coming when everything will make sense to you. You'll know the truth and it will set you free."

Felicia took another drink from her cup. When she looked up again, her grandmother was gone. Usually the dream ended at this point but not this time. She sat there for a while, waiting. A scratching came from the front door.

Felicia crept to the door and put her ear close to it. A slight scratching again from the other side. She leaned in closer.

"Come," a voice whispered.

A foreboding raced through Felicia's body as she whipped the door open wide and screamed.

Her brother stood at the door. Creatures, too many to count, dragged him into a waiting crowd standing in the darkness.

"NO!" Felicia screamed and bolted upright in her bed.

42

The conference room began filling with the residents of Mount Weather. They filed in and took their seats in front of the podium while Jim, Mick, and Sharon stood at the front of the room and conversed.

Sharon would speak first, confident that she had solved the riddle. After many months of study and dead ends, it all made sense to her now. It was complicated but she was prepared to explain in simple terms to everyone.

Sharon wheeled the chalkboard closer to the podium and then adjusted the microphone so she could talk and point out her findings on the board at the same time. The microphone squealed briefly as she adjusted it downward.

Once everyone was seated, the chatter stopped and she had their attention. She cleared her throat.

"I think I've solved the riddle of the plague," she said, and the chatter returned. She waited for it to subside before continuing.

"It's kind of complicated so you'll have to pay close attention to understand completely."

Sharon picked up a piece of chalk and drew everyone's attention to the chalkboard, where there were several drawings. To the left was a tadpole-shaped image labeled "Contaminating Virus." To the right of it were three oval-shaped images labeled "Healthy Blood Cells."

Sharon pointed to the tadpole image. "This single-celled organism is responsible and was very difficult to discover. In the human

187

body there are roughly one hundred billion cells. In a reanimate's body I estimate there are approximately one million of these organisms, ten of these cells per one million cells making up the body. I've also come to the conclusion that we all have the same number of this particular organism living in our own bodies. This organism alone caused the dead to walk again."

The room exploded with fear and shock on the faces of many, while others paled and turned to those next to them.

"No, wait!" Sharon shouted, trying to calm them. "There's no reason for fear. It won't affect us. Not while we are alive, anyway. Let me explain."

The room quieted and she continued.

"First, let me say that although I have found some answers, I don't know everything. I don't know what suddenly triggered this dormant organism to cause the dead to reanimate. With my limited facilities and resources, I simply don't have enough information to make that determination. I do believe, however, that I can explain it from this point forward.

"The process is two-fold. One way for the condition to develop is at the point of death." Sharon pointed back to the tadpole drawing on the board. "This is the original carrier of the disease and like I said, I believe we all have this organism hiding in our bodies but it is not designed to attack its host until death. The cell temperature must drop before it can carry out its function. Once the cell temperature is around ninety degrees or below, it will begin to mutate the cells that surround it. These cells in turn do the same thing in a swift chain reaction until the entire body is altered at the cellular level. The entire process happens very quickly. This I call the Assault Phase. Once complete, the body is recharged and reanimated.

"It is recharged through something that happens during this phase. Part of the process of altering the cells is to add something new to them. My study has shown that chloroplasts, or something very similar, are added to each dead cell and it's altered. A chloroplast is the part of a plant cell that allows it to gather energy from sunlight. It's something you may already be familiar with, called photosynthesis. That is why the hundred or so creatures who inhabited this facility were inactive upon our arrival.

"The people here were killed below ground and never saw the sun after reanimation. The organisms were able to draw enough energy from the host bodies to reanimate them for only a short period of time. When that energy was exhausted, they returned to a state of true death."

Sharon pushed the chalkboard away and returned to the podium. She took a sip of water before continuing. It was difficult to explain the phenomenon in layman's terms and she needed a moment to think.

"As everyone knows, this is not the only way to get infected and become one of the reanimates after death. A single bite that breaks the skin is deadly and will achieve the same result in the end. The mouths of these things are a breeding ground for bacteria and filth. Death occurs in a matter of days.

"The Komodo Dragon—I'm sure you all know what a Komodo Dragon is? It's a large lizard that kills its victim with an infectious bite. Its mouth contains four forms of deadly bacteria that no known antibiotics can cure. The bacteria causes major blood poisoning, which results in death in a week if the bitten animal gets away. Komodo Dragons are confined to a single area of the world and are an endangered species. Reanimates are in every corner of the Earth and we are now the endangered species."

Frank Thompson, a bald, portly man in his fifties stood up. "Where'd this disease come from? I mean, if you say we all have this…this *thing* responsible for the plague in our bodies, why hasn't it happened before now?"

Sharon nodded thoughtfully. "It's new. I don't know where it came from."

"How about space?" someone in the audience yelled. "Maybe it came here on a meteorite or something."

Sharon smiled thinly at the notion. "I don't think so. From what I've seen through study, the Earth is its point of origin. It's true that it's different than anything we've seen before but it still contains the basic makeup and structure of an earthbound organism."

Alice Johnson stood and asked, "Why can't they reason like we do? They're mindless zombies, more or less. They seem to have no recollection of their former lives."

"The period of time from death until the body is reanimated is now twenty minutes or more," Sharon explained. "Brain damage takes place in less than four minutes. By the time reactivation occurs the brain is damaged beyond the ability to reason, not to mention the damage caused by fever and changes that the cells, including those in the brain go through. They *are*, in effect, mindless zombies."

"Zombies who want to eat us!" another voice cried out.

"Yes," Sharon answered. "I believe that is a product of basic instinct–their instinct to reproduce. We, as living beings, are nothing more than a collection of cells doing their best to thrive and survive. Evolution is simply the process of one-celled animals changing the way they interact with each other to improve their chances for survival. Scientifically, our existence comes down to that simple equation. These creatures cannot reproduce through sexual contact so instinct has given them an alternative course of action: reproduction through contamination."

Sharon looked back at the chalkboard. "Of course, that is just my hypothesis. We have no way of knowing what motivates these creatures. It could be some latent instinct that the virus has reawakened during the process."

"How long, doctor?" Frank blurted out. "How long before this all ends? Will it ever?"

"If you mean, how long will the disease be here, I don't know. But on closing, I can tell you one thing. At first, I thought the creatures—and I use that term loosely, they're *not* human, you know, they don't function as such—would remain mobile for ten years, maybe more. But recent findings suggest that their lifespan may be much shorter."

"How much shorter?" another asked.

"As I mentioned before, sunlight powers them. That gives them their energy, not the consumption of flesh. But it's a double-edged sword. It will also be their undoing. Eventually, the sun and other elements will take their toll on the reanimate's bodies. I think it's possible that we might be seeing the last months of their existence. Hot weather is on the way so we must wait and see. That doesn't mean more can't be produced through infection, it's just that the ones presently walking our planet are burning out."

The chatter commenced again and Sharon took the opportunity to move aside and give Jim the podium.

Jim smiled at Sharon as he moved toward the podium. "Nice work, Doc."

"Nice work, hell," she smirked. "I have yet to find a cure."

Jim leaned forward and surveyed the crowd. They had become a family. Two years of surviving had made them that. In the front row sat Bob Deavers, a farmer-turned-floor-sweeper, his chore at the facility. Behind him was Shelly Sage. In her early fifties, Shelly still pined for her husband who was lost in the plague.

Several families had made it through the zombie onslaught. One such family corrected their unruly children in the back row. Others made new families once they had settled in. Brenda Welch was seven months pregnant. Her new husband held her hand as they both watched and waited for him to speak. Jim knew all of their names but he wasn't sure the next step was right for all of them.

"As most of you know," Jim began, "I just got back from Tangier Island and I'm pleased to say that we are not alone. There are many more who have survived this horror."

Applause broke the silence of the crowd. Some stood and whistled. Jim waited for them to express their pleasure before continuing.

"Tangier Island is located between Virginia and Maryland, in the Chesapeake Bay, part of a string of inhabited islands. The people there are happy, content, and would welcome us, should anyone want to relocate. There's plenty of food available by way of the bay. We could fish and do a bit of farming, too. There are plenty of houses for anyone who would like to take up residency for a nearly-normal life there."

A wave of chatter swept the gathering. He expected another round of applause at that point, but they waited, unsure. They had been safe where they were for more than a year but they had all learned the hard way that safety in this new world was a tentative thing.

"I don't want to worry anyone," Jim continued, "but there's something else you all need to know. I encountered more survivors than those at Tangier Island." Jim glanced at Leon. "I encountered a group of militia members, a particularly nasty group at that. This militia is well armed and from what I could gather, large in numbers. They are some of the worst our old civilization had to offer—racists, militants, white supremacists, Nazi's—however you want to categorize them. They were once a small part of our world's population, but things have changed."

He scanned the room, subconsciously making eye contact with the minorities in the room. "They are the ones who are responsible for Matt's death. They shot him in cold blood."

There were six blacks, not counting Leon, two Mexicans, an Asian, and a Pakistani out of sixty-three survivors. To the people of Mount Weather, they were part of the family but the militia would not see it that way.

"They killed Matt because of the color of his skin. Their idea of the New World Order is racial purity. If you're not white, they will kill you. I don't know if they are aware of our little hideaway but when they captured me, my map fell into their hands."

The room erupted again. "They know we're here?" Kelly Carley cried from the back. "They're coming here?"

"I don't know," Jim answered. "The map doesn't show this place as my starting point but it does come close."

"How close?"

"Route Seven."

"Jesus Christ, Jim. Are you saying that we aren't safe here anymore?" asked Bubby Wright, a short, plump black man known for his past job as the local weatherman. "Do we *have* to make the move to the islands?"

"No, I don't think so. For one thing, the map also shows the other end of my journey, so the islands may be unsafe as well."

Jim stepped out from behind the podium to address them on a more personal level. "I'm not here to tell you that we've got to move again, just to inform you of our options and our situation. I don't think we are in any immediate danger. Even if the militia should opt to storm this facility, they will need to plan carefully before doing it, and that means scouting the site and our numbers. It would be difficult for them to gain entrance but enough of them could. It is my intention to uncover their plans and make preparations accordingly. To pick up and move at this time would be premature."

Jim looked at the anxious face of Sharon Darney. "Doctor Darney says the zombies are burning out, that they may be nearing the end of their life span. From what I've seen out there, that may be true but we can't be sure. We have to operate and base our decisions on what we know, and right now that isn't much. So like it or not, some of us will have to leave the safety of this place again and go find answers."

Jim scanned the room. Things hadn't changed all that much. They were still the same downtrodden refugees of two years before. They were better fed and better housed, but fear still filled their hearts and minds—fear of the unknown, of what waits beyond the steel doors of the underground. He didn't see a room full of people, he saw a room full of ducks—sitting ducks.

"Tomorrow morning at nine o'clock, we want all of the men to attend a mandatory gun class. Should the need arise, we need each and every one of you to know your way around an automatic weapon. Any of you ladies who wish to do the same are encouraged to do so.

"The class will be held on the firing range in C-section. As most of you know, that's just down the hall from here, through the double doors." Jim looked around the room once more. "That's it for tonight. Thanks for attending."

As the crowd dispersed, some nodded their thanks to Jim as they left the room. Kelly Carley stopped to say to Jim, "I didn't mean to insinuate that you led them to us, you know? I didn't mean that," she said, worry lining her forehead.

"I know, Kelly. It's okay."

"If it weren't for you—"She looked past Jim to Mick. "If it weren't for all of you, we would all be dead now." She shuddered. "Dead or undead."

"We'll be fine. Don't let it worry you. We're safe here.

43

Turnout for target practice was better than Jim anticipated. Thirty-three people arrived to better their firearm skills. Ten of them were women who, to Jim's surprise, held their own with most of the men. It was a comfort to know so many were willing to defend their turf.

Two years ago they had been scared sheep waiting for a leader, unable and unwilling to stick their heads out into the sunlight for fear of the unthinkable horrors waiting for them. The sudden change in these survivors did wonders to ease the tension that had been pulling at the back of his neck for the last few days.

Members of his team were waiting when he entered the small conference chamber connected to the war room. Griz tagged along behind and plopped down in a seat.

These people were the heart and soul of their survival. They were the ones who risked their lives and forged ahead so that the others could follow. Jim's worry eased as he surveyed his comrades. He trusted them. He could count on them for anything. They were an impressive group, a collection of intelligent, heroic, determined people unwilling to give up.

Pete Wells chewed on a piece of jerky as he rocked back and forth in his chair close to the rectangular oak table. Jim noticed that Pete's hair had grayed a great deal in the past two years. When they had first met, Pete looked much younger. Obviously, this had been a difficult transition for him.

Pete knew his way around radio equipment but that knowledge couldn't help him fully repair the communications equipment at Mount Weather, not without the needed parts. Eventually, they had lost all possibility for outside contact.

Pete had spent hours listening to the endless stream of pink noise spewing from the prison radio when they were holed up there. After the move to Mount Weather, he had searched for live feeds, which, in the end, was dead air. They had finally come to the conclusion that they might indeed be the only survivors—until the signal from Tangier Island.

Sandwiched between Amanda and Felicia, Sharon Darney studied her notes. Mick chatted with Leon. When Jim entered the room, they all turned to face him, waiting for his next move, his plan.

Jim wasn't sure he liked the idea of so many depending on him for so much, or that they trusted him with their lives. He was only human and being human, he was just as apt to make errors as any one of them. Even Mick, who, in Jim's opinion, was every bit as competent as himself, leaned heavily on Jim for the final decision on most things. He and Mick were Captain Kirk and Mister Spock, flawless in the execution of every plan and able to get them out of trouble, no matter what.

Jim pulled the chair out next to Amanda. "We've talked it over," he said. "Some of us will be going back to Tangier to pave the way for anyone wanting to relocate. I'd like to take volunteers. No one is required to go but I'd like to have Mick, Griz, Amanda, and, of course, Leon, make the trip with me. Felicia, you need to stay. There's no way I'm going to take Izzy with us. She'll need you here. Pete, I want you here as well, to keep an eye on things."

Pete nodded and swallowed the last of his jerky. "No problem, Jim. I can do that," he said, chewing like a cow with a mouthful of cud. "If that militia shows up to make trouble, they'll find more than they bargained for."

"No," Jim said. "If they show up, there'll be no resistance."

Pete blinked. "But you said those people were dangerous, racist murderers. They will pose a definite danger to some of our people. Isn't that why we have everyone learning to handle a weapon?"

"Yes, it is," Jim answered, "but you can bet your ass that if they come here to attack, they'll be prepared. There's no point in risking all the lives down here. If they show up, you're to take the people they would target to kill up top and evacuate them to another location. I don't think they will want to kill us all. They're looking for a world to rule. They'll want people in that world. We're training everyone to use a weapon in case I'm wrong. Should they *need* to defend themselves, they'll know how."

Amanda fought to remain silent but failed. "And what about the people we so thoughtlessly relocate, Jim? What about them? Where will they go? Where can we take them to ensure their safety?"

Jim didn't like the solution anymore than he figured anyone else would. He didn't have all the answers, he wished they understood that.

"There's no other way right now," he said. "We've just got to work as fast as we can to remedy the situation. Hopefully, it won't come to that. If we can get things settled quickly, we'll have the support of a lot of people but if it does come to that, Pete, those people will rely on you to keep them safe. You'll need to use one of the armored vehicles to get them out of here and to Tangier Island. If the militia shows up here, I think it will be a good bet that it will be safer there."

44

Chris Smith covered the radio and scanned the area. He saw a house on stilts close to the beach that looked abandoned but livable. The yellow weathered board siding was loose in spots and a little worse from wear in the salt air.

The town was just on the other side of a knoll of sandy soil sparse with grassy vegetation. The knoll would protect the structures on the other side in bad weather by absorbing the impact of lashing waves. The house was a good place to set up his base of operations.

Chris walked toward town. He would try to blend in first, take in every detail of the inhabitants' daily lives and defensive capabilities. In the back of his mind he hoped they were too well armed to attack with any hope for an easy victory. Even if that was true, it may not be enough to stop Hathaway from carrying out whatever plan he had in store for these people.

The midday sun warmed his broad shoulders as he stood atop the knoll looking across the village. A moderate breeze blew his blond hair and pelted the side of his face with grains of sand. Squinting to keep the sand out of his eyes, he could hear the gentle tide as it licked the shoreline behind him.

A man worked on the roof of a house, hammering away to fix some shingles that had blown loose. Two more rode bicycles on the paved street. A woman stood at her front door, shaking a rug, dust particles flying in every direction. It was a welcoming sight. It erased years of horror. It was home to these people.

45

Jim slid the doors open and walked into the large warehouse as Mick flipped the light switch back and forth. "No lights," he said. Mick looked up at the darkened dish lights in the ceiling.

"There's no power on out here," Jim said. "I guess there's a breaker around somewhere. It's a good idea to find it so we can see what we've got in here.

Mick searched the walls for the breaker box. He found it halfway to the back. "Found it, Jim. Ready to power it up?"

Jim went to the wall switch. "Yeah, flip it."

Mick flipped the main breaker and Jim hit the switch. The lights crackled as they illuminated the large room. Mick was spellbound by what he saw.

"Don't pick out anything," Jim said. "I've already decided what we need."

Jim walked through the line of armored vehicles and Mick followed. They stopped in front of a large green tank-like thing with six wheels. A large gun was mounted on top, with a smaller, less menacing machine gun next to it.

"This is the one," Jim said, patting the angled front end. "It's heavy, fast, and will plow through just about anything." He climbed up next to the hatch. "It's called a Grizzly. It'll go almost sixty miles an hour." He moved behind the big gun. "It's a fifty caliber, with two banks of smoke grenade dischargers and a diesel motor pushing two hundred and seventy-five horsepower. There's enough room for all of us to fit inside for the ride to Tangier."

"You sure know your military trucks, don't you?" Mick said.

"I've had some experience with it," Jim said, sliding down. "It went into service in 1976. It's still in service today. At least it was."

Mick patted Jim on the back. "It still is, Jim, at least for us. How about fuel? Will we need to take extra for the trip?"

"We should carry some with us. It'll go a little over three hundred miles on one tank of fuel. The round trip is a little more than that. There's plenty here. We need to fill a few containers and strap them on." Jim walked back to the door. "We will essentially only have one thing to worry about in this thing. If it conks out, we're on foot."

Mick gave him a disapproving look. "Now why'd ya have to bring that up?"

Jim smiled. "Don't worry. I'll give it a good going over before we leave."

46

Robert Hathaway was sitting under a large oak tree when he saw Jake approaching. Ben Colby would not take his command, Hathaway thought, shifting his attention from Jake to Ben, who was talking to an assemblage of men.

The ignorant, uninformed bastard couldn't command a kindergarten class, Hathaway thought. He wasn't fit. He'd had no real training, no real combat experience. If he thought doing battle with those rotting piles of garbage was anything to be proud of, he was wrong. Dead wrong.

"Talk on, you ignorant bastard," Hathaway mumbled. "They won't follow you."

His jaw ached from gritting his teeth and he opened his mouth to relax the muscles.

Jake, who now stood by his side, spit and wiped his mouth. He never strayed too far from Hathaway. He felt secure close to him, like an older brother or even a father figure, even though there was only an eight-year difference in their ages.

"I've got almost a hundred men willing to make the trip, Bobby," Jake told him.

Hathaway stood. "I want more. We should have no less than twice that to do the job properly."

"It may be tough to get that many, Bobby. A lot of them are pretty pissed off at us right now, but these men are loyal."

"I know they're mad," Hathaway said, brushing the dirt from his trousers. "Colby's been trying to stir them up and turn them against me with his speculations and lies."

Jake followed as Hathaway walked down the gravel walk toward one of the small shelters. He watched Colby from the corner of his eye until they entered one of the small, previously unused rustic cabins.

Hathaway ran a finger through the dust on a wooden table and scanned the darkened room. Many of the larger buildings had gone up in flames when the explosion rocked the camp. He had not anticipated such destruction. How could he have forgotten about the gas tanks beside Bates' office? It was an amateurish oversight.

Jake watched Hathaway pace the room. He looked apprehensive, afraid even, but that couldn't be, Jake thought. Bobby Hathaway was fearless. He was in deep thought, that's all. He's devising a plan of some kind, making sure every detail was just right. That was it.

Hathaway moved to a small window and wiped away the layers of filth. Outside, Ben Colby was still talking to his men, bobbing his head as he patted one of them on the back. "Treacherous," Hathaway whispered. "Build your alliances, weasel. They can die with you." He turned to Jake. "Why do they listen to him? He's not really one of us. He's from the north, he's not a Freedom Fighter! College puke, that's what he is. He knows nothing. They're plotting against me, I know it!"

Hathaway went to the table and pulled the map from his pocket, the one with the yellow tracings. The one The Man had been in possession of the day he was captured. He spread it out across the table and studied.

Jake pretended to study the map, too, but he wasn't sure what he was seeing, except lots of lines and very small writing. It was confusing. It was one of the reasons he was never promoted during his military service. Sometimes he just didn't get it, but he was a good soldier. He could carry a pack and he could kill.

"Have you decided where we're going yet?" he asked.

"I'm waiting to hear from someone before I know for sure," Hathaway grumbled. "I'll make contact with him in two days. I'll know more then."

"That's that fella's map that we killed on the ship, ain't it?" Jake said. "Too bad he didn't tell us something before he died."

"That man wasn't going to tell us shit," Hathaway said. "He had plenty to hide, but he wasn't talking, goddamned FEMA man. I'll know his secrets."

"FEMA man?"

Hathaway refolded the map. "It's a federal organization, one that had way too much power. They're gone now with the rest of those federal pieces of shit. I just can't figure out what he was doing down in Fredericksburg. FEMA Headquarters is in Washington, D.C. I figure that he came from some island. I'd say he was a bleeding-heart, nigger-lover out looking for survivors. Well, he was obviously a nigger-lover, but that son-of-a-bitch was no bleeding heart." Hathaway shook the folded map in Jake's face. "You keep this shit under your hat, soldier. I don't want anyone knowing anything about this."

Suddenly the gnawing feeling Hathaway had struggled with for days revealed itself to him. Of course! There *was* another place! He remembered now. There was a FEMA center in Virginia!

He unfolded the map on the table again and stared at the yellow line. The southern end stopped at a place called Smith's Point. He was sure it wasn't there. No, it was in a secluded place, away from major population centers, much more secure than the Washington offices.

"It's here!" he pointed to the end of the line for Jake to see. "If memory serves me, there's a government base of some kind right there in Bluemont."

Jake listened and studied the map as best he could. "That there is where the Mount Weather station was, on top of Paris Mountain. It's something else now."

"How do you know that?"

"I've been by it before. It's right along the road that goes over the mountain. I don't think it's a weather station anymore, though."

"Why's that?"

"Because, there's a lot of buildings on top of that mountain right there in one spot. It looks like a little town all fenced in up there. It's called the ERC or EAC. Something like that."

"EAC? Emergency Assistance Commission?" Hathaway thought for a moment. "Sounds like FEMA to me."

47

"See here," Pete showed Jim, "the Grizzly has communication equipment we can use. It'll be on a military frequency."

"I know that but we have no relays or stations to carry the signal. It won't work."

"Oh, but we do!" Pete proclaimed. "We still have the one satellite working. We can bounce the signal off that. I just have to find the frequency."

"But the equipment in the war room isn't sending."

"I'll cut through the storage door with a torch," Pete said. "I'll get the needed parts and get it going."

Jim worked to strap two fuel canisters to the side of the vehicle. "We don't even know that it's storage behind that door for sure. And even if it is, how do you know it'll have what we need?"

"It's in the war room. We've haven't found the parts anywhere else. It has to be. They wouldn't put themselves in the position of not having replacement parts. Even if it's not, I'll strip one of the Grizzlies for the parts I need."

Jim shrugged. "If that'll work, fine. I want the radio working but we leave in the morning, regardless. I'll move the Grizzly up close to the gate so we can get it properly equipped."

Pete climbed out of the vehicle and wiped the grease from his hands on a rag, then tossed it on the floor. He studied Jim as he finished his task. "Jim, don't you think you're rushing things a bit? I mean, this has all happened so fast. Maybe if we wait a—"

"Wait for what?" Jim said. "For those maniacs to come up here and force themselves on us? No, I don't think so. Besides, we're not risking everyone. Only a few of us are going. If all goes well, we'll have a better life soon."

"Well, it was a thought. I had to say it, you know," he said with a grin. "Now I can say I *tried* to stop you if something goes wrong."

*   *   *

Amanda did her best to hide her anxiety. It wasn't anxiety exactly, it was more like excitement. She was excited to be going with Jim this time.

She couldn't help but feel their search for a normal life was almost over. If they made the move to Tangier, things would be different. They could actually live the way people were meant to live, in the daylight, above ground, and in a home again.

Home. How long had it been since the word had heart, real meaning? Home was a place you built your life around. Home was a place you lived with the people you love, a place full of dreams for the future. For so long she had known no such place. She closed her eyes and dared to dream. It would be good to have that again.

On the one hand, tomorrow could not come fast enough for her. On the other, it brought danger, maybe even death. "Not tomorrow," she whispered before reopening her eyes. They would not die tomorrow.

Amanda continued stuffing a bag with essentials for their journey until the zipper barely closed. She tossed it in the pile with the others.

Mick entered and placed two more weapons on the heap. They would be armed to the teeth, more than enough. Boxes of ammunition were stacked with the weapons and bags.

Mick's hair hung in his eyes and he brushed it away as he looked over the stack of guns, taking count in his head. Amanda walked over to the pile and picked up a rather nasty-looking pistol. It was heavy in her hand. "What is it?" she asked, turning it over and inspecting each side.

Mick took it from her and placed it back in the pile. "Micro Uzi 45ACP. It takes a clip, fully automatic. We're bringing six."

Amanda reached into the pile again, this time not for a gun, but for something else—eyewear, weighty with green lenses. She put them to her face. "I've never seen these for real before. Night vision aren't they?"

Mick nodded.

Amanda pushed the button on the side and the apparatus gently hummed. She suddenly tore them from her face, turned it off, and rubbed her eyes. Mick took them and returned them to the pile with the other equipment. "Sorry. I should've told you not to turn them on in here while you were wearing them."

Amanda squinted and blinked as though she'd just been caught in a camera's flash. "What *was* that?"

"They take what little available light there is at night and magnify it. It allows you to see in almost total blackness. Using them in a lit room isn't advised," he said with a laugh.

"I'll remember that."

*   *   *

Pete dropped the dark cover on the welding mask and continued to burn away at the door's hinges. Sparks danced in every direction as bits of the metal fell to the floor as glowing red particles. Jim watched from behind, wearing a mask of his own. He held a large crowbar and waited for Pete's signal to try again. The last hinge burned through and fizzled on the floor.

"Try it now," Pete told him.

Jim placed the end of the crowbar into the crack and looked at Pete. "What if we open this thing up and there's a horde of hungry ghouls on the other side, Pete?"

"Then we're fucked."

Jim applied pressure again. The door creaked, then broke free from the frame, hanging only by the locking system on the latch side. Jim and Pete stared in amazement.

"I'll be damned," Jim exclaimed, and shined his flashlight into the room. It was not a storage room as they had previously thought. "This is a whole new section. I wonder where it leads."

The door opened onto a corridor. Twenty feet or so in, there were two more doors, one on the left and one straight ahead. Jim eased himself in first and pulled his .44 from its holster. Pete followed.

They approached the door on the left first. Jim turned the knob and the door opened into a small room. He felt along the wall until he found a switch and turned on the light.

The room was small, with floor-to-ceiling shelves on the left and right. Some of the shelves held locked compartments.

Pete rummaged through several containers before finding what he needed. He held out a circuit board and strained to read the small print on the bottom edge. "Not the one I need," he said and placed it back in the box.

"How do you know?" Jim asked.

Pete continued his search. "Because that was a motherboard. I need a frequency processing board if I'm going to get the communications working properly. Got it here!" he said, holding the prized item high.

Jim walked back into the hall, Pete close behind.

"What's behind door number two?" Jim asked, pointing with the .44. "You ready to take a look see?"

"Might as well."

Jim turned the knob and to his surprise it opened.

This room was quite large. Directly ahead of them was a loading platform. A small blue and white train resembling a subway was parked at the platform, the Presidential emblem emblazoned on the side. "I'll be damned," Pete said, "so it *is* true?"

Jim moved to the edge of the platform and peered down the tracks. "What's true?"

"The rumors. This place was supposed to be secret but everyone knew it was here. One of the rumors was that there was an underground tunnel all the way to the White House. Once we got here, I never saw anything like that so I figured it wasn't true after all but here it is, bigger than life."

"You mean to tell me this thing goes all the way to Washington, D.C.?"

"Yep, to the White House, rumor has it."

"To the White House," Jim muttered. "Are you sure?"

"What's sure these days?" Pete answered.

"It could be of use to us but I want to know where it goes, with no doubts," Jim said. "Until we do, weld the door shut again. At the very least it may be a good escape route if the militia finds this place.

48

Chris Smith wrapped the radio in a burlap blanket and carried it into the small yellow house. He placed it on a small stand in the smallest bedroom, then covered it with the blanket. The house had no electricity but that was not a problem. A return trip to where he had stashed his gear and he would bring back the batteries to power it. The square batteries were heavy, awkward things, reminiscent of old World War II equipment. Hathaway would be expecting him to make contact soon.

Chris wasn't sure of Hathaway's plans. All he knew was what he'd been told: He was to blend in and simply report what he saw. So far, what he'd seen were people living their lives as best they could under the circumstances. They were regular people—young and old, sick and healthy, black and white, all shared the island. A melting pot, it was a tiny percentage of what had once filled the area. Chris was impressed that they had cleared the islands of the dead threat.

To the north there were several other islands, all inhabited, some much larger than Tangier. Now safe, the people kept a vigilant eye on the sick and dying.

The island proved to be self-sufficient. It was the perfect place to start over and wait out the apocalyptic rot of civilization across the Bay.

Chris stood by the window facing east and watched the gentle waves of the Bay lick the shoreline behind the house. The sight soothed his tired eyes and had an almost hypnotic effect. His vision blurred until only the blue of the Bay touching the blue of the sky filled his sight, a soft flow of blue movement.

Unwillingly, he refocused. He didn't like this mission. He didn't like the possibilities of what might happen should a well-armed militia move in and have their way. He was also constantly troubled with worry for his family, his mother and sisters. Where were they now? Alive? He hoped so. It had been years since he'd seen them. He had waited too long and then the dead came and there was no chance to seek them out.

Instead, the Freedom Fighters had saved his life and now he was indebted to them. He was a part of them and their plans.

But he was here now. He no longer needed the rogues to survive. He was safe from the murder across the water, safe as long as the militia stayed on that side of the bay. He knew they'd eventually come and that would be his undoing. One day he would fail to live up to their standards because he didn't hold their standards very high. It was just a matter of time. What could he do to prevent them from coming? He was just one man.

Chris left the house on stilts and made his way back to where he'd stashed his belongings. He'd get the batteries for the radio and then have a better look around the island. He would go fishing, he thought.

He looked across the water. The bay was very blue this evening.

49

At five A.M. the alarm clock rang and Jim Workman fumbled in the darkness and quickly put an end to the noise.

Amanda stirred next to him and he placed his hand on the curve of her hip and pulled her closer. The responsibilities of the day ahead played through his mind as he gently caressed her. The danger, the steps they would need to take to avoid them.

They were about to embark on an undertaking unmatched since they'd left the prison. It was a major move and they'd go right through the heart of hell to get there. Everything had to be thought through, every possible contingency prepared for if they were all to make it through this. A single bad judgment would cost lives.

He had reconsidered his decision to make the move more than once. Staying was the smarter thing to do, a bird in the hand type of thing. They were safe at Mount Weather but what happens in a year when there was no more food? What would happen if the militia showed up? They'd be on the run again, once again fighting to survive.

No, the move was the right thing to do, he reasoned, but that didn't make it any easier to accept. This would be the last time, though. Once on Tangier, they'd have a home until the world was safe again.

Amanda stirred and rolled over toward him. She kissed his neck with soft, hot breaths, then moved down to his chest, where she lingered just long enough to make sure she had his attention before moving on.

A moan of pleasure rose in his throat.

*   *   *

Pete barely had time to install the computer board before Jim entered the war room. He grabbed the unit by the handles on each side and pushed it back into its rack mount, then flipped on the switch. The readouts lit up and made three beeping sounds before settling into a quiet hum made by the cooling fan.

Pete moved to the center of the room and took a seat in front of one of the computer screens and typed in several commands. Jim quietly observed his actions.

Pete did a reset of the system and allowed the new hardware to install. When that was finished, he went to the setup screen and programmed it to do a frequency search. Numbers flashed endlessly on the screen as the system searched for a signal.

Pete turned to Jim. "Is it on?"

Jim nodded. "Mick's up there now in the Grizzly. He's keying the microphone. If this thing works, you'll hear him."

Pete returned his attention to the screen. It had stopped scanning and static spewed from the speakers. A voice was barely audible within the pink noise. Jim moved closer. "Is that Mick?"

"I don't think so. That signal is very weak. It could be coming from anywhere on the planet."

"Can't you zero in on where it's coming from?"

Pete studied the screen. He was good with electronics but he'd never used a system like this. He moved the curser to the top of the screen and clicked several command links before finding the LOCATE command. A small box appeared that said LOCATING PLEASE WAIT.

The caption blinked. When it stopped blinking, a new caption said UNABLE TO LOCATE.

"It must be too faint to lock in on," Pete said.

They listened a while longer until the signal faded and the computer automatically began scanning again, only to stop on a clear signal. "Mick to Base. Do you read?" He repeated the message.

Jim pulled a walkie-talkie from his belt. "Mick, we're reading you. Stop sending. We'll see if you can hear us."

"Ten-four."

Pete spoke into the microphone attached to the console in front of him. "Mick, this is Pete. You getting all this? Over."

"Ten-four. Loud and clear. Looks like you did it."

"That's a big ten-four. You're ready to go. Over and out." Pete switched off the microphone and swiveled his chair around to face Jim. "Is that clear enough for you?"

Jim nodded. "How far will it reach?"

"Your guess is as good as mine. I'm not that familiar with military gear but it should serve you well for your trip to Tangier. It's been a while since I was an enlisted man.

"Yeah, me, too."

50

Chris walked into the bar with the bright blue sign overhead and tried to adjust his eyes to the darkened room. As the room revealed itself, he found his way to the bar and took a seat.

A short scrawny Hispanic man came from the kitchen and rambled on in his native tongue as he placed clean wine glasses in an overhead rack. After he hung the last glass he stared at Chris, then raised a finger at him. "You are new here. I've not seen you before. Where are you from?"

"That's right. I just got here yesterday," Chris told him.

Julio made his way back to the kitchen, stopping halfway. He turned to face Chris. "You want something? I get you something to drink."

Chris smiled. "A drink would be nice. How about a beer?"

"No beer."

"Okay, a shot of tequila, then."

"No tequila."

"Okay, what *do* you have?"

"We have wine."

"Fine. Give me a chardonnay."

"No chardonnay."

"Any kind of wine is fine."

Julio pulled the cork and poured until the glass filled to the halfway point. "Apple wine. All we got."

"It'll do," Chris mumbled, and took a sip. The wine was surprisingly good and it showed on his face as he savored the flavor. "So who's in charge around here?"

"That would be me," Julio answered.

"No, I mean the islands."

"Ahh, that would be Carolyn Mayes. She makes the decisions for the islands. It was her husband who did it, but he was killed shortly after the islands were made secure. Sad, sad, so sad. He was a good man. He is the one who coordinated the effort."

"What do you have here in the way of protection?"

"What do you mean? Protection from what? The islands are clear of danger."

"Invaders."

Julio laughed out loud. "Invaders? There's no one left to invade us." He chuckled on his way back to the kitchen.

51

Jim placed the last of the weapons in the rack and connected the buckles on the straps to secure them. Mick made sure the passengers were in their seats and then stepped out to where Felicia stood with Izzy.

Leon grabbed Milly by the collar and made her sit next to him. The dog's movement irritated Griz.

"Does that damned dog have to go with us? It smells."

Leon looked at Griz. "Have you taken a whiff of yourself lately?"

Griz raised his arm, sniffed, and made a face. "Well what do you expect? There ain't no Right Guard around anymore."

Felicia's eyes filled and her lip quivered as Mick approached her. "I want to go, too," she said.

Mick smiled and wiped away a lone tear that rolled down her cheek. "I'll be back soon. Remember, it may take as long as a week. We have a lot to do once we get there. We'll be able to talk over the radio, but don't get worried if we lose communication. There's no guarantee that the radios will work once we get away from here, or that they won't just stop working because they are held together with chicken wire and chewing gum."

Felicia moped. "I understand."

Mick's attention was drawn to Izzy, who held out several strings of beads. He took them from her, five necklaces in all, each with an assortment of colored beads made from shiny plastic.

Felicia smiled. "You're supposed to wear them," she said.

Izzy pulled Felicia down to her and whispered in her ear, stomping her foot to make her point.

"She says you are to wear them always," Felicia said. "Never take them off, ever."

Mick stared at Izzy in wonderment as he put the necklaces on and tucked them inside his shirt.

"No!" Izzy said, reaching up. Mick bent over and Izzy pulled the beads out from beneath his shirt so they hung free around his neck. "They have to be out, like this. It's important, very important," she said, patting them with her hand.

"You'd better do as she says," Felicia said.

Mick smiled and lifted the child up in his arms. He simply stared, unsure if the beads were a gift of love or something else. The "something" related to the strange gift she possessed.

"Don't worry, Izzy. I will wear the beads always, out like this."

Izzy smiled and kissed his cheek.

*   *   *

Jim drove past the spot where he and Matt had cut the tree out of the road, past the small town of Marshall, and then south on to Route 17. Except for small viewing slots, there were no windows for the passengers to see the desolate world outside.

Creatures dotted the landscape but Jim was the only one who could see them. He watched them as they performed their mindless waltz, the new residents of a dead world.

They were darker now and more horrible than before. No longer were they the gray faces of the recently dead in business suits, blue jeans, or uniforms. They were grotesque, awful things, rotting piles of blackened skin and teeth propped up by bony carcasses that moved about with quick jerks and thrashes. They were slack-jawed, sunken faces stinking of death. Walking masses of disease and evil. They were still very dangerous, and there were too many of them.

Mick kept an eye on all the gauges as Jim maneuvered the machine to avoid debris in the road. Tree branches and roof shingles littered this stretch of highway no longer removed by road crews and chain gangs.

This part of the trip would not take them into heavily-populated areas. After Fredericksburg, the trip would get perilous and anything could happen.

It would take more than a flat tire to bring the Grizzly to a stop. The six wheels and all three axles were active parts of the drive train; it could easily operate on five, or four, for that matter. That knowledge helped ease Jim's mind as he did his best to steer clear of danger.

Leon was happy to be returning to the islands. He knew they would welcome Jim and the rest of them with open arms. Food wouldn't be a problem because of the bay. Blasé as it might become, seafood was abundant.

Milly sat between Leon's legs and stared at Amanda, who sat on the opposite side. Little more than metal benches built into the tank-like vehicle, the seats ran along each side, facing each other. They were uncomfortable and made for a very bumpy ride.

Leon fidgeted in an effort to get comfortable. Milly stretched out and fell asleep.

52

The Grizzly moved slowly into Smith's Point. The trip had been uneventful, a pleasant change that suited Jim just fine. He had avoided Fredericksburg by taking the highway to the north, bypassing it altogether. He had been tempted to take his previous route to see if Matt was there, mindlessly milling about, but today was not the day for that. He made a silent promise to his fallen friend: "I won't forget. I owe you that."

Jim stopped the Grizzly before entering the gate to the harbor. He grabbed his rifle and moved to the center of the passenger area, where he pulled down the locking mechanism in the overhead hatch.

"What are you doing?" Amanda asked.

Jim pushed on the hatch. "It's hard to see what's out there through the ports. I wanna see what we're up against before we spill out of this thing."

Mick grabbed his own weapon and moved to the viewing ports on each side and opened all of them. He peered through the one on the driver's side, while Griz and Leon took positions at the other two.

Mick pressed his face against the small window. It was hard to see at an angle, but he did his best. "It's clear on this side, Jim," he said, and moved away from the port.

Jim shot a glance at Leon, who shrugged, then shook his head.

Griz watched through the port in the rear. He backed away from the window and tripped over Milly, who squealed in pain as the heel of his boot came down on her foot.

Griz's head bounced off the hard floor when he went down but he quickly scrambled back to his feet. "An ass-load of zombies!" he cried and pointed to the rear.

Jim moved to the port and peered out.

There were two groups, one on each side of the road. They approached from around the corners of buildings and abandoned cars.

"Fifty," Jim whispered. "Maybe more." He ran to the driver's seat and checked out the situation out front.

"We need to back off for a while," Mick said.

"Leon, what does it take to close the gate?" Jim asked.

Leon came up and sandwiched in between Jim and Mick.

"What gate?"

Jim moved out of the way to give Leon a chance to look through the opening.

"I never even noticed it was there," Leon said. "If I'd have known that, I would've..."

Jim moved to the hatch and Amanda grabbed his arm. "I don't think you should be doing this. There's too many. We can come back later."

Jim gently pulled her hand from his arm. "I'll be fine."

Jim flipped the hatch and sunlight streamed through the opening. "Get us through the gate, Mick!" he shouted. He handed his rifle to Amanda and pulled himself through the opening. When he reached down, she handed him the rifle.

Mick moved the vehicle forward until they were twenty feet inside the gate, then stopped. He slung his own weapon over his shoulder and climbed up to join Jim.

Jim stuck his head back through the hole. "If something happens, Amanda, go back to the mountain. Is that understood?"

Amanda nodded, her eyes fearful.

The creatures lumbered forward, one large group of lurching, stumbling walking dead that reeled and swayed in unison. A ghoul in front was a hideous-looking thing with shredded clothes and a left leg that was chewed to the bone from the ankle to the knee. It favored the bone leg as if it was made of wood but it hobbled on, determined.

The rest of the rabble hadn't fared much better. Darker and more frightening now due to decomposition and exposure to the elements, most were nothing more than walking skeletons with stretched skin and sunken, blackened eyes.

They should be easier to handle now, Jim thought. He looked over his shoulder and then went to work.

Entrance to the harbor was via a two-lane road, surrounded by a ten-foot chain link fence that separated it from a residential area. A large warehouse ended close to the docks. Six bay doors faced the water, where shipments were unloaded, stored, and later distributed.

Jim and Mick raced to the two-part gate that locked against the fence. The fence slid back on a track and locked against the sliding portion. Jim pulled the left section and moved it out another ten feet. Mick did the same with the other side until sixteen feet of the gate area was open, still jeopardizing their safety.

Jim pulled the rusted U-shaped hook outward and swung the gate around. Mick followed his lead and the two gates clanged together. The lock rattled and fell to the ground as the gate clanged shut. Mick picked it up and placed it on the gate.

"We don't have a key to open it," he said before pushing down the top to lock it.

Jim brushed the hair from his eyes. "No big deal. I can pick it or, if we're in that big a hurry, the Grizzly will get through, locked or not."

Mick pushed down on the lock and it clicked closed. Jim pulled two bars across to stabilize it and locked them into place. They backed away as the slow-moving rabble began to paw at the fence.

53

Jim scanned the area. No ghouls approached but several rotted corpses littered the ground. They didn't appear to be dead by attack. No longer functional, they simply ran out of energy or whatever it was that had kept them going.

The chain link fence and the warehouse surrounded the area of the harbor where they were. With the gate now closed it was safe from further occupation of the dead, at least for the time being, even though they continued to claw and dig at the gate.

Milly raced toward the ghouls, barking fiercely. They turned their attention on her when she got close and wailed their frustration at not being able to reach the object of their desire.

Leon pulled the dog whistle from under his shirt and blew the silent order for her to return. The effect was unmistakable as the ghouls frantically cried out and rattled the fence with all their strength, their dead eyes now focused on Jim and the others.

"Jesus Christ!" Jim shouted, and took the whistle from Leon.

He looked at the whistle then at the horrid mob. "They can hear this thing," Jim said, "What's more, they're attracted to it, even riled by it."

Jim trotted away from the ghouls and blew hard on the whistle. Just as he expected, every rotted face turned toward him, their rage stoked once more. They moved closer to him.

"Jim, look out!" Amanda shouted.

Jim turned and saw several creatures moving toward him inside the harbor compound. He pocketed the whistle and ran back to the group as Griz raised his weapon to fire.

"No!" Jim said. "Use the silencers. No more noise."

Mick disappeared into the vehicle and returned with two pistols with silencers attached to the barrels. He gave one to Jim and kept the other. The strays were dealt with quickly and joined the other carcasses littering the ground. There were no others inside the fence as far as they could tell. Jim inspected the area before relaxing.

They found a fire department near the warehouse, a two-story structure with a siren in an enclosed bell tower on the roof. On the other side, a police station and a convenience store, both in ruins.

Jim handed the pistol to Amanda. "It looks like we're okay for now, but we'd better move fast. We're attracting too much attention. Mick, you stay with Amanda and Griz while Leon and I find a boat."

Leon grabbed a toolkit from the Grizzly and ran with Jim to the docks. Milly followed, more interested in the safety of her master than yelping at the ghouls at the gate.

They ran past several boats that were either damaged by storms or in a state of disrepair until they came to a blue and white Stingray tied to a pier. It was close to the fence that ran all the way to the water. A pedestal seat was attached to the motor cover in the rear. Jim tried to remove it but the pole was rusted into place. He left it there and swung open the motor cover that smashed into the seats in the front of the boat as it dropped.

The battery terminals were covered with corrosion and a gritty white powder. Jim sprayed it with cleaner and most of it disappeared. Everything else looked to be in pretty good shape. He moved to the cockpit and began cutting wires under the dash, working quickly.

Leon knelt on the deck and watched through the windshield as Jim held two wires inches apart.

"Which one is gonna cause this thing not to start, the battery or the old fuel?" Jim asked.

Leon cracked a grin. "You gotta have faith, my friend."

Jim touched the wires together. The motor sputtered and came alive and he twisted the wires together.

Leon jumped into the cockpit as Jim revved the engine "See? Ya gotta have faith!"

54

The canvas-covered personnel carriers abandoned by the army during the early days of the plague were almost loaded with the supplies Hathaway and his men would need. Five trucks were required to transport the ninety-six men to their destination. The trucks were not reinforced, but the men were heavily armed. If all went well, they would be leaving in the next two days.

Hathaway had hoped for more men. Less than one hundred was cutting it close for a job of this magnitude but it was all he could muster under the circumstances.

The camp had split into two factions. Ben Colby had publicly accused Hathaway of the bombing. There was no proof to support Colby's accusation but somehow he had garnered the support of most of the camp. Things hadn't worked out the way Hathaway had planned. He'd underestimated Ben Colby's desire to take command and his ability to achieve that goal.

Hathaway was checking off items from his list when Ben Colby and several men approached. Colby waiked with a confident swagger. He had the numbers on his side.

Colby stopped a few feet short of coming face to face with Hathaway. He watched the men loading the trucks, then said, "I'm not going to let you take our supplies and run out of here, Bobby."

Hathaway planted his feet and folded his arms across his chest. "And just what do you plan to do about it?"

"I don't know what you have in mind but I can tell you that it's not in the group's best interest," Colby said, taking a step closer. "These supplies belong to the force as a whole, not to a select few."

"These supplies go where I want them to go. It's you who's out of line. You're the one who circumvented normal protocol by assuming command here."

"I didn't assume command; you did it to yourself. You made your bed and now you don't want to sleep in it. Well, I won't let you take those supplies, or the men."

Hathaway grinned. "You have no proof. What gives you the right? These are *my* men and they'll follow *me*. They recognize proper procedures. Are you willing to have our people shoot each other over this? The casualties will be high."

Colby stood his ground. "Are you? They're your people, too."

"Not anymore. I have my men. The others are your people now, aren't they?" Hathaway stiffened. "I'll do it, and so will my men."

Colby searched Hathaway's face for signs of a bluff. Was it possible that he was willing to carry out his threats? His determination was unmistakable. He had blown up half the camp already. "If you leave here, you're out. There will be no coming back."

Hathaway smiled. "It'll be you that's out of the loop once we leave."

55

The nose of the Stingray bumped against the pier on Tangier Island. Jim throttled down and let the motor sputter into silence and Leon tied the boat so the starboard side was against the pier.

Amanda stepped out of the bobbing boat, then turned to help the others out. Jim was the last one out and Amanda breathed deeply of the clean sea air. She had been locked away for so long she had almost forgotten the feeling of freedom.

A flock of seagulls swooped low over the water, calling raucously to each other. One of the gulls took a hard dive into the bay with a loud splash. Amanda whipped around, pistol in hand, her heart pounding.

Jim took the gun from her. "I don't think you'll be needing this here."

Amanda grabbed the gun back from Jim. "I'll be the judge of that."

Leon led them to Julio's bar first. It was his turn to show them a little hospitality and he couldn't think of a better way to do that than to have Julio serve them a glass of his apple wine and allow them a moment to relax.

Jim resisted the idea at first. He was always thinking of what had to be done and how fast he could do it. Amanda had insisted, though. She, more than anyone, wanted a glass of wine or two to adjust to her new surroundings.

The five of them entered the dark room and made their way to the bar. Jim took a seat and the rest followed suit.

Leon smiled as he waited for Julio to serve them. It was his favorite place to be. He'd always liked the bars, but this bar wasn't like those of years past. Julio's was more laid back. The jukebox in the corner was always playing, never too loudly, and only what Julio wanted to hear.

Julio was a Credence Clearwater Revival fan and that was good. Credence Clearwater was one of those groups whose music never failed to make Leon want to sing along. It wasn't flashy and crisp like the new stuff, it had soul and heart. Leon appreciated that. He was never one for the new stuff anyway.

Julio finally made it over to them. "I'm thinking you make lots of friends, Leon, but these are people I've not seen here before." He looked at Jim. "Except for you. I remember you. You are new to the islands."

Leon smiled. "They sure are. How about hooking all of them up with a glass of wine?"

"For you, I do it," Julio said.

Jim scanned the dimly-lit room. Two people sat at a high table in front of a small window and sipped from their glasses and ate cracked peanuts, letting the shells fall to the floor. An old man with the tiniest bit of hair on top of his head read an old magazine in the center of the room, aided by the light from a lantern. In the shadows of a far corner, a young man sat by himself.

Julio placed the glasses in front of them. Mick took the first taste and his face puckered at the tart flavor.

Julio noticed his wrinkled nose. "That is from my newest batch. It's not as sweet as the other wine. If you don't like it, I can—"

"No," Mick said. "It's fine." He took another sip. "I'm afraid we don't have anything to give you for it, though."

"That's not a problem here," Julio said. "Money's no good anymore."

Mick nodded, taking in the surroundings. "Is this all you do? Work here in this place and serve people wine for free? Why?"

Julio smiled thinly. "Why not?"

"He does his part," Leon added. "Everyone here does. We see to it that everyone has what he or she needs. Julio's job is vital, maybe the most important on the island. This place gives us a chance to unwind, relax."

"What about the other islands? Is it the same there?"

"More or less."

Jim stood and walked over to Leon. "Who's in charge of the islands? We should be seeing them soon to pave the way for us to move the others who want to come."

Leon thought for a moment. There were several who thought they were in charge but when it came down to it, there was only one who was. "That would be Carolyn Mayes. She's the one you want to talk to. Her husband's the one who led the invasion. I guess you could call it an invasion. He's the one who came up with the plan to clear the island of danger and evacuate those who still survived on the mainland to safety here. He was killed making sure we all got here safely. His wife Carolyn finished the job. She's a strong woman. She'll help you."

"Is she here on Tangier or on one of the other islands?"

"She's here. There are a lot of people here on Tangier. It seems everyone wanted to be on this one. It has a real tourist feel to it. You kind of feel like you're on permanent vacation and that's a good thing, considering what's across the bay. Know what I mean?"

Jim nodded and he went back to his barstool. He subtly watched the young man in the corner. He wished he could get a better look at him but his face was in the shadow. There was something he thought he recognized. He watched from the corner of his eye as he sipped his wine. It wasn't long before the young man stood and his face was revealed.

Jim reached over and grabbed Mick's arm. "Cover my back."

"What?"

"We've got trouble. Watch my back."

Mick's hand went the grip of his pistol. He stood up but remained at the bar as Jim moved toward the man in the corner.

Jim studied the man for any sign that he may be prepared to draw a weapon. "What are you doing here?" Jim demanded.

The question startled the young man. He stepped backward and stumbled over the chair behind him. On impulse, Jim drew his weapon and trained it on the man's head. Mouth agape, the man stared at the end of Jim's gun barrel.

"You know me, don't you?" Jim demanded. "I know you, too. I saw you on the *Nimitz*."

Chris tried to speak but his throat had tightened. Only his lips would move.

"Where's Hathaway? Is he here, too?"

"No," Chris finally managed. "Not yet."

"When?"

"I'm not sure. I'm supposed to radio him tomorrow. I don't even know why *I'm* here."

"I know why you're here," Jim said. "Who else is here with you?"

"No one. Just me, I swear."

Mick moved close to Jim but kept a vigilant eye on the room. "What's going on, Jim? Who is this guy?"

"He's part of the militia who killed Matt and tried to kill me. I saw him on the aircraft carrier when I was there."

"Why is he here?"

"That's obvious. He's a scout."

Jim held out his hand to Chris. "Give me your weapons. All of them."

Chris removed his holster and handed it to Jim, then took his hunting knife from his pocket and tossed it at Jim's feet.

Jim bent down and picked it up, all the while maintaining eye contact.

"Where are you staying?"

"In a little house down by the water," Chris said.

"Is your radio there?"

"Yes."

"Good. Take us there."

56

Chris entered the house first and the others followed. Jim kept the gun trained on him as they moved through the small house. When they got to a bedroom in the back, Chris removed a cover to reveal the radio equipment.

"That's it," he said, pointing.

"Where are your other weapons?" Jim asked.

"There's a rifle over there." Chris pointed to a corner in the room. Jim motioned for Mick to get the rifle.

Chris wiped away the sweat that had beaded on his brow. "What now?"

Jim pointed to a chair by the bed. "Sit down."

Chris did as he was told. He didn't want to make any sudden moves and get himself shot. This man was not fooling around; he would shoot.

"I want you to tell us everything you know. Why are you here? What are your plans for this island?"

Chris thought hard. This was a definite crossroads for him. He could give them his name, rank, and serial number like a good soldier, which might get him killed, or he could tell them what they wanted to know. They weren't going to like his answers because he had no answers.

Hathaway was a dangerous, ambitious man who would stop at nothing to get what he wanted, including killing every last person, himself included, on this island if he felt the need. Chris prayed silently for guidance—a sign, anything.

"I don't know anything other than I was told to come here to check things out and wait to be contacted."

"He told you to come to Tangier?"

"Not exactly. I was told to go to Smith's Point first. If there were live people there, I was to blend in. If not, then I was to come here, to the islands."

"To blend in?"

"Yes."

Jim studied Chris. He was twenty-five, maybe twenty-six, but no older than that. "What's your name?" Jim asked.

"Christopher Smith."

"How long have you been with the Freedom Fighters, Chris?"

Chris shifted in his chair. "Only a while. I didn't meet up with them until after those things started showing up and everything went to hell. They saved my life."

"So you felt it necessary to share in their dirty deeds in return for them saving you?"

"Yes...I mean, no! There were no dirty deeds that I was aware of, at least not that I saw. Yes, I saw you on the *Nimitz* but I didn't know anything about you other than you were a prisoner."

"But you had to know what they stand for."

"Now how the hell would I know that? I knew they were militiamen. But being a militiaman doesn't necessarily make you bad. This country was freed from England's tyranny with the help of militias. For all I knew they were the only ones left alive. I didn't have much of a choice."

Maybe the boy wasn't privy to Hathaway's plans after all, Jim thought. It did seem unlikely that everyone associated with the militia would share Hathaway's views and hatreds, especially if they were made up of plague survivors. Still, he was here, spying for him.

Jim holstered his weapon. "Where are you from?"

"From the mountains, a little place called Browntown. It's in the Shenandoah Valley."

The reaction was unmistakable. Chris saw recognition in their faces. "You know where it is?"

"What did you say your last name was again?" Jim asked.

"Smith. Why?"

"Felicia's last name is Smith," Jim told Mick.

Mick came closer. "And she grew up in Browntown," he added, looking at Chris. "You're not *that* Chris?"

Chris snapped to his feet and Jim's hand tightened on his weapon.

"My sister's name is Felicia! Do you know her? Is she alive?" Chris demanded.

"Wait a minute. Slow down here," Jim cautioned. "This could be a trick."

Chris became frantic. "No! I'm not lying. My sister's name is Felicia. I also have another sister. Her name is Rebecca. We call her Becky. Do you know her, too? My mother…is she okay?"

"Felicia is okay," Mick said. "She's been with us throughout this nightmare. We don't know about your mother or sister."

"Where is she? Is she here? Can I see her?"

Jim pushed Chris back into his chair. "She's not here, but you'll see her soon, assuming you're telling the truth. This seems like quite the coincidence. A bit too much of one for my liking."

"I swear to you, I'm not lying. Ask me anything."

"Tell us a little about Felicia," Jim told him. "What's she look like? What is special about her?"

Chris covered his face with his hands to hide his emotional state. Unable to speak, he slumped back into the chair and struggled to regain his composure. This was so unexpected, so unreal. "She's tall, blonde. Thirty-one, I believe, and, yes, she is special. She has a gift. She sees things that others don't. She's very special."

"I believe him," Jim said.

Mick sighed. "I do, too. So what do we do now?"

Jim paced the floor, his hands in his pockets. He felt the metallic shape of the dog whistle there and pulled it out. He stared at it and in that moment it all became clear to him, as though God himself had shown him the way.

He turned his radiant face to them. "I know what we do next."

57

The radio crackled with static as Hathaway tuned in to the proper frequency, Jake watching over his shoulder. Hathaway shivered at Jake breathing down his neck. He disliked having someone's hot breath on him, but he said nothing.

It was almost time for the call from Chris Smith, if he had made it alive. Regardless, dead or alive, he would make the move, but the information he got from Chris was important. It would give him a definite course of action, thus cutting down on the number of casualties.

He was confident of his men's abilities. In his opinion, they were the best of the bunch. They believed what he believed, not what the others had ultimately grown to be. They had become soft in their thinking. His men were strong, pure.

Hathaway glanced at his watch for the third time. Chris was ten minutes late. His anger grew. He hated incompetence and it was incompetent to be late. Having the proper information now was vital.

Maybe Chris was dead, he thought. Better dead than incompetent. At least dead was an excuse.

Maybe the radio wasn't working properly. That couldn't be. He'd checked it himself. It was more than adequate to do the job, even at this distance. No, he thought, Chris is dead. He's dead and now we have to make the trip blind, with no recon.

Suddenly, there was a voice and Hathaway jumped for the microphone. He listened again before answering. He had to be sure it was Smith.

Hathaway turned to Jake. "Watch the door. Let me know if anyone comes near."

Jake moved to the window beside the door and spread the filthy curtains just enough to see outside.

The voice came again. "This is Smith to Lieutenant Hathaway. Come in. Do you read me?"

Hathaway keyed the mic. "Go ahead. I read you."

"Well, sir, I'm here. What is it that you need to know?"

"First things first. Where are you?"

"I went to Smith's Point just like you told me to. It was overrun with those damned things so I went to the islands. I found people here."

"How many?"

"It's hard to tell but I'd say several hundred. Mostly women and children."

"Are the men armed?"

"They have weapons. Hunting rifles and handguns, but most of them don't carry them around."

Hathaway could hardly keep his widening smile from turning to full-blown laughter. "What island are you on?"

The radio was silent for a moment, then, "Tangier."

"Do they have boats on the island?"

"Yes, sir. They have fishing boats. Most of their food is brought in from the bay."

Hathaway leaned his head against the microphone as he thought. "Are there enough boats to carry a hundred men?"

Again there was silence. Hathaway reasoned it was because Chris was calculating the numbers in his head. "Yes, sir. There's a big fishing boat anchored here. It should carry that many, if we throw unneeded items overboard."

Hathaway grinned. "Okay, now listen carefully. I want you to get the guy who captains that boat, at gunpoint if necessary, and the two of you bring it over to Smith's Point on Thursday. That's two days from now. I want you to have it there at exactly fifteen hundred hours. Do you understand?"

"Yes, sir, but that won't work."

"Why not?"

"There are too many people around at that time. They take the boats out during the day to fish. They don't return until around six o'clock. It's too risky."

Hathaway snorted. "Too risky. Too risky for us." He mused to himself. He keyed the mic again. "Can you have it there by eighteen-thirty?"

"Yes, sir. Six–thirty. I can do that, I'm sure of it."

"You'd better be sure, mister! If you're late, it's really going to piss me off and let me tell you, that's not something you want, is it?"

"No, sir, it isn't. Don't worry, I'll be there."

Hathaway was secure in the belief that his plan was coming together. "That's it, then. I'll see you at Smith's Point at eighteen-thirty on Thursday. Wear a watch. It's thirteen-fifteen now. Synchronize it."

Hathaway turned off the radio and looked at Jake standing guard at the window. Hathaway's face beamed with confidence.

Jim patted Chris on the back. "You did that very well. Even I believed you."

Chris released the breath he'd been holding. "I hope so."

Jim tossed the dog whistle to Mick. "Don't lose that. I hope to hell you can do what you said you can do."

Mick pocketed the whistle. "If it can be done, we'll do it."

"The fading light will be to our advantage," Jim told them. "We'll need every little bit we can get."

58

"The sun will be setting soon," Jim said. "I'd rather wait till tomorrow to do this but we just don't have the time to spare."

Mick set down the toolbox and raised his binoculars to his eyes. He studied the area around the gate just up the hill. There were two creatures roaming about but they had not taken notice of them yet.

He lowered the glasses and turned around to face the bay. "They'll assemble there, by the water," Mick said, pointing to an open area of the parking lot close to the docks. "They'll be able to see the gate from there. We need to do something to block their view of it."

Jim looked up the hill to the gate. The zombies were visible from only the shoulders up. The ridge of the hill obstructed most of the view from where he stood. He drew Mick's attention to the warehouse.

In a grassy area at the far end, Jim counted nine temporary construction office trailers ranging from twenty feet to over thirty feet in length. "If we place those trailers on the crest of that hill, they'll hide that gate from sight once the militia gets down here."

Mick considered his plan. "Yeah, but once they get down here, won't they realize that and either set up lookouts or move the trailers?"

"I'm betting that they'll think it's unnecessary. In their minds, Chris will be on the way with the boat."

Mick nodded. "This has to go just right, doesn't it?"

"It does," Jim replied. "Let's go check out the firehouse."

The firehouse was wrapped in red brick with four large doors across the front that allowed the trucks to get in and out. Jim stood on his toes and peered through the windows in the door closest to the personnel door. It was hard to see past the trucks with only ten or twelve feet between each one parked there.

He dropped down so his feet were flat on the ground. "It looks okay." He said and pulled a crowbar from the bag he'd been carrying.

The small door was solid metal. With no way to see inside, his adrenaline pumped as he slid the crooked end of the crowbar into the jamb and pried.

His arm muscles flexed and bulged as he pulled back with all his strength. The knob broke loose and dangled loosely from the hole, then the door broke free and flew open. The sudden release of pressure nearly sent him off his feet.

Suddenly, a body was on him and he was on the ground. The creature's hands grabbed Jim by the shirt collar, its rotting face leaking a thick liquid down on him. He shifted his face to prevent the vile fluid from making contact with his nose or mouth. Its weight was intense because of the heavy brown jumpsuit and oxygen tanks strapped to the dead fireman's back.

Jim brought the crowbar up and placed it crossways into the creature's mouth as it moved in closer. With a final hard thrust, he sent the ghoul up and off to the left. Shattered teeth showered down like brown Chicklets as Jim scrambled to his feet.

Mick moved in to help but Jim had already regained his feet. So had the creature. Mick backed off to give Jim room to work.

The creature wore a fireman's helmet held in place by the chinstrap, the brim cocked to the left. With his first swing of the crowbar, Jim hit the helmet and sent it flying. He swung again and brought the creature to his knees. On the third swing, the impact cracked its head like a ripe melon and it fell face down on the asphalt. Brain pulp spilled out from the open cavity. Now almost liquefied, the smell was ungodly.

Mick waved a hand in front of his nose. "Phew! That one's past its sell date."

Once inside, they checked out the rest of the building. On the second floor, another ghoul stagger-stepped in a circular motion, unaware of their presence. It was very tall, lanky, and bald. It also wore the jumpsuit and jacket of a fireman.

It continued to walk the circle. They noticed its name emblazoned on the back of the jacket: LURCH.

Jim got a better grip on the crowbar and moved in, ready in case it attacked. It didn't. It continued its loopy dance and Jim brought it down with the first swing, then wiped the weapon clean on its jacket.

They needed to find the generator first; every firehouse had one in case of a power failure. They found it on the first floor, a big diesel-powered monster. It started as though it had been used yesterday and hummed evenly. They allowed the generator to warm up and closed the doors.

Outside, the noise was barely audible, almost silent, over the small breeze that blew their hair.

"They won't hear it down there where they'll be waiting for Chris," Jim said.

"Yeah, as long as they don't come over here."

"They won't. They won't have the time."

The generator tested and proven, Mick switched it off. "Now for the easy stuff. I get to invent a new fire siren." Mick grabbed the toolbox and headed upstairs. Jim followed.

They passed through a door behind the kitchen to a small storage area. To their right, a metal ladder hung against the wall. Eighteen inches in front of the ladder, a ventilation shaft ran down from the ceiling and across the room and disappeared into the wall.

Mick looked at the trap door at the top. "It's gonna be tight," he said. Giving the toolbox to Jim, Mick started his climb up the ladder.

Three rungs up, he had to shift to the side of the ladder to get past the ventilation shaft. He placed his feet on the side of the rungs and continued unsteadily. Near the top, he stopped. Jim climbed up as far as he could and handed the toolbox up to him. Mick turned around and placed it on top of the shaft and flipped open the trap door. Sunlight filtered down as he climbed up to the roof. Once there, Jim handed the tools up to him.

From the rooftop they could see the entire harbor. Outside of their gated refuge, the bodies of the dead roamed in scattered groups of three and four. They plodded slowly with steps that took much effort. Like winos who'd had too much to drink, they swayed and held on to things for support, conserving their strength for more profitable gains.

The siren was six feet high and positioned in the center area of the roof. Twelve horns adorned its cap. Mick twisted his head upward from beneath and located the bolts to remove it. Just under the horns, a heavy fan rotor pushed air up into the horns when it was activated. The fan was his horseshoe. It would tweak his mistakes. Close was good in horseshoes, hand grenades, and sirens.

With a little effort and half a can of WD40, he had the horn assembly loose and Jim helped him get it down.

Mick rubbed his chin. "I've got to remove all these. They won't work," he said, pointing to the horns. "It'll be too hard to modify them. I'll modify four to replace the twelve. Face one in each direction."

Jim looked at the contraption. "You're sure this will work?"

"Yes, if I do it right."

"That is the question, isn't it?" Jim said.

"It needs to be 5800 Hertz to 12400 Hertz to work properly. If I get it close, we can change the speed of the fan to get it right. But I've got to get it above 5800 Hz. That's important."

"Good. You and Griz work on getting that right tonight. In the morning, I'll get Amanda and Leon to help me do the rest. We have till Thursday."

59

Griz and Mick were at the airport hanger on the island the following morning. They had spent most of the night reworking the firehouse horns to suit their needs. Mick had split the dog whistle in half and was getting exact measurements to the cavities inside when Jim and Leon walked in. Griz flipped up the brim on his welding shield and turned off the torch.

Jim handed them a cup of coffee. "There's more over at Chris' house if you want it."

Mick took a sip. "You left Chris up there with the radio all by himself?"

Jim reached into his pocket and pulled out a small vacuum tube. "It won't work without this. I want to trust him but I won't risk our lives on it."

"My thoughts exactly," Mick said.

"What do you have so far?"

From the table Mick picked up a metal cylinder that was six inches long and an inch in diameter. He tilted it so the open end faced Jim. The inside was split into two compartments. Mick picked up a small piece of metal from the table and fitted it inside, against the piece that separated it in half, and held it there. "Three of these will get welded into each one of the four horns."

He threw the small piece of metal back on the table and picked up one of the old horns that had been cut just before it began to flare. An adapter had been welded at the small end and Mick slid it over the cylinder to create the new siren.

"We should be ready for a test around noon," Mick said, putting the invention back on the table. "We'll know then if it works. Are you going over to the harbor now?"

"Yeah, shortly."

"Where's Amanda?"

"At Carolyn Mayes' house, explaining our situation to her. If this doesn't work, we're hoping to get enough men to thwart the militia's attack here on the island. Once we do what we're going to do tomorrow, the secret will be out and we'll lose the element of surprise. If it works, we'll save some lives. If not..." He shook his head.

Mick thought about Felicia back at the Underground. "Do me a favor when you get over on the mainland, will you?"

"Sure."

"Call Felicia on the Grizzly radio and tell her we're okay."

"Of course. I have to check in with Pete anyway."

"One other thing, Jim. Don't tell her about Chris quite yet. If something happens to him, I'm not sure we should say anything to her about his being here."

Amanda was at the kitchen table with Carolyn Mayes. A heavy-set black woman in her early fifties, Carolyn had a strong but kind face, a trustworthy face. It was also the face of a person who had been to hell and back. Her eyes masked an unknown turmoil.

Over the course of the morning, Amanda had relayed the story of how she and the others had survived for the past two years and what had brought them to Tangier. She also told Carolyn about the militia and the dangers they posed.

Carolyn listened intently, weighing, as she always did, the greater good of the island community. When Amanda told her of the militia's wicked deeds and what they had done to Matt, her eyes darkened. A hard expression replaced her countenance.

"Why didn't you just lie to them on the radio? Tell them there was no one here? Wouldn't that have made things easier? Kept them away?"

"No," Amanda said. "Jim is convinced they would come regardless. If not here, then back at Mount Weather, probably both. Eventually, we'd have to deal with them. This way, we have the element of surprise. The only way to be truly secure is to eliminate the problem."

"I don't know," Carolyn said. "More killing. It seems so...avoidable."

Amanda leaned closer. "History has shown us the outcome time and again. Think about it. Raiders, conquerors, slavers. Did you hear about or encounter any gangs of criminals who terrorized communities when this thing started?"

Carolyn nodded.

"The horrible things they did? The gang rapes, the religious maniacs? How about the soldiers, stripped of friends and family with little hope of survival themselves? Do you remember their desperation and the terrible, terrible things some of them did?"

"Yes."

"Imagine that, only in greater numbers. Now add to that. These people were programmed with hatred even before the plague. That hatred has become a building block for their new religion, one driven by their hate and led by dictators. They will lay waste your tranquil community here and replace it with their version of how things should be. If there's no other way, then there's nothing wrong with killing to preserve our own lives and freedoms. And believe me, there *is* no other way."

Carolyn stood. "All right. I'll call an emergency meeting. We'll get the men you need but I won't send them off the island. We will make our stand here."

Amanda blew a sigh of relief. "That's all I ask."

60

Jim switched off the radio and climbed out of the Grizzly. He slid down to the ground and Amanda reached out to catch him.

Leon held two metal boxes in his arms and placed them on the asphalt. He flipped the latches on one and opened it. Chris pushed a cart filled with oxygen tanks from the firehouse, the wheels squeaking as it rolled.

"How is everything at home, Jim?" Amanda asked.

"Pete followed the tunnel we found the other day. It doesn't lead to the White House like he thought. It only goes a few miles, then comes out in a sub-basement of a barn on a back road just off Route 50. I thought it sounded a bit far-fetched that it went sixty miles to the White House. At least they'll have an escape route should the militia show up there. He's coordinating a movement of some vehicles to the inside of that barn, in case an escape becomes necessary."

Chris rolled the oxygen tanks to the middle of the open area of the parking lot and started randomly placing them in stacks four wide and three high. When he had finished, he walked to where Leon squatted with the metal boxes.

"You'd better make sure that those things are set to a frequency we won't be using," Chris said.

Leon held up a detonator. "Do you know how to do it?"

Chris took the detonator. "Yes."

"Good. I don't like fooling with that stuff."

"I don't mind," Chris said. "I used it all the time when I was on a bridge crew; I was certified. I'll try to set this up to detonate on a

246

frequency they won't use either. We don't want it going off before we're ready."

"No, we don't," Jim said, "and be careful with it. It's old and sweaty and been in humid conditions. When you get that done, move that one stack of tanks. It's too much in the open. We don't want to draw attention to them."

Chris nodded and went to work bundling dynamite from the other box.

Jim and Amanda used the Grizzly to move the office trailers. It had a hitch on the back and plenty of power to pull them up the hill in front of the gate.

One by one, he placed them in such a way as to obstruct the militia's view of that area. The road from the gate came down the hill and snaked to the left. Once the trailers were in place, the militia would not be able to see anything happening there. The gate and a two hundred-foot section of fence would be concealed. More than that was unnecessary because buildings closed in the rest. This was vital to their plan.

There were four bundles of dynamite on the ground in front of Chris. He attached the devices to trigger the explosions and then placed a bundle in the middle of each of the four stacks of oxygen tanks, hiding them.

Jim moved the last trailer into place. By now he had drawn the ghouls' attention. Twenty or so creatures had gathered at the gate to rake the chain link with their hands, leaving bits of flesh and clothing to cake the wire, their cries more like pleas than anger or lust.

They were pitiful things, with their blackened faces and rotted stumps. Ragged clothing barely covered their hideous bodies. Regardless, they were still deadly in large numbers. Their numbers would grow at the gate very soon.

Mick watched as Griz welded the last horn into place. He had been precise with each modification so it would work properly. Tiny tools for tedious work had made the job possible. He had filed each piece so they were exact replicas, only larger.

Mick poured a cup of water over the hot metal. Steam roiled up as the water cooled the newly-welded seams at the base of the horns.

Griz tossed the welding mask on the table and slicked the greasy strands of his unkempt beard back into place. They were ready to test it.

It was up to Jim and Mick to test the siren. Power had to be rerouted directly to the fan in order to bypass the relays and switches that made the fan speed up or slow down, raising or lowering the pitch. For their purpose, the pitch needed to remain constant.

When Jim turned the power on, a high-pitched whine emitted from the horns, then immediately disappeared once the fan was up to full speed. The few creatures at the gate became agitated. They flailed their arms and rattled the gate. They moaned and hissed. Their determination grew.

From the firehouse rooftop where Jim and Mick stood, the sounds the creatures made were barely audible. Tomorrow it would be different. This worried Jim. If the creatures created too much noise, it would alert the militia and upset the delicate balance of their plan. They had done their best to create alternate plans should the militia become aware of anything too soon, but nothing was guaranteed.

That night, they all sat around Chris's table, rehearsing each detail of their responsibilities. Each had an important job to do. If one person failed, the entire plan might fail. It would be dangerous, six of them against a hundred soldiers, but they would have help from an unlikely source. The odds were hopefully in their favor.

Chris was nervous and squirmed in his chair. "I'm not so sure this plan is going to work like you think it will," he said. "These men are well armed and trained. You think we'll get the help we need from a bunch of deteriorating bone bags but I'm not sold on that."

Jim understood his concern but his own personal experience had given him the confidence to go forward with this bold plan.

"When we were at the prison, we had everything we thought was needed for safety. We had weapons, a secure location, and fences that were stronger and bigger than those that surround the harbor. We made one mistake: We let those zombies know we existed.

"When we left the prison to find supplies, they saw us and they followed us. Just a few at first, but those few went on a seventeen-mile journey down the highway behind us. Though they lost sight of us, they followed the road. Eventually it led them to us. By the time they made it to the prison, their numbers had snowballed.

"You see, they are creatures of instinct more than anything else. Creatures who saw the others making their way to us instinctively followed. Maybe they had nothing better to do. Who knows?

"The closer they got, the larger their numbers became. By the time they reached the prison, they were a thousand plus. It was by accident, of course. We didn't intend to attract them but tomorrow we intend to do just that. We'll have a lot less time but we have a secret weapon. There are literally thousands of them around Smith's Point. I don't expect to draw in all of them, but I think we'll get enough. They will hear the whistle for several blocks, maybe more."

Chris leaned back in his chair. He finally understood but now he had a new concern. "What happens if your secret weapon works too well, Jim, and there are too many even for us to make our escape?"

"Then we pray."

PART

IV

Apocalypse End

61

It was five in the afternoon when they finished preparing for the confrontation. Everything was quiet.

Griz and Leon were stationed in a building close to the docks. They had barricaded themselves in a room with two windows that faced the parking lot. They would have a good view of the militia.

Two gray bazookas leaned against the wall by their respective windows, along with three refill shells for each of them. They wore two holstered pistols and a micro Uzi. Griz chewed his fingernails as he waited, spitting bits of torn nail onto the floor. Leon held his walkie-talkie, ready for instructions.

Chris waited with Mick close to the gate, which was open to make the area appear abandoned. Several creatures had meandered inside the perimeter, completing the picture.

The Grizzly was parked inside the firehouse.

Chris placed a radio device on top of an old truck tire and extended the antennae. When the time came, he would use it to detonate the dynamite.

Mick stooped behind a concrete wall and studied Chris, who was watching ghouls lumber mindlessly down the hill. His hair was blonde like Felicia's. Their eyes were the same, too, bright blue and bottomless. Both had that faraway look, the look of a dreamer. Mick felt the need to ensure Chris's safety for Felicia's sake.

Jim opened the hatch and climbed onto the firehouse roof. Amanda handed the weapons to him, then climbed up with him.

They trotted across the roof and took up positions behind a two-foot wall that bordered the roof. It would give them some cover.

"When they show up, it's important that you stay out of sight," Jim said. "If you have to move, stay low."

Amanda gave him a harsh look; she already knew that. She hated it when he treated her like a naïve child.

"I hope Carolyn has the island ready in case this doesn't work," Amanda said.

"She will. It'll be tough to get over there, anyway. They'll have a hard time getting to the island. Mick hid our boat and made the others inoperative. The harbor will be the end of the line for the militia. Even if we lose the battle, enough of their forces will be killed to prevent any kind of real offensive on the islands.

*   *   *

At six twenty-five Jim heard the sound of approaching vehicles. He scooted to the side of the roof and peered over the low wall to the gate.

A line of green canvas-covered trucks pulled up to the gate and stopped. Jim raised his binoculars and saw several men jump from the back of the lead truck and take up defensive positions. Four more trucks stopped in line behind it. Jim watched as Hathaway stepped out of the first truck to survey the area.

Three creatures moved toward them. A man raised a weapon but Hathaway stopped him before he fired. The man used the butt of his rifle to crush in the skulls of the intruders.

Jim couldn't hear what they were saying but it looked as though Hathaway was giving orders. Several men ran through the gate and past the construction trailers. They walked briskly down the hill, their rifles raised, sighting down the barrels as they moved. After a quick evaluation, the point man waved the others through and the trucks inched forward. Hathaway walked up to the gate as the others moved through.

The original lock hung on the latch. Hathaway took the bait and used it to lock the gate once everyone was inside. The lock was easily picked and soon Mick would reopen it.

Just as they had hoped, the trucks stopped in the open area by the docks. It was the most convenient place to be to wait for a boat or to use one to get across the bay. It was the same spot where Jim had met Leon almost a week before.

Two men were stationed at the gate to keep watch.

The sun was low in the west. Dusk arrived around seven-fifteen and the dimming light would help add to the confusion should the battle be prolonged.

Jim scooted back to Amanda and picked up his walkie-talkie. "Mick, come in," he whispered.

"Yeah, I'm here," Mick whispered back.

"As soon as you think they won't see you from below, use your gun with the silencer and take out the two guards. As soon as you've done that, I'll start the siren."

"Ten-four."

Jim watched as the two guards walked behind the trailers and out of his line of sight. A minute or two later, they returned. Jim raised his binoculars as one of the guards gave a slight hand gesture toward him.

Through the binoculars Jim saw that Mick and Chris. wore the jackets and hats of the guards they had just dispatched. From a distance, no one would know the difference.

Jim turned to Amanda. "Okay, it's time. Start the whistle."

Amanda crept across the roof to where they had rerouted the power to the siren and plugged the two ends together. The fan turned faster and faster and the high-pitched whine squealed from the horns for an instant. Jim took a quick peek over the edge to see if anyone had noticed.

Soldiers continued to unload provisions and weapons from the trucks, oblivious to anything but their job. Three militiamen walked the parking lot, using the butts of their rifles to destroy the brains of the ghouls that had gained entry before they had arrived.

Amanda returned to Jim's side. "Are you sure this will work? I can't hear a thing from that siren now."

"You're not supposed to, but the creatures will." Jim looked toward the gates. Ten or twelve creatures were there and others were approaching. "That siren will attract every vile monster within earshot of this place. In a short time, there will be too many to count."

Amanda pulled her jacket closed and sunk closer to the gravelly roof surface.

Jim gently touched her shoulder. "Don't worry. They can't get up here. We'll go down when it's safe."

"What about the others? What about Mick and the others?"

"They know what to do."

62

Mick backed away from the gate, pulling Chris with him, to a place out of site of the approaching hoard that was beginning to make a lot of noise. They moved to a place where they could see both soldiers and gate but the creatures couldn't see them.

The soldiers were more spread out now, their provisions stacked close to an open dock. A stack of oxygen tanks stood close by.

Hathaway leaned against a wooden post at the end of the dock and watched the bay. He checked his watch. It was six-forty. Still no sign of a boat or Chris Smith.

He despised tardiness. Even if he caught sight of the boat now it would take it ten minutes to reach shore. He wondered if Smith had run into trouble acquiring the boat. Maybe the boat's captain had put up a fight. Maybe he had been discovered. Those were good reasons for being late. Any other reason required discipline.

Mick turned around in his crouched position to face the gate. The mob of creatures had swelled unbelievably in the last fifteen minutes. They pushed noisily against the fence, bulging the meshed wire with their combined weight. Mick feared they would burst through before it was time. He stayed out of sight, not wanting to agitate them further.

Chris edged closer to Mick and peered out at the creatures from behind a concrete jersey wall. "Jesus, I've not seen that many things in one place for a while," he said.

"Neither have I," Mick said. "Let's just hope the fence holds. If it comes down, be ready to move fast."

Jim watched the gate and waited. From his position he could see only a small portion on either side of the fence but he could see farther out behind it. A huge mob of ghouls crowded the landscape. For blocks on end there was a steady stream that stretched down the road like a line of ants on their way to a picnic. There were simply too many to count.

The first large wave hit the fence with a fury. The sudden addition of their weight stressed it even further.

Mick and Chris moved away to a safer spot and waited.

Now even Jim could hear them as they cried out in frustration and hunger. It was only a matter of time before the militia took notice as their cries grew in strength and volume.

Another wave arrived at the gate and pushed against the ones already there. Some climbed the wire and hung over the top. Less capable ones were trampled and buried beneath the pressing mob.

Jim's radio crackled to life and he grabbed it.

"Jim, this is Mick," he whispered, his tone urgent. "They're going to come crashing through any minute. We need to move *now* and get this thing in gear."

Jim watched the militia for signs that they were aware of the coming danger. Hathaway ran from the dock into the crowd of men. The jig was up.

"How many creatures are there, Mick? Can you give me an approximate head count?"

"Jesus, Jim, there's a shitload! And there's a shitload more on the way!" Mick said, not whispering anymore.

"Open the gate and get the hell out of there!" Jim said. "Don't linger!"

63

Hathaway, breathless, his eyes wide, ran to Jake. For the first time in his life, Jake saw real fear in him.

"Something's wrong!" Hathaway cried.

"He's late, Bobby, that's all. He'll be here."

"No! No! *Listen!*"

Jake turned his ear into the light wind. He heard a faint, rhythmic sound. Kind of like bees but lighter and higher pitched. It came from the direction the wind was blowing, toward the gate.

Hathaway strained to see the gate but the construction trailers blocked his line of vision.

"It's a trap, Jake! Goddamn it, it's a trap!"

Hathaway turned around and scanned the entire area. His head felt light when the truth suddenly hit home: It was a setup and he was not in command of the situation.

"What is that sound?" he demanded. "It sounds like it's coming from the gate!"

Hathaway clicked on his radio. "Billy Ray? What the hell's going on up there?" Only static answered him. "Billy Ray, goddamn it, you'd better answer me now!" Hathaway belted the radio and panicked. He turned to Jake. "Get some men and go up there and…" His words trailed off as he stared toward the gate, his mouth agape.

Jake turned and saw creatures swarming all sides of the trailers, a multitude of hideous apparitions that outnumbered the militia four to one. They shuffled with uncertain steps down the hill, crazed even more by the sight of their prey.

Jim watched as militiamen hurried to take defensive positions. He pressed the button on his radio. "All right, people, let's let hell loose!"

Two flashes erupted on the other side of the harbor as Griz and Leon sent their first barrage of bazooka fire. The explosions hit dead center of the militia's position. They returned fire, momentarily ignoring the approaching mob of walking dead.

Griz and Leon ducked for cover.

Jim and Amanda sent their own volley next, then Chris detonated the dynamite. The resulting explosions sent the oxygen tanks blasting out in all directions and the militia scattered for cover. A quarter of the enemy went down in the mega firestorm amid flying shrapnel.

Hathaway dashed for cover behind a half-full water barrel by the dock. Jim saw him as he made his dash and hurried to load the bazooka. He took aim and fired at the barrel. The explosion sent the barrel flying amid a cloud of smoke and fire. When the debris cleared, he searched for Hathaway's remains.

Chips of brick and mortar blasted Jim's face as enemy bullets nearly hit their mark. Jim threw himself on Amanda and the two went down behind the small ledge. Ricocheting fragments rained down on them as they lay face down for safety.

Mick turned to wait for Chris. A second ago Chris had been right behind him, now he was nowhere to be seen. He backtracked and ran down a gravel walkway between the docks on the right and an eight-foot wooden fence on the left. The walkway turned to concrete and Mick ran up a ramp to a loading area with a locked gate. A dead-end.

Mick turned. "Chris?" he yelled above the rapid gunfire. He called again but there was still no answer. He wanted to continue looking for him but his friends needed him to be part of the battle.

He ran down the ramp and right into the first creature coming around the corner of the walkway. The sudden impact caused him to lose his grip on his weapon and it skidded away from him.

The creature lurched forward.

Mick stumbled back until he was against the locked gate of the loading ramp. Eight more ghouls turned the corner of the narrow walkway and made their way to him. He reached up to climb the gate and drop down the other side into the water but he was grabbed from behind. Two creatures moved in to cover him.

Mick wheeled around and sent a devastating blow to the jaw of the one that had pulled him back. It fell into the creature behind it and both went down. The remaining ghouls moved in and surrounded him with surprising speed. The two on the ground struggled to regain their footing.

A creature reached for Mick's collar. What it got was a handful of the necklaces Izzy had given him.

The creature yanked hard and the necklaces broke, sending a flood of the little beads bouncing to the concrete. They rolled down the ramp and under the feet of the advancing reanimates desperately trying to get to Mick.

The ghoul that had broken the necklace slipped on the beads and fell into the one behind it. Without so much as an attempt to keep its footing, it fell into the next one and so on until they resembled a row of dominos falling, each into the other, until the last ghoul lay squirming on the ramp.

At first Mick was too shocked to move. It had been a comical sight, like something out of a Three Stooges movie. Izzy's necklaces had saved his life! Somehow the little girl had known.

He stared at the pile of bodies until one of them got to its knees, then Mick scooped up his weapon and ran down the corridor.

The gunfire stopped after two more explosions. Jim peered over the ledge. Griz and Leon had fired their bazookas and the militiamen had scattered.

The throng of walking dead was within the soldier's ranks. Many fought for their lives in hand-to-hand combat. They were no longer able to fight both the army of undead and the small band of attackers.

Jim fired his Uzi, targeting only the living soldiers. The militia's numbers dwindled.

Leon lowered his Uzi and watched from the window. Most of the enemy had been dispatched by either weapon fire or the horde of undead ravaging their bodies. The creatures attacked both the remaining soldiers and the freshly-killed ones on the ground. The militia was no match for the enormously-growing number of the undead. Leon turned his face from the carnage.

Jim pulled Amanda across the roof and stopped under the siren. He jerked the power cords apart and sat down next to her.

"It's over, we did it," he said.

"It was horrible," Amanda said in a subdued voice. "So much death. Now we have to figure out how to get out of here."

Jim got to his feet, but stooped low in case any of the militia were left alive who might take a potshot at his head. "Go back to the ledge and start shooting the ghouls. I'm going to find Mick and the rest and get the gate shut again. Keep an eye out for anyone who might shoot back at you."

"Be careful. There's a whole lot of those things down there."

"Don't worry," Jim said. "I will. You just make sure you stay here. Don't go down there."

64

Jim shimmied down the ladder, jumping the last six feet to the floor. At the far end was a door that opened to a balcony on the opposite side of the action. He would go down the stairs there. It would be the safest route to the others.

Jim opened the door and stepped outside.

"YOU!" Hathaway screamed.

A foot apart, they both raised their weapons to fire. Unable to get a clean shot, Jim used his rifle to knock Hathaway's to the side as each rifle discharged. Both men grabbed onto the other's weapon and fought to gain the upper hand.

Jim bulled forward and pushed Hathaway hard against the railing. Hathaway's rifle went flying over the edge and clanged to the ground.

Jim's weapon was now between them and they wrestled to gain possession of it. Hathaway twisted the rifle until the butt was turned upward, under Jim's chin. "Where's your big oaf, Hathaway?" Jim spit. "There's no one here to fight your battle now!"

Several ghouls saw them and began climbing the stairs.

Hathaway gave a quick thrust and the butt hit hard on Jim's chin. The impact caused him to lose focus.

Hathaway took aim at Jim's head. He pulled the trigger. CLICK! The gun misfired but Hathaway thought fast. He flipped the weapon around, took it by the barrel end, and swung it against the side of Jim's head. Jim staggered back and teetered on the edge of the top step.

A cold hand grabbed Jim's arm and the blackened teeth of the closest ghoul bit into his left shoulder. Jim cried out and shoved the creature back down the steps. Hathaway laughed manically as Jim pressed down on the injury.

Enraged, Jim charged at him. He grabbed Hathaway by the collar and drove an upward kick into his groin. Hathaway exhaled and bowed. Jim sent an uppercut to his chin and with newfound strength tossed him down the stairs.

As Hathaway fell, he took the ghouls with him. Dazed and confused at the bottom of the stairs, he faced the awful truth as eight ghouls covered him. He was face to face with the same zombie that had bitten Jim in the shoulder.

As though bobbing for apples, the ghoul lowered its face and bit into Hathaway's nose. Warm blood flowed over his face as its teeth tightened their grip and it twisted its head back and forth. The fleshy part of Hathaway's nose tore free, leaving the open nasal cavity to fill with blood.

Jim listened to Hathaway's screams and watched as the creatures tore into him. He waited until others noticed him and started up the stairs.

Jim suddenly realized the injury to his shoulder, and his fate.

65

Jim met up with Mick, Griz, and Leon in the midst of feasting ghouls. They ran toward the docks, away from the dangerous feeding frenzy.

Chris bounded out from under one of the docks, his clothing drenched.

"Chris!" Mick smiled. "I was looking for you. What happened?"

"I had to take cover. I got shot in the arm."

Mick grabbed his arm and inspected his injury. "Hell, boy, it's only a flesh wound. You'll be fine."

Chris allowed a brief smile, which faded when he saw the ghouls tearing at the bodies of so many men. They had systematically killed almost a hundred men. Though their actions were justified, it didn't prevent the sickening feeling in the pit of his stomach.

Mick noticed the torn shirt and the blood on Jim's shoulder. He thought if he waited, maybe the explanation would be different than what he suspected. His heart sank. He'd seen that kind of injury before.

Jim saw the sadness and resignation in Mick's eyes. "Go close the gate and get the boat ready," he said. "I'll get Amanda." He turned toward the firehouse and ran back through the ghastly feeding zone.

Amanda had not seen the fight between Jim and Hathaway. She'd been too busy sending more than forty creatures to their final rest. She was still plucking away at them when Jim stepped out onto the roof.

Jim did his best to hide his wound but the blood still flowed and soaked his jacket. He slung his rifle over that shoulder by the strap, hoping Amanda wouldn't notice.

"Come on!" he called to her from the trap door. "Let's go. We're going to make a run for the boat."

Amanda picked up her things and eagerly ran to him. "You okay?"

"I'm fine."

Amanda swiped her hand across his shoulder. Her fingertips were red with blood. "No, you're not! What happened?"

"I'm fine," he assured her.

The look on his face told her a different story and she pulled the weapon from him. Before he could react, Amanda jerked back his jacket and exposed the bite. Amanda gasped and the rifle slipped from her hand. "Oh my god, Jim! We've got to get you to a doctor." Tears welled up in her eyes.

"It's all right. It really is. There's only one thing left to do and that's get all of us back to the island."

"No, Jim, I won't let you go. You can't leave me." The tears came harder and a knot formed in her throat. "You can beat this. God-damn it, you can beat this!"

Jim pulled her close and held her tight.

66

The next day Mick took a small group of men back to the Smith's Point and killed the rest of the creatures and cleaned up the bodies. It gave him time to use the Grizzly's radio to contact Felicia and tell her what had happened. He told her about the necklace and how it had saved his life.

He told her about her brother and let her speak to him. Chris and Felicia cried as they spoke to one another. They would be reunited in two days, when Mick returned to the mountain with Chris. Then they would make preparations to move everyone to Tangier.

Amanda was devastated. Unlike Felicia, who had found happiness in the post-plague world, Amanda was in danger of losing the love of her life. Her first marriage to Will had been a happy one, but Jim was her soul mate. The wound would soon take him from her and she would be alone again. He wouldn't even make love to her for fear of transmitting the infection.

The strain was too much for her and now she slept at Chris' house. A mild sedative had been given to her and she was finally getting the rest she needed.

When she awoke, Jim was gone.

Jim drove into Fredericksburg in one of the militia trucks. A strange thing was happening. He had come to find Matt and put an end to his unearthly existence. So far he had not found him, but something was happening to the creatures.

As he made his way through town, Jim saw that there was less activity from them. Many lay motionless on the ground. At one point he had left the safety of the truck to advance on a creature he thought might be Matt. A ghoul crept up on him, unnoticed.

Jim turned around to meet the menace, only to watch it slide down his chest and fall dead. Even the active ones were not very active. They were slower now and very weak. It was no trouble to pass large groups of them without much thought of a chase. On average, three out of five of the creatures he encountered had lost their ability to function.

Jim leaned against the front of the Humvee. He had been waiting for Matt for more than an hour. It was the same spot where they had first encountered the militia, the spot where Matt had died. The wrecked plane was a hundred yards up the road.

Jim was sure Matt would return. His malfunctioning body had probably returned many times, not sure exactly why it was drawn back to this place. It was just something the undead did.

Jim wasn't one for long good-byes. Mick had understood that and had done his best to keep his emotions about Jim's fate to himself, but Amanda had been grief stricken. He missed her now, wished she was there with him. Her love would be so much comfort.

His emotions were never close to the surface but deep inside they gnawed at his sanity now that death was near. He tried hard not to let it get the best of him. Not yet. Not until this one last responsibility was carried out.

The sun faded and darkness came. The Humvee was wrecked, damaged by the plane when it came down, but it afforded him better protection than the canvas-covered truck. He rubbed his shoulder as he sat in the front seat. It burned like fire and he hoped he wouldn't die before morning.

He held the .44 in his lap throughout most of the night, thinking that it might be best if he used it on himself before the inevitable happened. The doctor on Tangier Island had shot him up with penicillin but it would do no good, not against the plague.

His destiny was set in stone now. If he could make it through the night, just long enough to take care of Matt, then he would do it. He would take care of himself, but not until then.

Jim wiped the sweat from his forehead. His fever was getting worse. His body ached all over like a bad case of the flu and he faded in and out of consciousness. His eyes opened and closed as sleep drew him into its grip.

The scent of spring flowers wafted through the cracked window. Jim opened his eyes, yawned, and sat upright in his seat.

Matt stood in front of the vehicle. His glazed eyes stared into Jim and he leaned to one side, the palm of his left hand on the hood. His mouth moved as if to speak but no sound came.

Jim stepped out of the driver's side. Matt watched him as he raised the .44.

"Hello, Matt," Jim said. "It's good to see you again. I took care of everything for you. I got the men who did this to you."

The zombie-Matt groaned and stood away from the Humvee. He staggered, then straightened his posture.

Jim smiled at the almost human attempt by Matt for dignity. "Are you ready to go home now?"

Zombie-Matt moaned again, then staggered toward Jim in an aggressive manner.

Jim pulled the trigger and fulfilled his promise.

Jim had brought a shovel with him from Tangier. He pulled it out from the back of the covered truck. Birds sang in the distance, while large black buzzards hovered overhead, waiting to pick at the unburied corpses littering the ground. They paid no mind to Jim as he dug Matt's grave.

In an hour the job was done and the last shovel of dirt was thrown on top. Thankfully, no creatures had interrupted him. There were none to be seen when Jim scanned the area. There were more bodies on the ground now than there had been the night before. During the night more had come only to die.

For the first time that day Jim remembered his injury. It wasn't hurting as much now and the fever was gone. Less than twelve hours ago he was worried that he wouldn't make it through the night. Now it barely bothered him.

Was he beating it? This was the third day. By now he should be incoherent and too weak to walk. Instead, he felt good, alert, hungry even.

He hadn't eaten in more than a day. A nice thick, juicy steak would be nice, he thought. Rare, of course...

0-595-27165-0